Bolan slipp ... **e and lowere** ...

"Nice and easy, now," ... ...tter with the hidden Uzi. "Any deviations from the script could be hazardous to your health."

The ranks of the Klansmen parted for them, Ritter leading, nodding to the faithful as they called his name, some raising stiffened arms in salutation. As they mounted the dais, Bolan took up station on the steps, assuming a position where his field of fire would cover Ritter and the crowd.

"Brothers!" the Klan leader bellowed to his audience. "We have assembled here to celebrate a victory over the farmers' union.

"You all know why we're here, so I presume you came prepared." A murmur of assent rippled through the crowd as Klansmen dug beneath their robes, producing knives, razors, blackjacks.

"Are you ready, brothers? I won't waste any more of your valuable time, except to say bring out the prisoner!"

The sentries emerged from the shed, supporting Wilson Brown between them, a condemned man on his way to the gallows.

Mack Bolan ripped open the snaps on his robe and cut loose with the Uzi.

MACK BOLAN®

The Executioner

DON PENDLETON's EXECUTIONER

MACK BOLAN®

The Fiery Cross

A GOLD EAGLE BOOK FROM

W🌐RLDWIDE®

TORONTO · NEW YORK · LONDON · PARIS
AMSTERDAM · STOCKHOLM · HAMBURG
ATHENS · MILAN · TOKYO · SYDNEY

First edition March 1988

ISBN 0-373-61111-0

Special thanks and acknowledgment to
Mike Newton for his contribution to this work.

Printed in Canada

"He who passively accepts evil is as much involved in it as he who helps to perpetrate it. He who accepts evil without protesting against it is really cooperating with it."

—Martin Luther King, Jr., 1958

"I refuse to stand idle and thereby cooperate with evil. Let the savages take notice: one man, here and now, is fighting back."

—Mack Bolan

"The men of the USS *Stark* stood guard in the night. They were great, and those that died embody the best of us. Yes, they were ordinary men who did extraordinary things. Yes, they were heroes."

—President Ronald Reagan,
May 22, 1987

Doran Bolduc
Braddy Brown
Jeffrey Calkins
Mark Caouette
John Coletta, Jr.
Bryan Clinefelter
Antonio Daniels
Christopher DeAngelis
James Dunlap
Steven Erwin
Jerry Farr
Vernon Foster
Dexter Grissette
William Hansen
Daniel Homicki
Kenneth Januski, Jr.
Steven Kendall
Steven Kiser
Ronnie Lockett

Thomas MacMullen
Charles Moller
Jaffrey Phelps
Randy Pierce
James Plonsky
Kelly Quick
Earl Ryals
Robert Shippee
Jeffrey Curtis Sibley
Lee Stephens
James Stevens
Martin Supple
Gregory Lee Tweady
Vincent Lenard Ulmer
Joseph Watson
Wayne Weaver
Terance Weldon
Lloyd Wilson

PROLOGUE

The young man stumbled, lost his stride and nearly fell. A sapling saved him, kept him on his feet, although the rough bark flayed his palms. The pain was nothing. Less than nothing. He had suffered worse, and he was running for his life.

Behind him, voices in the darkness. Cursing. Calling after him. Demanding that he stop and take his medicine. He could not hear the dogs yammering—not yet—but they were sometimes trained to hunt in silence, and they might be closing on him even now.

He was winded, almost to the point of absolute exhaustion, but it would be suicide to stand and fight. Unarmed, he had no chance at all against the dogs, the men with guns, who were pursuing him. It was a miracle that he had managed to escape their clutches in the first place.

They meant to kill him, that was obvious. If they had simply meant to beat him like the others, they could easily have done their business on the street without abducting him and driving miles into the countryside. This had been an obvious disposal run, but he was not prepared to make it easy for them. Not if he could break away.

He knew their faces now, a scattering of names, and he would blow their stinking cover for them, given half a chance. Forget about indictments; they would alibi one another till the cows came home, and most of them had wives or lovers who would swear that they were watching television or humping when the shit went down. But there were other ways to turn the heat on, and he knew them all by heart.

Some of his would-be murderers were righteous members of the church, and their fellow Christians might be forced to take a second glance at killers in the congregation. Others in the mob were businessmen; picket lines would generate enough adverse publicity to hurt them. His unsupported word might not be adequate to land the bastards in the prison cells where they belonged, but he could make them wish that they had picked another guest of honor for their little necktie party.

First, of course, he had to save himself. Survival was the first priority. If he was taken by his enemies the story ended here, with no heat, no pressure, brought to bear against the men responsible. The young man did not fancy martyrdom. And so he ran.

The trees and undergrowth were thicker now, with creepers that conspired to trip him, thorny limbs that snagged his flesh and clothing. Skull and ribs still throbbing from the beating he had absorbed, the runner scarcely noticed new lacerations on his face and arms. If anything, the pain was welcome. It would keep him angry. Keep him moving as his energy reserves ran out.

He thought of Mona, knew she would have started making calls by now. The sheriff's office would be slow to respond, as always, but the others would be looking for him, scouring the town for starters, fanning out to launch a wider search when they came up empty. They would do their best, but they would be too late unless he kept on running, made the hunters work for everything they got.

How long since they had taken him? An hour? Two? The drive had taken twenty minutes, minimum, his face jammed against the floorboards of a station wagon, heavy work boots pressing on his neck and spine. Though no woodsman, he possessed a decent homing instinct, but the darkness and exhaustion, coupled with the ringing in his ears from one too many backhand blows, combined to leave him feeling disoriented. There was every likelihood that he had been "escaping" in a circle, going nowhere, but he had to keep on moving, give it everything he had.

Which, at the moment, wasn't much.

His nose was definitely broken, and the pain in his side was probably a broken rib. At that, he had been fortunate. The bastards had been drinking when they'd picked him up, and alcohol had made them clumsy. Sober men with murder on their minds would probably have taken steps to cripple him, eliminate the possibility of an escape. Instead, his captors had been content with knocking him around in preparation for the main event, and they had given him his chance.

The runner felt a surge of satisfaction now, remembering the satisfying impact of his fist after he had picked a target from the circle of attackers and launched himself without a second thought or any hint of warning. Whiskey and surprise had slowed the enemy's reaction. His man had gone down, and he had been away and running for the trees before the bastards had realized exactly what was happening. There had been a few wild shots, and then the leader had called them off and they had given chase on foot.

He wished that he could hear the dogs. At least he would know if they were closing on him, narrowing his meager lead. With so much noise behind him, heavy bodies crashing through the brush, it would be easy for the hounds to take him by surprise. One of them would be strong enough to drop him in his present state; the pair of them might finish him before the gunmen had an opportunity to join the fun.

He hesitated, found a fallen limb and weighed it in his palm. It wasn't much, but it would have to do. If he could ambush one of his pursuers, take the bastard's gun...

The thought of killing surfaced automatically, surprising him. He had been schooled to seek nonviolent answers in the face of sometimes violent opposition, but his life was on the line, and primal instincts swiftly overrode his training. There had been too many human sacrifices for the cause already. He was not prepared to make another. Not with Mona and the others waiting, searching for him, counting on him. The bastards who initiated violent confrontations had to learn that there were risks involved.

The runner might have laughed aloud, except that he was out of breath. The notion of himself as hero and avenger, standing tall and fighting fire with fire, appeared preposterous within the context of his circumstances. He was injured, near collapse, and being hunted like an animal by men with dogs and guns. There were no heroes here.

There might, however, be survivors.

He had been running for a quarter of an hour, though it felt like days. He had to be making headway. Every moment gained was in his favor; every moment wasted by the hunters shaved the awesome odds against his own survival. Some of them were sober now, he heard it in their distant voices. Sober and afraid. Their "simple" operation had already taken much too long, and they were running out of time. Delays increased the possibility of hazardous exposure. If they did not overtake him soon, a few of them, at least, would start to think in terms of giving up and turning back.

Already one or two might be considering a way to cut their losses, scrub the whole fiasco and pretend it had never happened. There was strength in numbers, and a single witness—let alone a radical with axes of his own to grind—was easily dismissed from serious consideration. No one would believe his story of abduction in the middle of the night by some outstanding local citizens. It would seem preposterous.

Except that *someone* might be listening. If not the sheriff, then the press, the networks, possibly the FBI. Who could predict what an investigation might uncover? Each of the enemy had secrets to protect, a multitude of sins that had to be hidden from the light of day. To save themselves, one another, they would stick awhile, continue the pursuit until they ran him down or saw that it was absolutely hopeless. While they had a chance to salvage something, anything, they dared not let him go.

The dog appeared from nowhere, crashing through the undergrowth immediately to the runner's left, a guided missile, lips drawn back from silent, flashing fangs. He raised an arm in time to save his jugular and felt long canines slicing through flesh and muscle, grating on the long bones, locking tight.

He brought his cudgel down across the German shepherd's skull. Again. At the third blow, something gave. The dying animal released him with a final gnawing twist that brought the runner to his knees. He struck the twitching, prostrate body one more time and struggled to his feet.

He heard the second shepherd coming through the trees and was ready when the hairy javelin erupted from its cover, hurtling toward his face. He swung the cudgel like Hank Aaron going for the record, and it shattered on the streamlined skull. The dog's momentum drove him backward, and they rolled together in the ferns, his fingers scrabbling for the throat and pinching off the windpipe. Weak resistance, stifled whimpers, and the hound at last lay still.

It took his last remaining strength to get back on his feet. Warm blood was flowing freely from his savaged forearm, but he scarcely felt it. He wondered fleetingly if this was what it felt like to die.

"You're covered, nigger!"

Turning slowly, almost apathetically, he watched his enemies approaching through the trees. He had no strength to run, nowhere to hide.

"Black bastard killed my dogs!" a second gunman bellowed. "Jesus Christ!"

"Don't matter. This is what we came for."

"Let's do it."

Stepping forward, first one member of the hunting party, then another and another readied rifles, shotguns, pistols, taking aim. Again, the young man wondered what it would feel like to die.

And then he knew.

1

The sanctuary of Bethany AME Church was about three-quarters filled, and new mourners were arriving in droves. The majority were dressed for Sunday meeting, though it was in fact a Tuesday afternoon. Others, who could not afford suits, had come in work clothes, faded and worn but scrupulously clean. Their casual attire implied no disrespect to the deceased.

From his position on the dais next to the Reverend Cletus Little, Wilson Brown sat motionless and watched the pews fill up with solemn faces. There were angry murmurings among the members of the crowd, a restiveness that threatened to explode if someone stuck a verbal match and lit the fuse. Other mourners, he knew, would be gathered outside on the steps and in the parking lot, unable to find seats inside. They would be content to stand and listen to the service on a pair of tinny speakers, under the watchful eyes of sheriff's deputies and state police.

The AME in Bethany's name stood for African Methodist Episcopal, a throwback to the antebellum days when churches—like the nation—had been split on racial lines, divided on the monumental issues of slavery and secession. In the aftermath of Reconstruction, no one had ever gotten around to changing the name of the church, and in fact the congregation had been solely "African" for another century, until the second civil war had started making inroads into the bastions of Jim Crow.

Today, all that had changed—a few of them familiar, Theo's friends and allies in the movement, others from the local media, with notebooks and tape recorders on their knees. In back, another line of stern Caucasian faces, uniformed officers of the state police standing shoulder to shoulder with two men in suits. The latter had the look of Washington about them, but they scarcely mattered. They were all too late to save his son.

Scanning the crowd while he waited, Brown looked for the one face he wanted to see. He came up empty, told himself that he should not have been surprised. It was too public here, with the police and journalists on hand, the network television cameras parked outside. And it was early yet. There would be ample time for Wilson Brown to savor plans of revenge against the bastards who had killed his only child.

He sensed a rising tension in the crowd and noted that the white mourners were attracting sullen and suspicious glares from the majority of blacks. For the most part it was an undeserving mistrust, symptomatic of the deep divisions that had brought Parrish and the rest of Chatham County to the brink of civil war. Those schisms in society had cost Theo his life. Others, too, had died, and Wilson Brown knew the worst was yet to come.

The church was full, the double doors were closed and flanked by officers in uniform with pistols on their hips. Beside Brown, Reverend Little checked his watch and said, "I think we should begin." His surplice shimmered under the pulpit floodlights as he moved to stand before the microphone. Brown willed his eyes to remain on the minister, not stray to the closed casket, which stood at the foot of the altar on sawhorses draped in black. He could not maintain his poise if he allowed his heart and mind to linger there, inside the box. Not yet.

It took a moment for the crowd to notice Reverend Little in the pulpit, but the murmuring subsided by degrees, replaced at last by ringing silence. Angry and expectant faces waited as the minister cleared his throat and straightened the foolscap pages on the lectern.

"My duty is a sad one, as you know," he began. "I'm called upon to say a word in parting for a young man cut down in his prime. His name is known to all of you. He needs no introduction here."

"Amen."

A single baritone pronounced the word, and other voices picked it up until a chorus washed against the pulpit, ebbed and died away.

"You all know Theo Brown, and I believe you all respected him. Your presence here today is testimony to your admiration of his work, his sacrifice. It would have pleased him, I think, to see this turnout. Not by any means because he sought your admiration or your praise. Our brother Theo was a self-effacing man who put his ego and his own best interest second to the needs of others."

"Tell it, brother."

"Rather, I believe that Theo would have smiled upon this gathering, because it symbolizes unity, commitment to the cause for which he gave his life. By your attendance here, you send a message to the enemies of brotherhood and freedom."

"Send it, Jesus."

"You have put the enemies of brotherhood on notice here today that dreams cannot be slain with mortal man."

"Praise God."

"You have announced your own intention to pick up the fallen standard and to bear it proudly in the days and weeks to come. By turning out today, you have become a part of Theo's dream for Chatham County and for all mankind."

"Yes, Jesus."

Toward the rear, Brown saw the troopers shifting nervously and studying the crowd. They felt it begin to simmer. Several of the officers kept anxious fingers close to blackjacks and batons, as if afraid weapons would be needed at any moment.

The minister was warming up, his enthusiasm easily communicated to the crowd. Reporters clustered on the sidelines felt it, scribbling furiously in their notebooks, twisting microcassette recorders toward the congregation for a sampling of the crowd's reaction to the eulogy.

"You don't need me to tell you Theo was a good man, that he worked and finally gave his life for others out of a commitment to their need. You don't need me to freshen up your memories about the circumstances of his cruel, untimely death."

"No, Lord."

"It's not my job to name his killers, though I have a fair idea of who they are. I won't name names today. I can't inform you to a moral certainty of who precisely pulled the trigger. But I know and you know to a moral certainty the names of those who gave the orders, those who had it done on their behalf."

"Yes, Lord, we know."

"It's not my function to detect and prosecute a murderer, but there are those who have that grave responsibility. To them I offer this advice: proceed. Push on and do your duty, without fear or favor. See that justice finally is served in Chatham County."

"Hallelujah!"

"Theo knew, and we know, that the yoke of bondage can be swept away if men of goodwill work together in a common cause. He knew, and we know, that the road will not be easy. We have miles and rugged miles to go before we reach the promised land of peace and freedom, but *we will endure!*"

"Praise Jesus!"

"Theo Brown did *not* lay down his life in vain."

"Amen."

"His sacrifice will *not* be proved futile."

"Hallelujah!"

"Say 'Amen!'"

"Amen! Amen!"

The Reverend Little waited, sipping at a glass of water that had stood beside his notes atop the lectern. A moment passed before the restless crowd could hear him, even with assistance from the microphone.

"It is my privilege to introduce a man who stood by Theo in his darkest hours, lending him encouragement and offering him the opportunity to be himself. Mr. Wilson Brown."

Brown's legs were suddenly unsteady as he rose and moved to take Reverend Little's place behind the lectern. He could not keep his eyes from resting briefly on the casket as he stood before the microphone. The thought of the casket's contents struck him like a fist in the heart, recalled all the pain of loss and sadness.

"I appreciate the Reverend Little's words," he said, and realized that he was whispering. Clearing his throat, Brown began again. "I appreciate the Reverend Little's words, but I must point out one mistake he made in introducing me. I wasn't with my son when he came up against his darkest hour. If I had been there, you might not be gathered here today. You might be going on about your lives. My son might still be going on about his business."

Many in the crowd were weeping openly. Wilson Brown ignored the tears that filled his own eyes, speaking to them from the heart.

"I failed my son—"

"No, Lord."

"—and I've come here to beg his pardon—"

"No, sweet Jesus!"

"—and to beg *your* pardon for my failure."

"You've not failed us, brother."

"I'm here to beg your pardon, and to promise you that Theo did not spend his life in vain. I wasn't there when he had need of me in life, but I'm here *now*, and I'll be here until his murderers are brought to justice."

"Hallelujah!"

"I'll be here until the dream my son conceived with all of you becomes reality."

"Praise God."

"I've got no time for anything, now, except the struggle. I've got no energy for anything outside the cause."

"Amen."

"If Theo's enemies believe the murder of my son can stop the movement, I'm up here to tell them that they're wrong."

"Yes, Lord."

"I'm serving notice on the killers now that I will not be turned around or frightened off by anything they do or say.

They've done their worst to me. I've got nothing left to lose.''

"Sweet Jesus.''

"I don't know who killed my son, not yet, but I intend to know. And may the Lord above have mercy on their souls—''

"Amen.''

"—because I have no mercy left in me.''

"That's right.''

"I'm here to tell you that my son's life stood for something.''

"Yes, Lord.''

"I may be too late to help him, but I'm here in time to see that justice isn't overlooked or swept aside. I'm here in time to see his killers brought to book, and that's exactly what I mean to do. If any of them want to try and take me out, I'm here.''

"Yes, sir.''

"I'm here.''

"Amen.''

"I'm here!''

"Amen!"

The crowd was on its feet as Wilson Brown retreated to his place beside the minister. He scarcely heard or understood the thunderous applause as he was ushered through a side door, through the sacristy and outside to the waiting Continental. He would ride with Reverend Little to the cemetery, following the hearse to Theo's final resting place.

It took nearly twenty minutes for the church to clear and Theo's casket to be loaded in the hearse. The Lincoln fell in line behind the hearse, other vehicles following behind them, headlights burning in the middle of the afternoon. The church stood on the east side of town, seven miles from Mount Holly Cemetery. The procession traveled north along Van Buren and east on Main, right through the heart of Parrish. The grief and loss of Wilson Brown were on display for all the world to see.

The procession gathered mixed reactions on the way. A group of shiftless whites on Main Street jeered and pointed, two of them extending middle fingers in mock salute. Brown wished them dead and turned away from their malice, trusting to the police escort to prevent serious incidents from marring the funeral. Farther along the route, a pair of aging black men doffed their hats and stood stiffly erect as the cortege rolled by. Most of the inhabitants they passed, however, appeared indifferent or uninformed.

It saddened Brown to think that Theo's death, for all its coverage in the media, had had so little impact on the people he had worked—and ultimately died—to help. The residents of Chatham County were no different, he supposed, from people anywhere. They went about their daily business with their eyes fixed on tomorrow, concentrating on themselves, their families, their private needs. It was asking too much of them to care about another human being, let alone a stranger, after he was dead and gone. They seemed to have no stake in Theo's struggle, and they seemed to feel no grief at his death.

Mount Holly Cemetery had been officially segregated for one hundred years, until the local law had been struck down in 1964, and it was still segregated now. The law provided equal rights for black and white to lie together in their last repose, but there were no Caucasians on Mount Holly's waiting list. If Theo's white friends from the church turned out to join the graveside ceremony, it would be the first time in history that Parrish whites had mourned in public the passing of a black. It was time.

The cemetery's wrought-iron gates were standing open, ready to receive the funeral cortege. It wound along a narrow gravel drive, meandered across the graveyard's seven-acre width and back again before reaching its destination. Fifty feet to the left of the stopped hearse, a strip of garish artificial grass concealed an open grave where trestles waited to support the casket during the graveside ceremonies.

Wilson Brown was not among the men who carried his son to his rest. Six of Theo's friends, local farmers, corded muscles rippling beneath their Sunday suits, conveyed the coffin from the hearse to the graveside, moving stolidly, head down, grief and anger mingled on their faces. Conscious of their feelings, struggling with his own, Brown followed and took his place on a metal folding chair beside the casket.

The other seats filled up immediately, leaving several dozen mourners on their feet, a final audience for Theo to inspire. The minister stood at the head of the casket, his well-thumbed Bible clasped against his chest, eyes closed, waiting for the stragglers to arrive and quiet down.

"To everything there is a season, Lord," he began. "A time to live, a time to die. A time to sow, a time to reap. This young man's time was not yet ripe, O Lord, but he has been cruelly cut off by those who stand outside your light and your forgiveness. Work upon their hearts, O Lord, and show to them the error of their sinful ways."

"Amen."

"Our brother Theo Brown has journeyed through the valley of the shadow, trusting in your promise, Lord, and fearing no man. He has earned his just reward, and we entrust his soul to you. In Jesus's name, amen."

"Amen and hallelujah."

Was he afraid? Wilson wondered. When they took him? In the final moments, when he knew that there was no escape, that he would surely die?

Of course.

His son was—no, *had been*—a human being, after all. A hero in his way, perhaps, but subject to the same emotions, hopes and fears as other men. What must he finally have felt, before the storm of bullets swept his life away?

Brown had been called upon to view the body in the Chatham County Morgue. A friend of Theo's in the movement had already made the technical ID, but next of kin was still required, and as the only living relative, the father had been summoned to identify and claim his son.

One thousand years would not erase the image burned into his mind: a prostrate form on the surgeon's stainless-steel table, shrouded by a sheet, a name tag dangling from one stiff toe.

Beneath that bloodstained sheet lay the final horror. Brown did not know how many rounds the enemy had fired at Theo; any one of half a dozen wounds could have been immediately fatal, and the coroner had counted forty-seven bullet holes, excluding the exit wounds. It took a firing squad to do that kind of damage. There had been other injuries as well. The autopsy report suggested Theo had been beaten prior to death, the evidence of trauma visible in spite of forty-seven rounds from rifles, shotguns, pistols. Several mutilated bullets had been extracted from his body for comparison in case a suspect was arrested later.

The question of an open casket never entered Wilson's mind.

His plan did not involve police, grand juries or the vagaries of courtroom justice. Scanning once again for the familiar face he sought, Brown suffered yet another disappointment. These people were farmers, with a scattered few from the professions—lawyers, teachers, an accountant who had quit his city job to keep the union's books. Unless Brown missed his guess, there was not an assassin in the lot.

And at the moment, he had desperate need of such a man.

The minister was finished, and the members of his audience began to scatter, many pausing first to offer their condolences to Brown and shake his hand. Some men and women wept, but most were stoic in their grief, refusing to expose their sense of loss. Brown knew the feelings behind their reserve were sincere. A hardscrabble farmer learned early to hide his pain and disappointment, and in Chatham County, sudden funerals had become a way of life.

He stood beside the casket, waiting for the final mourners to depart. A pair of diggers had appeared from out of nowhere, and as Wilson watched, they dragged the artificial grass aside, revealing Theo's open grave. The soil was dark and rich. Determined to maintain his composure, Brown closed his mind to the thought of worms.

The coffin, with his son inside, was lowered with assistance from a pulley, straps like strips of fire hose cradling the box. Brown watched until it was out of sight. He turned away before the spade men went to work, their shovelfuls of dirt impacting on the coffin with a hollow, thumping sound. A muffled drum.

And thirty yards away, a solitary stranger stood and watched in the shadow of a vintage monument depicting angels on the wing. Brown felt his stomach lurch, the short hairs rising on the back of his neck . . . and then he knew.

As Brown approached the stranger, his legs felt numb, like the prosthetic foot he wore. Mirrored sunglasses hid the white man's eyes, and there was nothing in the least familiar about his face, but there was something in his stance, his military bearing. Yes.

"Thank God you've come," Brown said, and gripped the tall man's outstretched hand.

"Let's take a walk," Mack Bolan said.

2

They walked together through Mount Holly, past the silent stones and monuments, while Bolan studied his companion. Wilson Brown was massive, six-foot-five and so broad across the chest and shoulders that his jacket seemed in danger of ripping at the seams. The passage of time had dusted his close-cropped hair with gray, but it made him look distinguished rather than old. The only sure sign of aging was revealed in Wilson's weary eyes. He hardly limped at all, despite the artificial foot he had worn since Vietnam.

Brown had been a young lieutenant in the U.S. Army during Bolan's maiden tour of Southeast Asia. They had hit it off all right, despite the differences in race and rank that lay between them, differences other men might not have overcome. They had been comrades in a higher calling: Bolan fresh from frontier duty in Korea, looking forward to a future as an officer and "lifer" in the military, Brown recently sidelined from a promising career in professional football. They had agreed intuitively on the need to stand and fight in Vietnam, despite the odds, despite the storm of criticism gathering at home. It was not their destiny, however, to stand and fight together. Bolan had been ordered up for duty on the DMZ, while Brown remained with his command, a recon unit fighting Charlie near Song Lai. Two months after they parted company, a claymore mine took Wilson's foot above the ankle, simultaneously shattering his alternative careers in football and the military.

"I was looking for the face you wore in France," Brown said when they had walked for several moments in reflective silence.

"Had to switch," the soldier told him, smiling. "That one had a bull's-eye painted on the forehead."

"I heard that."

"All things considered, I got lucky."

"Hey, don't look a gift horse in the mouth. I think you're getting younger."

"Doesn't feel that way."

"Forget about the feelings, man. They'll nail you every time."

Bolan tried another tack. "I didn't know you were a friend of Mr. Justice."

"I've been helping him with little things from time to time since Monaco. I guess you might say I was paying dues. Anyway, I'm out here now, with no place else to turn."

Leonard Justice was a federal code name, and the man behind its cover was another Bolan ally, Leo Turrin. After years of serving as an undercover agent in the Mafia, the gutsy Turrin had ascended to a desk in Washington, coordinating many of Hal Brognola's anticrime and antiterrorist campaigns. It had been a surprise, indeed, to hear a plea for help by Wilson Brown from Turrin's lips.

In the wake of Nam and half a dozen VA hospitals, where doctors had tried in vain to put his life back on its tracks, the former football lineman had fallen back on self-pity and a quest for easy cash. He had found the latter as a numbers runner—later banker—for the late Arnesto Castiglione, Mafia boss of the Eastern Seaboard. In those days, "Arnie Farmer" had been a moving force behind the outfit's hunt for Mack Bolan as they sought to repay in spades the damage the one-man army had inflicted on their operation in Pittsfield, Southern California, Arizona and Miami. Learning that the black he took for granted was an old acquaintance of the Executioner, Castiglione had offered Wilson Brown a deal: one half of all the money then on Bolan's head if he would plant a Judas kiss upon the soldier's cheeks. Their paths had crossed in Monaco, where Brown rediscovered pride and his priorities in time to help the warrior wriggle through a sticky ambush. Bolan had last seen Wilson Brown bobbing in the surf beside a pier, a firefight raging overhead, and he had wished the big man well. There had been rumbles later about the former lineman "going straight," enlisting as a football talent scout and putting his experience to work for others, but there had been no suggestion of a double life involving covert work for Justice.

One more small surprise in a world of surprises, and Bolan had long ago learned to take nothing for granted. The only thing a warrior at the front could properly expect was the unexpected.

"I'm sorry about your son, Lieutenant."

"Not your fault." The dark man managed to approximate a smile. "And you can drop the rank, okay? I've been out of uniform longer than most lifers have been in."

"Okay."

"How much did Justice tell you?"

"Bits and pieces."

"Mmm. I guess I'd better fill you in." They paused beneath the cover of a weeping willow. The few remaining cars and mourners from the funeral cortege were more than a hundred yards away. "You know that Theo was a union man, with NFU?"

"I heard."

The National Farmers' Union was a new—and some said radical—development on the labor scene. From what he knew of Wilson's son, the Executioner was not surprised that Theo had emerged to lead the fledgling group in Arkansas.

"I don't know what you've heard about the NFU. There's lots of bullshit circulating, all about so-called Red involvement, how the union is a front for civil rights groups, how the organizers advocate a socialized economy. I checked it out when Theo got involved, and most of what you hear is crap. The propaganda mills are working overtime, like in the sixties with those sex-and-segregation stories. You remember?"

"Vaguely."

"Hell, you ain't *that* young."

The soldier grinned. "You're right."

"Okay. So, once I put my mind to rest that Theo wasn't tying up with Communists and whatnot, I got interested in running down the propaganda to its source. It took a while, with all the bullshit cover names they use these days, but eventually everything led me back to Freedom Press, a local publisher in Little Rock."

"Go on."

"I'll let you have three guesses who owns Freedom Press, and the first two don't count."

"I give up."

"Jerome Freeman."

"The Aryan Vanguard? *That* Freeman?"

Brown nodded. "You know him?"

"I've heard some. He's new on the scene."

"New and *big*. What I hear, since he merged with the Knights he's the number one redneck around, with a nationwide network behind him. In public he sounds like Bill Buckley, with traces of old vintage Wallace for flavor. In private, away from the press, he makes Hitler sound liberal."

"Who are the Knights?" Bolan asked.

"A new Klan splinter group," Brown replied. "They call themselves the Teutonic Knights of the Ku Klux Klan, but I haven't seen a German in the bunch. The self-proclaimed Grand Wizard is a peckerwood named Mason Ritter. He's done time in Alabama for possession of explosives with intent, and now he's Freeman's shadow. You can't get a razor blade between the Vanguard and the Knights these days."

"A publisher needs backing."

"Freeman's got it, don't you worry. Bankers, landlords, anybody with a stake in keeping family farmers down or driving them completely off the land. The union is a nightmare come to life for all of them."

"Was Theo making headway?"

"Some. It's hard, you know. Besides the racial thing, so many of the locals have been beaten down financially they don't know who to trust. Last time a so-called organizer worked the area, he ripped off the farmers for close to thirty thousand bucks in dues and fees before he disappeared. They've got long memories around these parts.''

"I've heard. Some folks are waiting for a second opinion on the Civil War.''

"It's getting better,'' Brown confided. "Chatham County's not the promised land, but it could be a whole lot worse.''

"You make the Vanguard or the Knights for Theo's murder, Wils?''

"Who else?''

"Well, if the heavy money is against the union, they'd have access to professionals.''

Brown shook his head. "It's Freeman's game. If he and Ritter haven't got the in-house talent, they recruit from other groups around the country.''

"You've been doing homework.''

"Keeps me off the streets, I guess. Won't say it keeps me out of trouble, though.''

"What have you got?''

"There's nothing I could take to court. That's why I made the call.''

"I'm listening.''

"Since Theo started working for the NFU eighteen months ago, there've been twenty-seven major incidents of violence in the area. We're talking bombings, arson, beatings. Back in January, someone snatched the union's lawyer from his office, drove him out of town and shoved a broomstick where the sun don't shine. Oh, yeah—they drove nails through it first.''

"That's grim.''

"That's just for openers. A few weeks later, drive-by shooters crippled Theo's second-in-command. Another union organizer disappeared in April. Hunters found his car, burned out, a couple of miles from town. He's down as missing and presumed dead.''

"So Theo knew the risks involved.''

"Hell, yes, he knew! *I* knew, and like a damned fool I ignored it. Told him I was proud of him. Encouraged him to lay it on the line for people that I never even met before last week.''

''You're not responsible.''

''Hell, no. I'm irresponsible. It's easy to be reckless from the sidelines, when you're safe.''

''That's not your style.''

''Oh, no? I didn't used to think so, either, but I've had it on my mind.''

Bolan changed the subject. ''These other incidents. I take it they didn't worry Theo?''

''Not enough to scare him off. He had his mother's stubborn streak when he believed in what he had to do. The calls and letters never fazed him. Oh, he took precautions when he could, but he refused to hire a bodyguard because the other members of the union didn't have the luxury. If anybody wanted Theo Brown, he meant to meet them on his own. But it didn't work.''

''Was he involved with anything specific, just before?''

''We weren't in touch a lot, the past few weeks. I had my scouting, and the sideline out of Wonderland. I try to tell myself there's nothing I could have done.''

''It's true.''

''Maybe, but I'm not buying it.'' The man shook his head. ''To hell with that. He *was* on something special, right before…before he died. A couple of his people in the NFU tell me Theo had a pigeon lined up in the Vanguard. Someone who was sick of Freeman and his people, primed to split, but Theo talked him into staying on, reporting back on what was going on. He had in mind to build a case against the Vanguard and the Knights for some of the outrageous shit that they've been laying down in Chatham the past few months. I'm told he had a file damn near completed. He was going to deliver it to someone—locals, FBI, I can't be sure.''

''What happened to the file?''

''The night the bastards took him, someone turned the union office upside down, made off with all the papers they could carry, trashed the rest. If Theo had a case, it died the same time he did.''

Bolan scanned the silent rows of stones and crosses. Cemeteries were the same throughout the world, regardless of differences in religious symbolism. Hopes and dreams were buried there, along with the remains of human beings. Visions of an afterlife could mitigate the pain of loss, but they could never wipe it out completely.

"What's the story with police?" he asked.

Brown shrugged. "The sheriff is a 'good ol' boy.' You know the type? He's not a Kluxer that I know of, and the chances are he wouldn't take a bribe, but he respects the 'decent citizens' of Chatham County, and he's not about to issue warrants on the unsupported word of hardscrabble farmers. His investigators have been 'looking into' the harassment, bombings, all of that, but so far all they've got is questions."

"And the FBI?"

"They take our calls and talk to witnesses, they keep an eye on Freeman and the Klan. But things are different from the old days. Congress keeps a sharp eye on surveillance, and the last I heard, the Bureau didn't have a man inside the Vanguard or the Knights. I guess they follow Freeman when he travels, make notes on his speeches, all of that. But no one ever said he pulled the trigger personally. He's the brains, if you can call it that."

"Who pays the tab?"

"Specifically?"

"If possible."

"The Southern Bankers' Conference has a solid interest in the farm recession hereabouts. They cut their major deals with big agribusiness interests, but they also hold the mortgages on damn near every farm in Arkansas and six or seven other states. If they foreclose on small-time operators, turn around and sell the land to larger clients . . . well, they win both ways."

"This conference have a chairman?"

"Natch. They're based in Georgia, but the local honcho is a fat cat by the name of Andrews, Michael Andrews, also out of Little Rock."

"Connections with the Vanguard or the Knights?"

Brown shrugged again. "I figure, but I can't say for sure. Whatever proof my boy had disappeared the night he died."

"Okay. It's obvious we need a man inside."

"I guess, but Theo never passed his contact's name around."

"That's not exactly what I had in mind."

"Well, what . . . oh, hell, it figures."

"Any other thoughts?"

"Unfortunately, no."

"All right, then."

"Listen, Sarge, the tab on this one's high already. I don't want to raise the ante."

"Sometimes that's the only way to play the game."

"I didn't make that call to find myself another martyr, understand?"

"I know that, Wils."

"I want the killers punished—hell, I want the bastards *dead*—but I'm not asking anybody else to put their future on the line."

"You didn't have to ask. Besides, who's got a future?"

"Jesus."

"Listen, Wils...I never met your son, but everything I've heard about him tells me he believed in living large."

The former lineman thought about it for a moment, staring into space. When he turned to Bolan once again, his eyes were glistening.

"I'd say so, yeah."

"All right. Then he deserves a monument."

"What do you have in mind?"

"Oh, I don't know. A bonfire, maybe."

"Could we fix that up to be a funeral pyre?"

"You read my mind."

"I don't know how to say this, man. When I put through that call . . . I was afraid you wouldn't come."

"I didn't hear that, guy."

"Well, hear it, then. I'm trying to apologize."

"Unnecessary."

"Don't tell me. I know what's necessary."

"You've been carrying some weight around that isn't yours," the soldier counseled. "Might be time for you to lay it down."

"Not yet. I'll think about it when we're finished."

Silence hung between them for a moment, each man dealing with his private thoughts. When Wilson spoke again, his voice was firm and resolute.

"What can I do to help?"

"Stay hard. Watch your back and take it easy. I'm not here to make a martyr, either."

"I won't knuckle under to these sons of bitches."

"No one asked you to. That doesn't mean you have to meet them in an alley after midnight."

"Yeah, I hear you."

"Fine. I've got some calls to make, and then I need to have a look around. Might be I'll find myself some friends among the local Aryans."

"I hope you've had your shots."

The soldier's smile was grim.

"Not yet," he said. "Not yet."

3

Although he had not shared the fact with Wilson Brown, Mack Bolan was, indeed, familiar with the Aryan Vanguard. He had been briefed on the telephone by Leo Turrin, but prior to that call the Executioner had already been a killing-close acquaintance of the Vanguard's parent organization, the so-called Aryan Brotherhood.

Founded in the late seventies by "survivalist" Gerry Axelrod, the Brotherhood had offered the embattled farmers of America assorted scapegoats, in the form of immigrants, minorities, the "Jewish bankers" who "control America today." Ironically, the neofascist group had been a sort of twisted ancestor of Theo Brown's National Farmers' Union. Both had cast their nets among the people of the land, although the Brotherhood had been more discriminating in its final choice of members. Only whites had been welcomed to the fold, and once inside the racist clique they had been bombarded with the sort of propaganda that historians would recognize at once as originating in Hitler's Germany. Inflation and foreclosures were said to be the work of Communists and Jews. America was said to be undermined by enemies within, most often recognizable by pigmentation. The Brotherhood's response to the threat lay in endless angry talk about the need for a revolt against the government in power, and the collecting of weapons in preparation for the revolt. Silent revolution would bring back an approximation of the "good old days" to America, when men were men and blacks were free to use the service entrance.

If the vaunted revolution seemed a trifle slow in coming, few among the Brotherhood would have considered blaming Gerry Axelrod. A handful of his aides had been conscious of the business he operated on the side, supplying arms to terrorists of various persuasions, dipping greedy fingers in the cocaine traffic, handling murder contracts. The superpatriot had come to Bolan's notice while the Executioner was stalking a Soviet-backed international terrorist, Julio Ramirez—a.k.a. "The Raven." Their paths had crossed in Switzerland, within the very shadow of the Matterhorn. By a fluke, Axelrod had managed to escape the cleansing fire that finally consumed Ramirez and his lethal look-alikes. He had not been heard from since, and of late Bolan had allowed himself to hope that tardy justice might have run its course. Whether through a double cross within the convoluted world of arms and drugs, a bungled border crossing or a clash with greedy "friends," all that mattered was the result, and Axelrod's protracted absence from the scene had given Bolan cause for optimism.

With his disappearance and public speculation on the possibility of his death, the Brotherhood had withered on the vine. No sooner had it been laid to rest, however, than a new association had sprung to life and taken its place, absorbing treasury and membership, producing leaflets similar—if not identical—to flyers circulated by the Brotherhood. For all intents and purposes, the Aryan Vanguard was Axelrod's Brotherhood reborn, more strident now, reputedly more prone to sudden, unexpected violence. A scattering of incidents throughout the South and in the Rocky Mountain states had sounded new alarms with law enforcement, and investigations were proceeding, undercover agents butting heads against the Vanguard's tight security procedures.

It came as no surprise to Bolan that the Vanguard were flirting openly with members of the Ku Klux Klan. There had been Klansmen in the Brotherhood, attracted by its litany of hate, and the association of the KKK with native Nazis was nothing new or startling. The Klan had marched with German Bundists during World War Two, and several of its members had done time on charges of sedition. Later, in the violent sixties, hooded knights had cast their seedy lot with various factions of the fascist fringe, including Rockwell's Nazi party. The result had been more hate, more blood, more time in jail.

Bolan had no solid information on the new Teutonic Knights, but from appearances they fit the pattern of the countless factions that had cut themselves a slice of bigot pie across the past four decades. Unlike their Reconstruction ancestor or the monolithic "Empire" of the 1920s, modern Klans appeared to spend as much time quarreling among themselves, competing for the income of their members, as they did in fighting for "white rights." Many self-proclaimed Klan leaders proved, on close examination, to be felons, deviates and swindlers, scrambling for a buck, milking loyal believers in the rank and file and getting off on their cherished illusion of superiority and power. At the grass-root level, the recruitment of unstable personalities perpetuated violence, racking up a cost in lives and human suffering that no financial analyst could ever quantify.

Through the early 1970s, FBI surveillance had been effective in curbing Klan violence, but tightened Congressional oversight and the complaints of civil liberties groups had weakened law enforcement to the point where terrorists were free, for the most part, to do their work in private. Taps and bugs were virtually nonexistent now, except in cases dealing with the Mafia or foreign spies. Racist groups had learned to screen their applicants for membership and weed out probable informers. Infiltration, therefore, would be a problem, but Mack Bolan never drew the easy jobs. And if police and the FBI were handcuffed by their rules and regulations, there were still assorted avenues open to the Executioner.

He placed the call, long-distance, from the pay phone at a local self-service station.

"Justice."

"That's exactly what I need."

"Hey, bud . . . I trust this line's secure?"

"It's public, but I have no reason to believe it's leaky."

"Fair enough. What can I do you for?"

He smiled at Leo Turrin's ever-present sense of humor. More than a decade serving undercover in the syndicate, and Leo had come out clean, to join the covert war on crime and terrorism under Hal Brognola. In the years that Bolan and Turrin had known each other, through the worst of it, Bolan thought he could count the little *paesan*'s truly solemn moments on the fingers of one hand, with a few left over. Somehow, Turrin kept it all together, thriving on a job that would have broken other men and sent them looking for a desk to ride until retirement.

"I need more on Freeman, Mason Ritter, the Teutonic Knights."

"Okay. It won't take long, because we haven't got that much." A muffled clacking, as the little Fed keyed up a file on his computer terminal. "Freeman, Jerome. No middle name. Born 1/13/47, in St. Louis, Missouri. He says. There's no record on file. Four years in the Marines, with a tour in Nam, he says. Again, no record."

"I assume that someone's looking into that?"

"We're looking, sure, but there's nothing to see. Unfortunately, it's no crime to impersonate a veteran, unless you're falsely claiming benefits. Which Freeman isn't, by the way. We figure he just likes the military aura. Helps him sell himself these days."

"Go on."

"Where was I?" Turrin hesitated, found his place again. "All right, I've got it. IRS reports that income taxes have been paid by Freeman for the past seven years. Beyond that, they can't say, but he lists his occupation as public relations, self-employed. Social Security lists him as paid up to date, with a card issued twelve years ago. We have no prints on file, nothing with NCIC or the FBI. Nothing, in short, worth a damn."

"If we pass on the taxes for now, what's the first public record of Freeman's appearance?"

"Let's see...it's a bit hard to say, but our definite sightings go back eighteen months, give or take. Around the time the Vanguard organized."

"Around the time that Gerry Axelrod went missing in Zermatt?"

"It's close. There was an interval, of course. You looking at connections?"

"I'm just looking," Bolan told his friend. "Describe the führer for me, will you?"

"Six foot two, blond hair and beard, athletic-looking. Widowed, so he says, although there doesn't seem to be a record of the marriage or his dear departed."

"Girlfriends?"

"Nothing steady. Our surveillance is restricted, as you know. We haven't got the PC necessary for a tap, and so far no one in the Vanguard seems inclined to spill their guts."

"What word on Theo Brown's inside connection?"

"Zip. I couldn't say there's no such animal, but we've got nothing to suggest a leak."

"I'm interested in Mason Ritter, Leo."

"The Teutonic Knights? We've got a little better information there. The FBI maintains a vested interest in the Klans, but this one's relatively new."

"Would that be new, as in approximately eighteen months?"

"You guessed it, pal. Within a month or so of Freeman firing up the Vanguard, Ritter had his Knights in gear. Nobody here is buying a coincidence."

"I wouldn't, either. What's the scoop on Ritter?"

"He's a hard case, but at least he's got a past that we can work with." Leo started reading from the Klansman's file. "Arrested in Atlanta, August 1969, assault and battery. He decked a sixty-year-old minister who tried to buy a sandwich in a downtown coffee shop."

"The minister was black?"

"You guessed it. Ritter paid a hundred-dollar fine and walked. He's been picked up on weapons charges half a dozen times in Georgia, Alabama, once in Indiana. He's a traveler, I guess. Convicted in September 1982 for the attempted bombing of a synagogue in Birmingham. He drew five years for that and served a little over two. Paroled to Arkansas on the condition that he stay away from politics and racist groups. He finished off his time last year and organized the Knights to celebrate."

"A prince."

"I had another term in mind."

"He's tight with Freeman, though?"

"Like shit and flies. There's no official link between the Vanguard and the Knights, as far as we can tell, but they've got overlapping membership, they meet together twice a month for rallies, both groups run their propaganda out of Freedom Press in Little Rock. Their offices are half a mile apart, but we believe that's basically for show. If you find Freeman, Ritter won't be far away."

"That's what I'm counting on. What do you know about the Vanguard's backers?"

"We're a little shaky there. No reason for a judge to order banking records opened yet, so we're confined to hearsay, with a dash of observation."

"What about the Southern Bankers' Conference?"

"Bingo! You've been doing homework, guy. A couple of their honchos have been seen with Freeman, social like but if you think they're talking baseball averages, I've got some lakefront property I'd like to sell."

"What goes with Michael Andrews?"

"Anything, and nothing," Leo answered. "He's the mouthpiece for the conference there in Arkansas. Statistically he's number four in order of succession to the chairmanship, but two of those ahead of him are in their seventies, with one foot in the grave and one on a banana peel. A miracle or two could put him at the helm inside a year."

"What kind of weight would he be carrying?"

"That's difficult to say. The conference is regional, of course, but you can buy a lot of juleps with the yearly net."

"They're heavy into agribusiness?"

"Bet your life, but that's not half of it. There's light and heavy industry, recording studios—including most of Nashville, by the way—and half a dozen other areas, from chemicals and oil to shipping. If it operates in Dixie, chances are the SBC has interests in the deal. A bold new farmers' union definitely would not make the bankers' day."

"Agreed. But it's a giant step from being pissed to paying terrorists and hit men."

"Granted. No one here believes the conference as a whole is compromised. Selected members have been linked to Freeman and the Vanguard—Andrews among them, by the way—but others wouldn't let the bastard have the time of day."

"What kind of leverage does that give us?"

"Well, it's touchy. Proof of Andrews's link with Freeman could produce some major heat inside the conference, but you never know who might get burned. If Justice wound up tied to the exposure, there'd be hell to pay."

"All right, forget it. I've got other plans for Freeman and the Vanguard."

"I was waiting for that."

"Can you build me a jacket?"

"Of course, within reason."

"Of course. What I need is a background like Ritter's . . . or worse, if you can. Make it rabid, but leave in the greed."

"Prison time?" Leo asked, taking notes.

"Might as well. Make it federal, and move it out west. I don't want any cellmates to show up on *This Is Your Life*."

"We can swing it, I think. There's an offshoot of Rockwell's old bunch in L.A. that the Bureau keeps tabs on. They're mostly informants these days, taking notes on one another, with two or three head cases thrown in for flavor. They'll cover your action if someone inquires, and I'll rig something up in the files."

They discussed Bolan's cover in detail, agreeing on fine points and working the bugs out. Before they were finished, the soldier was certain his legend would stand up to a casual scrutiny, possibly even to in-depth feelers. If he had to stay under too long, though, there were risks he could not anticipate, could not provide for until they arose. Every time he went under, the risks were unique, with the bottom line always the same. Life or death.

He was counting on speed, but he could not predict what could happen—assuming in the first place, that he got past the Vanguard's security screens. It would not be easy, but Bolan was skilled at role camouflage, with years of experience under his belt in presenting an image for others to swallow. In Nam, in his war with the Mafia, during his later campaigns against terrorists, Bolan had proved that skilled men and women, professional killers, could be deceived by appropriate means. The eyes were inclined to observe what the mind had been trained to expect, and Bolan had sharpened his skills to a fine cutting edge in the course of his war without end.

"Listen, Sarge . . ." Leo's voice sounded distant, distracted. "I know there's a personal angle on this, but be careful, okay? We've got martyrs we haven't used yet, and I don't need another one."

"Martyrdom isn't my style."

"Pull the other one, will you? I know how you live: on the edge, all the way."

"It's a living," the warrior replied.

"Maybe so, but it could be the other thing, too."

"Not to worry."

"Who, me? Hell, I grow these gray hairs for a hobby, you know that."

"Okay."

"Once you're in there, I can't do a whole lot to help you, all right? Hal would choke if he knew you were pulling this."

"Maybe we shouldn't disturb him."

"Oh, sure. I can hear it all now. 'By the way, Hal, I don't know how to break this to you, but . . .' He'd have my butt, I guarantee you that."

"I'll leave it up to your discretion then."

"Terrific. Dump it all on little Lenny Justice."

"Hey, you knew it was a dirty job—"

"Before I took it. Yeah, I know. So spare me, will you?"

"Roger."

"Listen, guy... I know it goes against the grain and all, but if you wouldn't mind too much, a little caution in the clinches, okay?"

"My pleasure."

"Bullshit. If you need me, I'll be standing by to help you all I can. Which won't be much."

"I'll see you, Leo."

"Yeah. I hope so."

Bolan cradled the receiver, backtracked to his rented Chevrolet. Little Rock was an easy thirty miles away, and he was in a hurry now. He had so much to do.

Like infiltrating Freeman's Vanguard, the Teutonic Knights or both. Establishing a contact in the upper echelons as soon as possible. Investigating Michael Andrews on the side, and running down connections between the Southern Bankers' Conference and the racist underground in Little Rock and Chatham County.

In the process, he would have to think a bit about the missing Gerry Axelrod, whose fallen empire had become such fertile soil for hate and violence. If the missing fascist's heir was following in his footsteps, there would doubtless be a price tag on the mayhem the farmers' union had experienced. Proving that, with enough evidence to lay before the conference board, was half of Bolan's present battle. Failing that, it might not be enough to simply ice the local führer and his second-in-command. While there was money to be made from bigotry, another greedy redneck would be standing by to fill the leader's empty shoes, and yet another after that.

This time, it might not be enough to simply cut off the serpent's head, as in other antiterrorist campaigns. The Executioner might be required to run his adversaries down, destroy them root and branch, before their special brand of poison could take root, give rise to twisted growths of hatred, inhumanity and bloodshed.

First, however, Bolan had to win the confidence of savages, become accepted as a member of the fold.

It should be simple.

Just like falling in an open grave.

4

It was a thirty-minute drive from Parrish to Little Rock, and Bolan held the rented Chevy at a steady sixty miles an hour as he crossed the line from Chatham County, homing on the capital. He kept an eye out for highway patrolmen in the rearview mirror, letting his mind free-float, drifting from one aspect of his latest campaign to the next, randomly selecting problems for consideration, either solving them or shelving them for later and moving on.

It was the kind of dusk that falls only in Dixie: sultry, sullen, painting angry bruise-tones on the sky. Full dark within another hour. He had just time enough to reach his destination, settle in and turn himself into a piece of furniture before the nightly rituals began.

He had spent the early afternoon touring Parrish, memorizing streets and landmarks, charting country roads that led away from town through gently rolling hills and swampy flats. When he was finished, Bolan felt that he could navigate the town and the surrounding countryside by night or day, without a map or guide. If it became urgent to move from A to B without delay, he had no fear of driving into dead-end alleys, getting lost on shortcuts leading nowhere. He did not know the area like a native, by any means, but well enough.

That done, he had consulted Wilson Brown again, this time by telephone. The ex-lieutenant and onetime football pro had been surprised to hear from him again so soon, but he had been accommodating, answering the soldier's questions when he could, referring Bolan to another likely source when he couldn't. By the time he said goodbye to Brown,

Bolan knew the name and address of a hangout in Little Rock favored by the rougher members of the Vanguard and the Teutonic Knights. He also knew the business addresses of both organizations, along with the home addresses of their leaders. The information ought to be enough. For now.

His destination was a down-and-dirty honky-tonk establishment that had been christened the Blackboard, for reasons no one living could remember. Bolan thought a visit might prove educational, and if he played his meager cards correctly it might open up an avenue of entry to the Vanguard, the Teutonic Knights or both.

The latter phase of Bolan's plan might prove a little sticky in the clinches, so to smooth the way, he had enlisted Wilson Brown. The big man had heard him out and had agreed to help without hesitation, despite the glaring risks.

"We'll be there," Wilson had promised, and the soldier had never doubted for an instant that the hulking pro would keep his word. He would be there on schedule, ready for the worst, and he would do his part because it mattered to him. The pursuit of justice in the murder of his son would not allow the man to do a job halfway. It would be all or nothing, damn the cost. Bolan thought the trick might be to make him disengage once battle had been joined. He hoped Brown would not forget himself and turn a manufactured incident into a holy war before the time was ripe.

In Little Rock he found the Blackboard easily. He made a drive-by, checking out the neighborhood, the parking lot and access from the rear. He planned no major operations at the bar, but he had not survived this long, against the odds, by leaving anything to chance.

He parked the Chevrolet and locked it, scanned the darkened parking lot before sauntering toward the bar. The suit he had worn to the funeral had been replaced by denim jeans and work shirt, heavy boots with steel-capped toes. He was unarmed, his paramilitary hardware locked in the rental's trunk, away from prying eyes and sticky fingers.

The interior of the saloon was loud and smoky. Country and western music twanged from a jukebox in the corner, Johnny Paycheck mourning love gone wrong. A few states farther west, the Blackboard would have been a cowboy bar, but here in Arkansas it drew the patronage of cabbies and mechanics, factory workers and hardscrabble farmers. The spotty crowd was mostly male and uniformly white, the scattered females sporting heavy makeup and hairdos five or ten years out of style.

You did not need a scorecard to identify the players in the Blackboard. The beefy barman wore a vest that had been fashioned from the Stars and Bars, the battle flag of the Confederacy, and bumper stickers bearing pointed messages were plastered on the wall behind the bar. Support Your Local Police; Get U.S. Out of the UN; Sure, I'll Give up My Gun...When They Pry My Cold, Dead Fingers from the Grips; Kill 'Em All, and Let God Sort 'Em Out. A sticker fastened to the register proclaimed: I Am a Secret Member of the KKK. Mounted on a plaque above the rows of whiskey bottles, the rubber likeness of a black man's head stared down with marble eyes at the patrons of the bar. The plaque bore an inscription, but Bolan had to squint to make it out: A Nigger Tried, A Nigger Died.

Tried what? the soldier wondered. Voting? Drinking at the Blackboard? Organizing farmers to resist a land grab by the big conglomerates? It was not worth his time to try to penetrate the minds that had devised the grinning "trophy." Later, if those sick minds needed airing out, he had the tools in hand...or rather, in his car. For now, he was a mere outsider, studying the layout, trying to belong.

He ordered beer and took it to a table near the door, examining his fellow patrons as he put the suds away. Gruff men with callused hands washed none too recently, their names stitched on the breasts of uniforms and coveralls. At the Blackboard short hair was definitely in, as was hair oil, slick and shiny. The skin of many of the drinkers had been darkened by prolonged exposure to the sun until their pigment fairly matched the dark complexion of the trophy on the wall. Strong forearms, here and there exposed by rolled-up sleeves, were thick with hair and decorated with tattoos.

He drank and eavesdropped on the conversation of his nearest neighbors, seated at the bar. They aired complaints about their jobs, told jokes involving sex and race.

Bolan drained his beer and flagged the barmaid for another, watching her retreat in the direction of the bar. He had a firm fix on the label of her tight designer jeans when another supple body intervened and blocked his field of vision.

"Buy you a drink, stranger?"

Tracking upward from curvaceous hips, lingering appreciatively on a well-filled tank top, Bolan settled on a pretty face that would have benefited from removal of half its makeup. Honey-colored hair had been trimmed to shoulder length, and framed the smiling face with what appeared to be natural curls.

"I think that's supposed to be my line," he replied.

"Well, fine. I thought you'd never ask."

The shapely new arrival settled in an empty chair at Bolan's table, making certain that her knee made contact with his own in the process.

"I'm Vicky. Who are you?"

"I'm Mike. Mike Bowers."

Bolan paid the barmaid for his beer when she returned and ordered a Scotch and soda for the lady. He had not been looking for companionship, but if the opportunity arose to gather information on his quarry, he could not afford to turn away.

"I haven't seen you here before," she said. "I would have noticed."

"I just got in town this afternoon," he told her.

"Transfer?"

"Mmm?"

"Your job?"

He shook his head. "No job. I'm looking, but it isn't an emergency. Not yet."

"You don't look like a family man to me."

"You've got good eyes."

"I don't waste time on family men."

"Me neither."

Vicky laughed at that and sipped her drink, pronounced it satisfactory. "They water down the whiskey, lots of times. I guess they're feeling generous tonight."

"My lucky day."

"Could be."

He glanced around the smoky room. "You come here often?"

"Often as I can. Sometimes I get burned out on nothing but the same old faces, if you follow me."

"I know exactly what you mean."

"I'll bet you do, at that."

He nodded toward the rubber trophy on the wall. "Another satisfied customer?"

Vicky's smile turned brittle. "Only coon you'll ever see in here's the rubber kind. The Blackboard's strictly out of bounds to shines. You got a problem with that?"

"I wouldn't have it any other way."

"All right. I knew we'd get on fine."

"Fact is," he told her, "I've been hearing tales about the Blackboard."

"How you spelling that?"

He smiled. "I'm told this is the place to make connections if a man is interested in standing for his race."

Vicky's smile slipped a notch. "That's not for me to say."

"I was told to ask for Mason Ritter."

"You one of those Kluxers?"

"Let's just say I'm shopping."

"Mason isn't here tonight. Not yet, anyway. If it's night-riding you're interested in, I might be able to help you out."

"That so?"

"I'm always in the market for a wizard under the sheets."

"That's pretty near the best offer I've had all day."

"Pretty near?" She pretended to pout as he ordered more drinks. "Now you're making me jealous."

"No call."

"It's too noisy in here. Why don't you and me go for a ride?"

"In a bit," Bolan said, stalling. "No point rushing things."

"Damn, you're a strange one."

"How's that?"

"Most fellows would've had me in the parking lot by now, or tried to, anyway. You're not as sudden."

"Were you going somewhere?"

"Might."

"Then I'll doubtless hate myself in the morning for missing my chance."

"Smooth talk."

"I'm trying."

"You've had practice. I can tell."

"Not lately."

"Oh? Why's that?"

"I've been away."

"Like out of state or something?"

"Something."

"Somewhere without girls?"

"I didn't notice any."

Vicky frowned. "Have you been doing time?"

"Let's just say I was a prisoner of conscience."

"What the hell is that supposed to mean?"

"My conscience didn't bother me when others thought it should have."

She laughed. "That's pretty good." She sobered, adding, "I don't have a thing against a fellow who's done time, as long as he comes out the same way he went in. You follow? I mean, sometimes boys who go in feeling macho come out acting sweet, you know?"

"I haven't got a sweet bone in my body," he assured her.

"I believe that I could find one if I tried."

"That sounds like fun."

"Your place or mine?"

Before he had a chance to answer, angry voices sounded from the corner near the jukebox. Bolan turned in time to see two patrons squaring off, fists raised. The taller of the two was red in the face from drink or anger or both, and weaving on his feet. His shorter adversary had a cooler head, or maybe just a better tolerance for alcohol; before the burly barkeep made his way across the room, the little guy had landed half a dozen blows that left his opposition stretched out on the floor, blood streaming from his nose.

The barman waved a sawed-off pool cue in the winner's face and ordered him outside. Two spectators from ringside scooped up the loser and half carried, half dragged him in the direction of the door.

"Nice crowd."

"You meet a better class of gents inside the walls?"

"Not necessarily."

"What were you in for, anyway?"

"You sure you want to know?"

"I'm asking."

"Well, let's say I had a difference of opinion with some fellows of the African persuasion. They were looking for a fight, and I was handy."

"So you beat them up?"

"I shot them."

"Shot them?"

"Three. I would've got the fourth, but he was clocking better time then Jesse Owens."

"Who?"

"Forget it."

"Did you kill them?"

Bolan shook his head. "My aim was off. One of them limps a bit these days; another sings soprano."

"Jesus."

"Best I recollect, he wasn't there."

"I don't know how to take you, mister."

"Waiting for suggestions?"

"You've got business here, remember?"

"I remember."

"Listen, I don't like to drink and run, but if you wrap it up by closing time..." Vicky flicked a glance in the direction of the entrance as she started to get up, froze halfway out of her chair and settled back again. "Well, speak of the devil."

A hard-looking middle-aged man with a crew cut had entered the bar, trailed by two younger men in their twenties. They settled on bar stools at one end, away from the door.

"Mason Ritter?"

"And friends."

"He looks pissed."

"That's his normal expression. I hear that he smiles when he's out with the wrecking crew doing his thing, but you sure couldn't prove it by me."

"What's the wrecking crew?"

"Never you mind."

Bolan glanced at his watch: 8:14.

"Well, I guess there's no time like the present."

"Good luck, man. You'll need it."

"I make my own luck."

Bolan knocked back the last of his beer, took his time about rising. If Brown was on time, he should be in the parking lot now. He might well have observed Ritter's arrival.

Bolan was halfway to the bar when he heard the door creak open. A hush fell on the patrons of the Blackboard. Turning, Bolan watched as Wilson Brown approached the bar. Three other large black men followed him in single file.

"Niggers!" someone whispered, pointing out the obvious to anyone who might be blind as well as drunk.

Behind the warrior, Mason Ritter set his rum and Coke down with force enough to spray the bar. His bodyguards were on their feet before the wizard rose, but Bolan had a stake in getting there before the Klansmen could connect.

"Say, boy!" he called to Wilson Brown, eliciting a glare of pure contempt. "You lost, or what?"

"I'm thirsty," Brown replied, dismissing him. "Go on and mind your business."

"We're fresh out of everything," the barman drawled, evoking nervous chuckles from the regulars.

"That bottle looks right full to me," Brown answered, pointing toward a fifth of Seagram's on the shelf behind the bar. "They all look full."

"That's what they call an optical illusion," Bolan sneered, moving to intercept Brown, placing himself between Brown and the bar. "Sometimes it seems like what you see's not what you get."

"We came in here to have a drink, not look for trouble."

"Well, I'd say you can't have one without the other, boy."

Brown glanced across his shoulder toward the barman. "Law says if you're open to the public you serve *everybody*."

"Law?" the Executioner cut in. "Which law is that?"

"The Constitution. Ever heard of it?"

"Not recently."

He had the rednecks now. A snicker of appreciation ran around the room and back again. He felt the wizard and his henchmen watching, interested.

"Well, that figures," Brown replied. "Most peckerwoods I know can't even read."

Bolan pulled the punch, but it was solid, even so, and Wilson rocked backward on his heels. The blow that Bolan soaked up in return was hard enough to throw him back against the bar, but he rebounded swiftly, slipping beneath the black man's guard to hit him with a flying tackle.

"Help him!"

"Kick their asses!"

They were grappling, falling, as the room exploded into chaos. Bolan clung to Brown and braced himself for his collision with the hardwood floor.

5

Within the time it takes to drain a shot glass, blacks and whites were grappling in hand-to-hand combat. The odds were long against the new arrivals, but Wilson Brown had chosen three hulks for his backup, and some of the Blackboard's regular patrons hung back from the fray, content with their roles as observers at ringside. The mournful lament of the jukebox was drowned by the harsh sounds of battle.

Bolan ducked a flying beer mug and heard it crash against the wall behind him. Feinting to his left as Brown fired off a looping roundhouse punch, he took it on the shoulder, jarred by the impact, even though the former lineman must have pulled it at the final instant. Bolan had a new respect for movie stuntmen as he jabbed a right at Brown, avoiding contact with his chin by a fraction of an inch.

A reeling body caught Bolan from his blind side, staggering him as he spun to face his new assailant. Bleeding from his flattened nose, a chunky regular was pawing at the air with ham-size fists, retreating as he realized he had collided with a white man. One of Brown's companions, taking advantage of the guy's confusion, stepped in close and threw a vicious sucker punch that took his adversary down and out.

At the bar, Mason Ritter was perched upon a stool, cheering on his bodyguards as they began to double-team a burly black man, pummeling him simultaneously from both sides. Their target tried to dance away out of reach, but they were after him like jackals, weaving, jabbing, timing measured blows for maximum effect. It was apparent to the Executioner that they enjoyed their work.

He wondered, fleetingly, how fully Brown had briefed his men. In an instant he had his answer, as a big hand grasped his shoulder, spinning him around, and a hard fist hurtled in to block his field of vision. Bolan saved his eye by shifting slightly to the left, but he could do nothing to block the punch. He took it on his cheek, relaxing just enough to let the impact drive him backward, arms flung out to cushion his collision with the nearest wall. Rebounding, dizzy, Bolan braced himself to spar with the enraged behemoth, but he never got the chance.

From out of nowhere, Ritter's bullyboys tore into Bolan's adversary, firing kidney punches, slamming him behind the ear with heavy fists. The black man staggered, grimacing with pain, and turned on the two attackers like an angry bear. A backhand rocked the taller of the Klansmen on his heels, crimson geysers spouting from his nostrils as he stumbled out of range. The other dug inside a pocket of his jeans, produced a switchblade knife and snapped it open in a single practiced movement. He feinted left and right by turns, alert for any opening.

Bolan scooped up a beer bottle from the floor, spilling the last of its contents over his hand and forearm as he weighed it in his palm. He gauged the distance, cocked his arm and let the empty bottle fly. It missed his black assailant's ear by inches, spinning in its flight, and struck the sneering Klansman squarely in the forehead with a hollow clonk. Unlike the breakaways used in Hollywood, the bottle did not shatter, but it did not need to. Velocity and impact did the job, as Bolan's target dropped his knife and folded like a rag doll to the floor.

As Bolan took time to glance around the milling barroom, he saw Mason Ritter heading for an exit. The soldier turned—and ran directly into Wilson Brown. The ex-lieutenant wrapped him in a bear hug, hoisting him off the floor and swinging him around like a child. It was a rough maneuver, but it gave Brown time to speak.

"I'm too damned old for this," he hissed. "I hope to hell somebody's called the cavalry."

As if in answer to his words, the Blackboard's door slammed open to admit a stream of deputies in riot helmets, nightsticks drawn and ready as they waded in. Brown hurled Bolan sideways through a short 360, sending him tumbling across a table that collapsed beneath his weight. Bolan came up staggering, saw Brown and company retreating toward the alley exit, where they met another team of riot troopers.

It took a few minutes for the officers to put the cuffs on Brown and his companions, for they had to stop several times to club and pummel whites who found a final cheap shot irresistible. Finally the blacks, and half a dozen Blackboard regulars, were lined against the wall in manacles.

When Bolan realized the deputies were almost ready to depart, he charged on impulse, a riot billy glancing off his shoulder as he threw a punch at Wilson Brown. He grazed the big man's cheek and was rewarded with a hammerlock that choked off his wind and brought him gasping to his knees. He offered no resistance as handcuffs were tightened on his wrists and he was wrestled upright to his feet.

A scowling deputy jabbed a nightstick under his chin. "You want it, boy, you got it. One more fancy move and you'll be pissing blood for a week."

"I hear you," Bolan growled.

"I thought you might."

The deputy patted Bolan down for weapons, came up empty and directed him to follow the last prisoner in line. A sheriff's van was waiting in the parking lot. The whites were marched inside and told to sit on benches, while the blacks were muscled into cruisers for a segregated ride downtown. Bolan found himself seated next to one of Mason Ritter's muscle men, the purpling goose egg on the bodyguard's forehead offering the Executioner a modicum of satisfaction in his own discomfort.

He was not concerned about the prospect of a night in jail. The records from his brief incarceration in McLary County, Texas, had been lifted and expunged with an assist from Hal Brognola's Justice contacts. If the deputies in Little Rock were interested enough to put his prints and picture through the national computers, they would call up the cover jacket prepped by Leo Turrin for "Mike Bowers." At the moment, he was clean—no wants or warrants—but his fabricated record would reveal a history of violent crime with racial motivations worthy of attention from the Vanguard or the Teutonic Knights.

The Executioner was counting on it.

At the sheriff's station, they were rousted from the van and ordered into single file, conducted through a metal door that slammed behind them with a grim finality. The corridor was painted beige and lit by overhead fluorescents, institutional and cheerless. Bolan followed Ritter's stooge, with other prisoners behind him, led and driven by the deputies until they reached a holding tank.

In fact, there were two pens, adjacent to each other, with a narrow walkway in between. The occupants of one cage had an unobstructed view of persons in the other; they could carry on conversations, jeer at and curse each other to their hearts' content, but they could never touch. Not quite. It was a simple but effective isolation system, made to order for the separation of combatants from a riot.

Like tonight.

He saw that Wilson Brown and his companions were already lodged inside one holding cell, their manacles removed. As Bolan and the other whites approached, the blacks formed a line against the bars, reviling their assailants from the Blackboard.

"Well, now, lookee what the cat dragged in."

"You like them bracelets, white meat?"

"Step on over here, you want a piece of me."

One of the jailers raked his stick across the bars and drove them back a pace. "Shut up in there," he drawled, evincing no great interest in the conduct of his charges.

His cuffs removed, Bolan entered the cage and found himself a bench against one wall. The others followed singly, some rubbing their wrists, several drifting toward the bars that faced the other holding pen, picking up verbally where the brawl had left off.

"You niggers better count your blessings."

"Sheriff save your asses, that's for sure."

"Next time, boy. Next time."

"We'll be looking forward to it."

Each new gibe elicited an angry answer from the blacks, but with their prisoners confined, the deputies were satisfied to let them waste their breath on empty threats. Three-quarters of an hour passed before the jailers started booking one man at a time, beginning with Brown and his comrades. As each returned from the booking room, catcalls and curses greeted him, evoking responses in kind. Several black men who had been in the holding cage prior to the brawlers' arrival were inspired by the white's ethnic slurs to support Brown and company, shouting derision at Bolan and his fellow jailbirds. By the time the jailer got around to booking rednecks, angry pandemonium reigned in the pens.

Bolan held himself aloof, retreating to a corner of the cage, resisting an impulse to join in the verbal melee. Any drunken idiot could curse and shout; to impress the members of the Vanguard, it would take deeds, not hasty words. His judgment was vindicated when Ritter's muscle broke off from the jeering group and took a seat beside him.

"Do I know you?"

Bolan shook his head. "I don't think so."

"Bobby Shelton."

Bolan took the offered hand and felt the Klansman 'est his grip. "Mike Bowers."

"Glad to know you."

"Come here often?"

Shelton snickered. "I've been in and out. They know me."

"Well, I guess they'll know me now."

"Is that a problem?"

Bolan made a show of thinking that one over, taking his time. "Shouldn't be."

"Have you got paper out?"

"You ask a lot of questions."

"It's my nature."

"It could be unhealthy."

"I've lasted this long."

A deputy was eyeing Bolan from the entrance to the cage. "Next man," he barked. "That's you, boy."

Bolan let himself be guided along the corridor, turned left on orders from the jailer, halted at the booking desk. There his prints were rolled for posterity, and after he cleaned his hands with liquid soap he stood before a stationary camera. The wall behind him had been calibrated so that a subject's height was automatically displayed in every mug shot. Bolan took the numbered slate that he was offered, held it under his chin for the full-face shot, then turned on command to offer the lens a profile.

Standing once again before the booking desk, he emptied his pockets, watching as a jailer picked through crumpled bills and scattered change, examining his wallet.

"Name?"

"Mike Bowers."

"Mike, or Michael?"

"Suit yourself."

"Don't sass me, boy."

"It's Michael."

They ran through the litany of vitals, while the booking sergeant pecked, two fingered, at an IBM Selectric, filling in the necessary forms in triplicate. When he was asked about prior arrests, the soldier answered, "None." A background check would show that he was lying, but it would not hurt for them to do their jobs. In any case, "Mike Bowers"—had he existed—would certainly have lied in an attempt to spare himself further scrutiny.

Bob Shelton was taken for booking, departing with his bully's swagger more or less intact. After twenty minutes he returned, favored Bolan with a cocky smile and rejoined him in the corner.

"Piece of cake," he said. "I reckon we'll be out of here inside an hour."

"Yeah?"

"I've got a couple friends outside."

"That's nice."

"The bond on bullshit raps like this is never more than two, three hundred dollars."

Bolan grimaced. "Well, that leaves me out. Or I should say it leaves me in."

"You broke?"

"I figure I could scratch up a hundred if it was life or death."

"Sounds like you need yourself a job."

"That's easy said."

"What kind of work you interested in?"

"You hiring?"

"I might know some people."

"Well, in that case, make it something with travel, adventure, all the right fringe benefits."

"Sounds like the service," Shelton cracked.

"No thanks. I've been there. Special Forces."

"Any combat time?"

"I did a couple tours in Nam."

"Gook-killer, huh?"

"I bagged my share."

The Klansman tapped his chest. "Marines. I had a cousin in Grenada, but I never got the chance myself. The way these politicians pussyfoot around today, the fighting man's a damned fifth wheel." He paused. "I take it that you didn't like the military?"

Bolan took his cue. "I liked it fine, the times we were allowed to do our job," he growled. "Seems like my second tour was mostly wasted kissing up to ne-groes, running errands for a bunch of faggot officers who never spent a weekend in the field."

"I guess you saw a lot of that."

"Enough to last a lifetime." Bolan glowered, playing to the military records inserted in his jacket by the man from Justice. "If it hadn't been for dark meat, I might still be in."

"How's that?"

"My second tour, they stuck us with a spade lieutenant." Bolan glanced across at Wilson Brown and caught the big man glaring at him through a double set of tempered bars. "He liked to send the white boys out on recon while he kept the soulmates safe and sound in camp. The second time I lost a squad, I kicked his ass and drew a general discharge."

"Nigger lovers stick together."

"Tell me something new."

"No promises," the Klansman said, "but I might know a place where someone with your kind of military background and experience could find a steady job."

"How steady?"

"If it flies, you'd be full-time."

"What kind of work?"

"Some training exercises, this and that. If everything pans out, there might be free-lance business on the side. You up for night work?"

"I don't mind."

"All right. So let me check it out when we get done with all this shit. I wouldn't be surprised if you were just what the doctor ordered."

Bolan fought the urge to smile, remaining deadpan. A display of zeal was out of character, and Shelton clearly did not have the final say on his acceptance by the Vanguard or the Klan. There would be precautions, screenings, an initiation if he was accepted. Once inside the paramilitary clique, he still could not aspire to membership in the inner circle. As the new boy on the block, he would be treated with reserve, perhaps a measure of suspicion. Infiltration by informers was a constant problem for domestic terrorists, and no group had been so beset by federal agents as the Ku Klux Klan. If Ritter and his partner Freeman had learned anything at all from recent history, they had to be aware of the necessity for caution in recruiting members.

It was Bolan's task to sell himself, to present the image of a proper bigot who could serve the Vanguard and the Teutonic Knights to good effect. It would not do to overplay his hand, to appear too rabid in the early stages of recruitment. Spies and plants might come complete with swastika tattoos and well-rehearsed speeches, but Bolan had a subtler course in mind. He would allow his prey to do the courting, demonstrate enough reserve to make them understand that he could take or leave their fellowship. If they were hungry, shopping for a man with Bolan's expertise, the bait should be sufficient. Either way, it was the only plan that seemed to offer any prospects of success.

The door of Bolan's cage slid open, and a meaty jailer used his bulk to bar the way. He held a clipboard in his hand, referring to it as he rattled off a list of names.

"McCullough. Jackson. Thorndyke. Shelton. Carlyle. Bowers."

Ritter's man was on his feet, all smiles. "Come on," he beamed. "That's us."

"What's going on?"

"We're out of here."

The soldier kept his seat. "I told you, I can't make the bail."

"It's covered," Shelton told him, "or they wouldn't call your name."

"Who's buying?"

"Wait and see."

"I've never cared much for surprises."

"Live a little, Mike. You owe it to yourself."

With feigned reluctance, Bolan followed Shelton past the scowling jailer, past the second holding pen. He caught a glance from Wilson Brown in passing, hesitated as the black man rose to face him through the bars.

"This isn't finished, whitey. I'll be seeing you again."

"Count on it," Bolan growled, and followed the grinning Bobby Shelton down the corridor toward freedom.

6

Outside the jail it was a crisp, clear midnight. Bolan wished he had taken time to fetch a jacket from his car. *His car.* It was a long walk back, unless...

"You coming?" Shelton asked. The Klansman was already halfway to the courthouse parking lot.

"I've got to get my wheels."

"Don't sweat it. We leave cars around the Blackboard all the time, and no one messes with them. We've got business."

"Oh? What kind?"

"You want that job we talked about, you've got to meet the man."

"Tonight?"

"Why not?"

Because he was unarmed and outnumbered—but the Executioner voiced none of those concerns. Instead, he merely shrugged and said, "Why not?"

Two cars were waiting for them in the parking lot, a station wagon and a middle-priced sedan. Their recent cellmates filled the wagon, then its driver made a sharp, illegal U-turn, taillights fading in a moment as he headed west in the direction of the Blackboard. Bobby Shelton took a seat beside the driver of the dark sedan, and Bolan sat in back.

"Where are we going?"

"Like I said, to see the man. We're going to his office."

"You expect to find him there at midnight?"

"He'll be there, don't worry." Shelton grinned at Bolan in the rearview mirror. "Don't you know a wizard never sleeps?"

"A wizard?"

"*The* wizard."

"I see."

"Not just yet. But you will."

Fifteen minutes in sparse midnight traffic, the dark sedan winding past storefronts and offices, all closed for the night. Bolan ticked off the streets as they passed, burning the names in his memory, filing the route away for future reference. He might be coming back this way again without a tour guide. For all he knew, he might be walking home.

Except he had no home in Little Rock—or Parrish, either, for that matter. Finding a room had taken second place to contact with the enemy, and he would have to look for one after his unscheduled interview. Assuming they didn't spot him as a ringer instantly, see through his cover like a pane of glass and solve the problem with a bullet in his brain. He had no backup this time, no weapons but his own two hands if it came down to killing in the next few hours. He was vulnerable, and he knew it.

It was not a pleasant feeling.

Shelton's destination was an office building that had obviously seen better days. A mile or so from downtown, the structure occupied a corner lot, with entrances on the north and west. Its neighbors were a Laundromat, a one-stop market and the office of a "painless dentist," who appeared to specialize in dentures for the toothless poor; on his plate-glass window his credit terms were euphemistically described as "reasonable."

Bolan followed Bobby Shelton through the north entrance, while the driver waited in the car outside. The lobby was illuminated by an ancient ceiling fixture that created more shadows than it dissipated.

"Stairs," his guide decided. "Elevator's too damned slow."

Six flights, three floors. Then a corridor with threadbare carpeting and doors on either side. Outside one door, halfway down on Bolan's left, stood Shelton's companion from the Blackboard.

"How'd it go?" the sentry asked.

"No sweat."

"All right."

The office waiting room was every bit as dingy as the outer corridor. A secretary's desk sat unattended facing half a dozen plastic chairs, which apparently had been designed without thought to comfort. Light was visible behind the frosted glass of Mason Ritter's door, a sign of life within the inner sanctum.

"Take a load off," Shelton offered, waving at the plastic chairs. "I have to let him know we're here."

The Executioner sat down and was surprised to find the chair even less comfortable than it looked. With minor alterations, it could have served the Inquisition. Shelton crossed the anteroom, knocked once on Ritter's door and waited for the wizard's summons. Once inside, he closed the door behind him and stood framed in silhouette against the frosted glass. Bolan heard the murmur of voices but couldn't make out their words.

Five minutes passed, and then another five, before the Klansman reappeared. "You're up."

As Bolan entered, the brains of the Teutonic Knights was lighting a cigar. He blew an aromatic smoke cloud toward the ceiling, waved the new arrival toward another of the space-age plastic chairs.

"Mr. Bowers...can I call you Mike? You did all right back at the Blackboard," Ritter said by way of introduction.

"Not so good. I didn't need another bust."

"It happens. Let it go." The wizard studied Bolan for a moment, measuring him with his eyes. "I'm Mason Ritter. Name mean anything to you?"

"I'm new in town."

"How new is new?"

The soldier checked his watch. "About six hours."

"Where you staying?"

"Nowhere yet."

"First thing in town, you hit a bar?"

"Not any bar. The grapevine told me I might make connections at the Blackboard."

"Grapevine's useful sometimes. Other times it trips you up and dumps you on your ass."

"It wouldn't be the first time."

"Understand you're looking for a job."

"Depends."

"You've got a military background? Special Forces?"

Bolan nodded, waiting.

"But you had a bit of trouble." It was not a question this time. "Trouble with a nigger officer."

"That's right."

"I like to think I'm a decent judge of men," the wizard said. "Unless I miss my guess, that general discharge ain't the only trouble you've been in because of niggers."

"You could say that."

"Want to talk about it?"

"Why?"

"You need a job; I need a man who fits my needs. I don't go in for hiring strangers."

Bolan shrugged. "I've done some time. A three-spot at MacAlester."

"What charge?"

"Attempted murder."

"Don't be bashful."

Bolan glanced around the office, feigning hesitation. "Listen, if you don't hire ex-cons, okay. Don't waste my time."

"Go easy, boy. I never judge a man until I know his story."

"I was in a bar, all right? I had a few too many. Or a lot too many. Either way, these spades were waiting when I started for my car. Four of them. Liquor slows reaction time, you know? They got my wallet—forty, fifty dollars and some plastic—and they worked me over pretty good before a squad car happened by. They were identified, but you know how it goes, one thing and then another. I was waiting for the bastards when they posted bail."

"You said *attempted* murder."

"They got lucky."

"Jesus Christ, I sometimes wonder what this country's coming to." The wizard shook his head in evident disgust. "Time was, the streets were safe for decent folk. A thing like that sounds more like self-defense."

"The D.A. saw it differently."

"Was he a white man?"

"More or less. He called himself Levinsky."

"Ah."

The Klansmen shared a knowing glance, commiserating at the fate of Aryans adrift in a world controlled by blacks and Jews. Behind a rising cloud of smoke, the wizard studied Bolan's face more closely.

"I'm in need of military personnel who have a knack for training others. Small arms, demolitions, hand-to-hand. The basics of survival in uncertain times. You follow me so far?"

"Yes, sir."

"You know of the Teutonic Knights?"

"A little."

"And?"

"I take Dan Rather with a grain of salt," he said. "The things I've seen and heard so far, I like."

"We're on the verge of a momentous turnaround in the United States," the wizard told him, warming to his favorite theme. "There's revolution in the wind, and I'm not talking any bullshit we-shall-overcome Red dogma, either. People in America are sick to death of being walked on by minorities and hyphenated immigrants. They're sick to death of schools where homosexuality is taught in place of Christian values. Men and women all across this land are waking up to the realities of race and reason, organizing to resist the mongrelizers while they still have time."

He paused to catch his breath and suck on the cigar. Mack Bolan wore a properly respectful face, appearing to hang on Ritter's every word.

"Unfortunately, revolutions just aren't what they used to be," the ranking Klansman said. "We don't have any minutemen today, and from appearances, our enemies have got the upper hand in numbers, weapons, the technology of mass communication. We require a dedicated hard-core group of patriots who will not flinch from their appointed duty in the hour of need. You might say we're assembling a group of men who take life . . . seriously.''

Silence hung between them. Bolan nodded slowly, letting Ritter know he got the message.

"Our numbers have been growing in the past two years, and we have access to the necessary hardware. Now our recruits need proper training in the proper skills. . . ." Ritter looked steadily at Bolan, as if inviting him to speak up.

"On my second tour in Vietnam, I helped train Montagnards and South Vietnamese to fight the Cong and NLF. I figure teaching white men ought to be a breeze."

"You're not intimidated by the thought of standing in open opposition to the government?"

Bolan's smile was ice. "The government has been opposing me for years."

"Of course, enlistment with the Knights would be mandatory if you held this post."

"Seems fair."

"A background check would be required." The wizard noticed Bolan's frown and hastened to explain. "We have a problem with informers, infiltrators—local, state and federal, take your choice. I have this office swept for bugs every morning, regular as clockwork."

"And you figure I'm a plant?"

"I didn't say that, Mike. There's no offense intended. On the other hand, I have a grave responsibility to all the other knights, the movement. Every new recruit is screened as carefully as possible. If that's a problem for you . . ."

"No. You put it that way, it makes sense."

"All right." The wizard fished a business card out of his vest pocket, sliding it across the desk toward Bolan. "You find yourself a room for a night or two, then call that number, leave a number where you can be reached. I'll be in touch with you."

The interview was over. Bolan rose. "I hope we have a chance to work together, Mr. Ritter. Either way, I want to thank you for your time."

"My pleasure. Bobby, if you'd help Mike fetch his car..."

"It's done."

They rode the elevator down, with Shelton whistling tunelessly. Outside, the dark sedan was waiting where they'd left it.

"Did I pass?" the soldier asked.

"That's not for me to say." The Klansman glanced at him and grinned. "Relax. You pass the background check, you've got it made."

"And if I don't?"

"Well, then, my friend, I'd say you still won't have a problem in the world. You'll just be dead."

So simple. Life or death determined by a madman's phone call, his acceptance or rejection of the data in a manufactured file. Bolan wondered briefly if the Klan had ties with local law enforcement that would let them tap computer records, call up information from the central file in Wonderland. If so, it would not be the first time that a "superpatriotic" group had managed to seduce police or military personnel with platitudes and pledges of support.

In fact, he knew, the neofascist movement took little interest in the cause of law and order. Chaos was the movement's goal, apocalyptic violence the modern bigot's end that justified all means. From coast to coast, police and federal agents who attempted to curtail subversive actions by the Klans and modern Nazis had been harassed, threatened, shot and killed. Their epitaphs were silent testimony to a grass-roots movement gone berserk, inflamed by blood lust and the creed of hatred.

Bolan had an opportunity here and now to strike a blow against that twisted movement. Provided he passed the entrance test administered by Mason Ritter. Once he was inside it would be his task to wound the serpent when and where he could, as often and as mercilessly as he was able.

Bolan harbored no illusions that he could change the world, blot out the strain of racial hatred that had dogged mankind forever. He could not aspire to change the hearts and minds of men. What he could do was deal with savages in language they understood. He could and would provide them with the heat of cleansing fire . . . if he got the chance.

For now, his fate rested in the hands of Leo Turrin. If his manufactured cover stood up under scrutiny, he would be one step closer to his goal. If it failed . . . well, he was one step closer to the grave already, with the night wind at his back.

The view from graveside was familiar, but he never grew accustomed to it. Never.

Driving through the darkness with his newfound comrades of the Klan, Mack Bolan set his eyes on life and kept his fingers crossed.

Mason Ritter sipped his bourbon-laced coffee, set the steaming cup aside. "He seems all right to me."

"That isn't good enough."

"I understand we have procedures—"

"And they will be followed in this case, as always."

Freeman was not giving him an order, not exactly, but the chief of the Teutonic Knights resented having his best judgment overruled this way. He understood his placement in the pecking order; he did not need to have that understanding reinforced at every turn. It should be good enough for Freeman this time that he chose to take on a new man in time of need.

Across the glass-topped desk, his nominal superior leaned back in a reclining chair, examining his tented fingers. Ritter never ceased to wonder how a man of Freeman's size could have such tiny hands. Not soft, exactly. Not precisely feminine. But they were tiny, more like a child's hands, with pudgy sausage fingers and meticulously tended nails. Freeman preferred to keep them in his pockets when he could, but that was awkward when he sat behind his desk. Noticing now that Ritter was regarding his diminutive digits curiously, he hid them in his lap.

The wizard tried again. "We need a new instructor right away, before the training program falls apart. We've been six weeks without a man who knows his business, and the boys are getting itchy."

"Let them itch." There was a sudden edge to Freeman's voice. "I'm not about to jeopardize the program, everything we've worked for, on a hasty welcome for a jailbird."

"I've explained what he was in for, *and* his trouble in the Army. He's a natural, I'm telling you."

"You've told me what you heard from him," the leader of the Vanguard countered smoothly. "I'll feel better when ı've heard the same thing from a more official source."

"You think he's running down a sting?"

"I didn't say that. Chances are he's clean. But if he's not, if he's a plant, I want to know about it in advance, before he gets inside."

"He seems all right to me," the Klansman said again, aware that he could push no further once the chairman had his mind made up. Like now. A stubborn streak was part of Freeman's nature, and it did no good to butt your head against the stone wall of his determination. All you got in the end was headaches and a battered ego.

"I understand the program's need." Freeman seemed to have relaxed a little once his hands were safely out of sight. "I'll put the query through as soon as possible and make it top priority. We should know something by tomorrow or the next day."

"Well, I hope so. The way he sounded, Bowers could develop itchy feet most any time. He hasn't got the cash to hang around and wait for very long."

"A day or two. If he's the man you think he is, he'll stick. And if he's not . . ."

"Okay." There was no point in arguing. Freeman had his mind made up, and he would not be swayed by anything his second-in-command might say.

That "second-in-command" bit galled the Klansman. He had the status of a leader with his own Teutonic Knights, but what the hell good was that when every move he made had to be cleared through Freeman and the Vanguard? Sometimes Ritter thought he was nothing but a goddamn puppet, and he did not like the idea. No, he did not like it in the least. Someday, he thought. Someday . . .

"What else?"

The chairman's voice recalled him from his reverie, and Ritter had to think a moment, scanning the old memory banks for new business. Finding none, he shook his head.

"That's all I have."

"How are we covered on that other business?"

Ritter did not have to ask what other business Freeman had in mind. Five days since they had dealt with Theo Brown—since *he* had dealt with Brown on Freeman's orders—and he heard the same damn question every day.

"We're fine," he answered, as he always did. "The boys are hanging in. I don't expect a problem."

"It's the unexpected that we need to watch for," Freeman chided, frowning deeply. "One of them gets nervous, he might try to cut himself a deal. The law gets mileage off of frightened men."

"They'll stand the heat. Don't worry."

"Someone has to. You remember Mississippi? Bogalusa? Selma? Birmingham? Each place, each time, the FBI found someone who was looking for a deal, a quick way out. Each time, a weak man sold out his brothers for money and immunity."

The wizard shook his head. He knew the stories, had known some of the men, but he was not terribly concerned. He had learned from the mistakes of others. He had the problem covered.

"Like I told you, everybody's implicated. Everybody took a shot, all right? If someone talks, he puts his own ass in the chair along with anybody else he names. I don't think anyone will risk it."

"Maybe not." The chairman did not sound convinced, by any means. "But with immunity, the way these bastards work, I'd still feel better if we had insurance."

It was Ritter's turn to frown. He did not like the sound of that at all. "What do you mean?" he asked, afraid to hear the answer, frightened that he might already know.

"I don't mean anything. Not yet. We'll need to keep a sharp eye out for any signs of weakening."

You mean I will, the wizard thought. He seriously doubted whether Freeman would be standing watch on any rowdy Klansmen. He had better things to do, arranging payoffs from the banks and heavy-duty farmers who were covering their overhead in Chatham County and around the state.

But never mind. The Knights were his concern, and he would hold his end up, rain or shine. If someone tried to cut and run . . . well, he would deal with that one if and when it became necessary. There was no point fretting in advance. Fretting caused ulcers, and the wizard did not need that kind of damn white-collar problem.

"I've been thinking we might ease off a little," Ritter mused. "Give things a chance to cool."

"No good. Our sponsors want the union broken yesterday. We have to keep the pressure on."

"They ought to understand we can't work miracles."

"The kind of cash they're laying out, they look for miracles. We can't afford to keep them waiting."

"Still, the more we push right now, the more risk we run of someone getting busted."

"Strategy," the chairman snapped. "Plan every move before it's made and double-check the consequences. Keep the details to yourself and share the necessary minimum with members of the wrecking crew."

"I do that now."

"All right, so what's the problem?"

"Law of averages," the Klansman answered sourly. "We run too many operations and it stands to reason someone's got to take a fall. You've got to figure on some bad luck somewhere down the line."

"We make our own luck, Mason. Chance and circumstances are the excuses offered up by failures. Winners have no need for explanations."

"That's all well and good, Jerome, but—"

"But nothing," Freeman snapped. "The locals can't be everywhere at once; the FBI has even less manpower to work with. A professional strike force should be able to go on indefinitely, choosing targets with discretion. We just need a few more weeks."

"I'll tell you what we need." Ritter's face was flushed and his voice had a rough edge as he tried to make Freeman see his point. "You talk about professionals, and all I have are amateurs. Okay, a couple of the boys are fair with dynamite, they all know how to shoot, but that's the limit. If they don't get decent training soon, as promised, we'll see losses in the rank and file. Who knows? I might start losing members of the wrecking crew.''

"See that you don't.''

"Or what? You reckon I should wipe them out? Does that make sense to you? You figure I should threaten seven hundred Klansmen on my own?''

"I hardly think that's necessary, Mason.''

"Maybe not, but promises were made when we recruited some of these old boys, and they've been waiting for the payoff. They were promised weapons, military training, action. They won't sit around forever, jerking off, while we play word games with them at the monthly meetings.''

"I've been working on the weapons, you know that. I expect a shipment later in the week.''

"That leaves the training.''

"What you mean is, that leaves Bowers.''

"Him, or someone like him.''

Freeman heaved a weary sigh. "I'll see what I can do. But I'll be damned if I'll abort the screening process. If he can't stand up to scrutiny, he's not our man.''

It was the best that the wizard could hope for, and he let it go. If Bowers could not pass the test, then he would have to look for someone else, and quickly. There were mercenaries to be found, if one knew where to look; some of them even advertised in magazines these days. Of course, they might not be committed to the cause. Not like a man who had been betrayed by niggers more than once already.

The wizard liked to put his faith in hard experience. A man who had been burned was cautious when he handled fire, but he also knew its uses and its value. Freeman had the caution down, no question there, but sometimes Ritter wondered what had happened to his nerve.

What did he really know about his nominal superior, when it came down to that? Freeman had appeared as if from nowhere when the Brotherhood had been floundering, and had pulled the scattered troops together, promising they would be better, stronger, than before. He had the PR angle covered, but you had to wonder sometimes what was going on behind his steely eyes.

Sometimes Mason Ritter wondered what it would be like to sit in Freeman's chair behind the glass-topped desk, instead of killing time in his dilapidated, roach-infested office half a block away in the slums. These days he thought about it more and more.

One day soon, the wizard thought, he might find out. In fact, he would be looking forward to it.

FREEMAN WAITED for the outer office door to close before he raised the telephone receiver, punching up the number for the sheriff's office. Despite the hour, he was confident that he would reach his party at the other end.

"Zverbilis, R and I."

Records and identification. He was in.

"How are you, Gary?"

He could imagine the overweight deputy glancing around at the otherwise empty office, terrified of being overheard.

"You're not supposed to call me here."

"I know that, Gary. I apologize, but this is an emergency."

"Oh, yeah? How's that?"

"Your people had a fellow in the tank last night. I need some background on him, quickly."

"One of yours?"

"Potentially. Not yet."

"What's his name?"

"Mike Bowers. He came in with Bobby and the others from the Blackboard."

"Yeah, I figured. It'll take some time to run him through."

"This is a matter of some urgency, you understand?"

"You can't rush Washington. I'll do my best."

"Of course you will. And I appreciate it, Gary."

"Yeah. You at the office?"

"Just as usual."

"Okay. I'll be in touch."

Freeman listened to the dial tone for a moment, frowning, finally replacing the receiver in its cradle. He had done his part, and it was up to the computers now. If Ritter was not satisfied with their performance, that was *his* problem.

It was bad enough to rush security procedures; he refused to scrap them altogether, even if the chief of the Teutonic Knights was running short of patience. Freeman knew from grim experience the price tag that inevitably came with carelessness and sloth.

Before the Vanguard, in another life, he had been brash and overconfident, self-satisfied. He'd thought that no one could touch him, that nothing could go wrong with any of his plans. Success had been preordained and therefore guaranteed. He had been wrong, of course. Disastrously, apocalyptically mistaken. Smug self-confidence had very nearly cost him his life; it would have cost him everything if he had not been prepared for a failure he was positive would never occur.

When Freeman looked around his office now he missed the opulence of other days, but he was thankful for his life, for the remnants of an empire that allowed him to begin anew, from scratch. In eighteen months he had established a base of operations, he had gathered fifteen hundred men around his standard, with another seven hundred in the ranks of the Teutonic Knights, and he had earned the confidence of men with money, power, the respect of governors and presidents.

No small task, but as with everything, he had been forced to compromise along the way. His name was not his own, a minor inconvenience when he thought about the price of clinging to his former life. He could live with the change. As for the rest . . . well, he was a professional, a master in his chosen field. He had long ago decided that it did not pay to argue with the money men.

He would provide the services for which he had been paid, because he had no choice. The motives of his various employers meant no more to Freeman than the color of their skin. If there had been a bullish market for black militants, he would have dyed his skin and learned to breakdance overnight.

He placed his small hands on the desktop, studying the nails, which from time to time he chewed. Expensive manicures had solved the problem for the moment, as a ready fund of cash had eased his other hungers, kept his demons momentarily at bay. Destruction of the farmers' union would ensure that cash remained in plentiful supply. A failure to deliver would destroy him.

Mason Ritter would not be a problem. He was anxious now, Freeman thought, but he could be manipulated with a minimum of difficulty. The Klansman was a brawler, but he had the passions of an adolescent and the intellect to match. If necessary, he could be eliminated and replaced.

The thought of murder led back again to Theo Brown. Freeman grimaced. He had not been present at the execution, could not be connected with the crime except by Ritter, but he did not share the wizard's faith in the dependability of underlings. Subordinates were rarely to be trusted, never absolutely, and he worried that the Knights might spring a lethal leak at any moment. He would happily have silenced every member of the wrecking crew, but that meant finding other killers, placing other men in a position to betray the movement. If it came to that, he would demand that Ritter do the job himself, and after he was finished . . .

Freeman pulled the reins on his imagination, cutting short the homicidal fantasy. It would not come to that. The background check on Ritter's chosen drill instructor, Bowers, would be clean. And if it wasn't, a polite rebuff would do the job in place of messy violence or a disappearance that would have to be explained away. A simple no would do the same job as a bullet, and with fewer complications.

Since forming the Vanguard, Freeman had become obsessed with safety and simplicity. The two ideals were often incompatible, but with a little effort, harmony could often be achieved.

He smiled. For someone who had staked his future on the propagation of unrest within society, it was ironic—even humorous—that Freeman's private vision of success revolved around a state of blissful inactivity. An island setting came to mind, with brown-skinned natives with perfect bodies frolicking on deserted beaches beneath the tropic sun.

The natives in his fantasies were always male, athletic, busting with vitality and youth. Freeman had no use for women save as window dressing to maintain his image as a rugged all-American, possessed of raw machismo. Otherwise, he found their touch repugnant, something to be shunned at any cost.

Six months of celibacy had done nothing to improve his temperament, but Freeman was accustomed to self-sacrifice. There would be time enough for recreation when he finished the present job with cash in hand. When it was time, he would not seek companionship among the members of the Vanguard or the Knights. Exposure would be self-destructive, and there were so many other ways to find release without involving members of the cause.

The murder of Theo Brown had been a tactical maneuver, aimed at silencing his criticism of the Vanguard's backers rather than destroying the union he led in Chatham County. The elimination of Brown's private files had plugged a crucial leak and had also furnished Freeman with the name of one who had betrayed the movement, selling precious secrets to the enemy. Within a day of Brown's removal, Freeman had arranged the permanent eradication of that leak—a tragic auto accident had done the trick—but the experience had only confirmed his gut suspicion of the men who worked beneath him.

No one could be trusted absolutely.

No one.

During transitory episodes of paranoia and depression, Freeman did not even trust himself. He questioned his ability to lead the movement, to succeed where he had failed before, had come so close to losing everything. Might he betray himself unconsciously, through momentary weakness of the flesh? Was *he*, in fact, the weak link in the chain?

Disgusted with his own self-doubt, the Vanguard's führer drew a bottle of expensive whiskey from a lower desk drawer, topping off his coffee mug. The liquor scorched his throat at first and quickly lit a fire inside him, smothering his doubts and purging them with liquid heat.

Eliminating Theo Brown had left the farmers' union leaderless, but only for the moment. There were rumors even now of Theo's father stepping in to fill his son's position, taking up the fallen standard, as it were. The elder Brown was still an unknown quantity, but Freeman had his own paid eyes and ears inside the NFU—no movement was secure from traitors, after all. He gathered that the old man had no union background. Some kind of an athlete, ruined by the war, who had retired from play to scout the colleges. A football pimp of sorts.

The story was encouraging, if true. It pleased him to believe his enemies could do no better in their search for a replacement. Sentiment had surely played a role in the selection—yet another weakness he could turn to his advantage when the time was ripe. Soon, now.

He recognized that Ritter's plea made sense, that they wait awhile, allow the heat to die down. But Andrews and the others, rich men all, were pressing him for fresh offensives, hot new blood. Ensconced in lavish offices, their money safe in vaults, they had grown restless, anxious for the final conflict to be joined. It was imperative that farmers who had worked the land for generations be driven into poverty and hounded from their homes. For Freeman's part, he did not care or wonder why.

It was enough to know the truth concerning Andrews, cocky spokesman for the moneyed clique that paid the Vanguard's bills. That truth had not been easy to uncover, and Freeman would have bet his life that no one else in Little Rock possessed the knowledge that he held.

It was his secret ace, the hole card he would play when it was time to cut and run. A final coup that would surprise the smirking banker, teach him something of humility as he began to pay in earnest.

Freeman savored the idea and poured himself another drink. It might be hours before he got the word on Bowers from his contact in the sheriff's office. In the meantime, there were confrontations to be organized, "spontaneous" events to be anticipated, planned in detail. There were hopes and dreams to be demolished just across the line in Chatham County, and he had no time to waste.

It would not do to keep the buyers waiting.

8

"You're in. Be out in front of your motel at eight o'clock."

The call from Bobby Shelton had inspired a host of contradictory sensations for the Executioner. First of all, he was relieved to know his cover had survived the scrutiny of Mason Ritter and his cohorts. Bolan had no way yet of knowing their connections with state or local law enforcement, but he had to figure his jacket had been studied, in whatever detail, and had passed inspection by the Klan.

You're in.

Immediately after satisfaction, Bolan felt a certain apprehension. Could it be a trap? A setup? Had his cover failed somehow, provoking Ritter and his Knights to jury-rig a plan for the elimination of Mike Bowers? Bolan knew there was a chance, however slim, that he was being led to the slaughter...but he had to keep his date with Shelton, all the same. The purpose of his drive to Little Rock had been a bid to infiltrate the Vanguard or the Klan, and having come this close, the Executioner would not allow himself to turn away.

He would be ready, though, for anything that happened. The Beretta and the AutoMag were out, of course. Too ostentatious, too sophisticated for the likes of ex-con Bowers to be carrying around on his nocturnal errands. Shelton would expect him to be armed, might be suspicious if he wasn't, but the Klansman would have questions if the new recruit arrived bearing state-of-the-art military hardware.

Bolan chose a Browning Hi-Power semiautomatic pistol for his head weapon, checking its load and easing off the safety before he snugged it into shoulder rigging. Three rounds less than the Beretta's maximum capacity, without the selective-fire option for 3-round bursts, but it was still a decent weapon, capable of killing on command. More important, it was a weapon readily available through legal outlets, plentiful throughout the country and the world. The Browning would not raise an eyebrow if its presence underneath his arm should come to light.

The odds were good that Bolan would be asked to hand his weapon over, even if his invitation to become a Klansman was legitimate. Accordingly, he opted for a backup, buckling on an ankle holster that would grant him easy access to a second, smaller gun. His choice from the selection in his special suitcase was a Colt Mustang automatic, chambered in .380 caliber. Less than six inches overall, the snubby side arm held five rounds in its magazine, with a sixth in the firing chamber. Bolan loaded it with hollowpoints to take maximum advantage of the firepower available.

Six rounds might be enough, allowing for close range, a limited number of participants in the initiation ceremony. At the very least, it might give Bolan time to seize another weapon, increase his firepower. In close-up killing situations, the advantage of surprise meant more than caliber and muzzle velocity.

The soldier hoped he was being an alarmist, that he would not have a need this night for either weapon. His plan did not involve an early confrontation with the Knights. He sought instead to infiltrate their ranks—their hierarchy, if he could—and catch a glimpse of Ritter as he worked with Freeman and the Vanguard. The Teutonic Knights were secondary in importance, though their strength in numbers could not be discounted. Jerome Freeman, by all accounts, was the brains of the operation, its guiding hand. A decimation of the Knights that left the Vanguard and its chief intact would accomplish precisely nothing.

Bolan double-checked his chosen weapons, locked the surplus in the rental's trunk and engaged antitamper devices. A first attempt to open doors, trunk or hood would produce an earsplitting shriek of ten seconds' duration.

Further intrusion, including any contact whatsoever with the interior of the trunk or engine compartment, would immediately detonate a plastic charge suspended from the gas tank, wiping out the vehicle and frying any would-be thief before he had a chance to cut and run. It was overkill, perhaps, but Bolan could not contemplate the horror of his weapons and explosives falling into hostile hands. Klansman, street gang member or collector for a chop shop, they would gain no contributions to their private caches of weapons from the Executioner.

At 7:50 he stepped outside, bought an evening paper from the sidewalk dispenser and sat down at the bus stop to read it while he waited. Theo's funeral got a mention on page three, together with a recap of the murder and some background on the farmers' union. Bolan thought the coverage fair enough, although it lacked the slightest trace of sympathy. The author clearly had no love for midnight vigilantes, but he saw no need for unions, either. The editor expressed himself on the opinions page, denouncing "rabble-rousers" in the same breath with the rabble that was roused. "We need no Klan to keep the peace in Arkansas," the editorial declared. "We need no outside 'unions' to manipulate our farmers and deplete their small amount of cash on hand with wasted 'dues.'"

He heard the car before he saw it idling at the curb. He made a point of browsing through the paper until Shelton had his driver tap the horn. It was the same sedan that had been waiting at the jail last night.

"You ready?"

"As I'll ever be."

"Get in."

Bolan climbed in back with Shelton, scarcely glancing at the wheelman or the stranger who was riding shotgun.

"Guess you checked out fine."

"I'm glad to hear it."

Shelton grinned. "You should be. Mason doesn't care for being conned. He might've had us put you through the beltline."

"Thanks, I'll pass."

"You wouldn't have much say-so in the matter." Shelton tried for an apologetic face and missed it by a mile. "I hate to do this, but I've got to pat you down for hardware, Mike. You understand?"

The soldier feigned resentment. "What's the deal? You told me I was in."

"You're almost in. You passed the background check, all right, but you still have to be initiated. No one but initiated members are allowed to carry iron inside the klavern."

"That makes sense, I guess."

"Okay. We'll make this nice and easy."

Shelton ran a hand inside his jacket, found the Browning and removed it from its holster, passing it to the shotgun rider. A cursory pat of Bolan's jacket pockets finished the routine.

"You'll get it back as soon as you're initiated," Shelton said. "Now there's just one other little thing."

"What's that?"

"You'll have to put this on." The Klansman drew a blindfold from his pocket with a flourish, handing it to Bolan. "The location of our den is confidential, get it? New recruits don't see the outside of the place until they leave."

"I wasn't counting on this kind of hocus-pocus," Bolan growled.

"Security, you know? We've had a few guys come this far and get cold feet before they took the oath. This way, the losers don't know where they've been, and they can't give us any trouble down the line."

"Okay."

With obvious reluctance, Bolan slipped the blindfold on, adjusting the elastic straps for comfort. Shelton watched him, made a small adjustment of his own and asked, "How many fingers?"

"How the hell should I know?"

"Fair enough. Let's roll."

They drove for fifteen minutes before the driver parked and killed the engine. Bolan let himself be trundled from the car and led across a field of broken asphalt like a blind man, one arm linked with Bobby Shelton's.

"Each of the following questions must be answered by you with an emphatic yes. First: Is the motive prompting your ambition to be a Klansman serious and unselfish?"

"Yes."

"Second: Are you a native-born, white, gentile American citizen?"

"Yes."

"Third: Are you absolutely opposed to and free of any allegiance of any nature to any cause, government, people, sect or ruler that is foreign to the United States of America?"

"Yes."

"Fourth: Do you believe in the tenets of the Christian religion?"

"Yes."

"Fifth: Do you esteem the United States of America and its institutions above any other government, civil, political or ecclesiastical, in the whole world?"

"Yes."

"Sixth: Will you, without mental reservation, take a solemn oath to defend, preserve and enforce same?"

"Yes."

"Seventh: Do you believe in clannishness, and will you faithfully practice same toward Klansmen?"

"Yes."

"Eighth: Do you believe in and will you faithfully strive for the eternal maintenance of white supremacy?"

"Yes."

"Ninth: Will you faithfully obey our constitution and laws and conform willingly to all our usages, requirements and regulations?"

"Yes."

"Tenth: Can you always be depended on?"

"Yes."

Ritter cleared his throat before continuing. "The distinguishing marks of a Klansman are not found in the fiber of his garments or his social and financial standing, but are spiritual: namely, a chivalric head, a compassionate heart, a prudent tongue and a courageous will. All devoted to our

"Three steps here. Be careful."

Bolan heard a heavy door swing open, close again behind them. Footsteps on a concrete floor reverberated from the ceiling overhead, conveying an impression of size. He counted twenty-seven steps before his guide brought him up short. Shelton released his arm and moved away, leaving Bolan alone. Around him, rustling cloth informed him that the members of the Klan were suiting up.

"Remove the blindfold." Ritter's voice, muffled but unmistakable.

When he could see again, the soldier spent a moment letting his eyes adjust to the fluorescent lights. He stood before a folding table draped in satin to create a makeshift altar. On the table sat a sword, an open Bible and a pitcher filled with water. He was flanked by two Klansmen robed in white with pointed hoods, masks lowered to conceal their faces. Three more stood behind the altar, dressed in robes of purple, red and black respectively.

"What is your name, sir?" Ritter's voice again, behind the purple mask, at center stage.

"Mike Bowers."

"The Teutonic Knights of the Ku Klux Klan, a great and essentially a patriotic, fraternal, benevolent order, does not discriminate against a man on account of his religious or political creed when same does not conflict with or antagonize the sacred rights and privileges guaranteed by our civil government and Christian ideals and institutions.

"Therefore, to avoid any misunderstanding and as evidence that we do not seek to impose unjustly the requirements of this order upon anyone who cannot, on account of his religious or political scruples, voluntarily meet our requirements and faithfully practice our principles, and as proof that we respect all honest men in their sacred convictions, whether same are agreeable with our requirements or not, we require as an absolute necessity on the part of each of you an affirmative answer to each of the following questions."

Ritter hesitated for a moment, eyeing Bolan closely before he continued.

country, our Klan, our homes and each other: these are the distinguishing marks of a Klansman, and this man claims the marks. What if he should prove himself a traitor?''

On cue, Bob Shelton answered. ''He would be immediately banished in disgrace from the invisible empire without fear or favor, conscience would tenaciously torment him, remorse would repeatedly revile him, and direful things would befall him.''

''Does he know all this?''

''All this he knows,'' Shelton replied. ''He has heard, and he must heed.''

''A Klansman speaks the truth in and from his heart,'' Ritter growled. ''A lying scoundrel may wrap his disgraceful frame within the sacred folds of a Klansman's robe and deceive the very elect, but only a Klansman has a Klansman's heart and a Klansman's soul. Let us pray.''

The man in red stepped forward as their heads were lowered, offering the invocation in a voice like velvet-covered steel.

''God give us men! The invisible empire demands strong minds, great hearts, true faith and ready hands. Men whom the lust of office does not kill; men whom the spoils of office cannot buy; men who possess opinions and a will; men who have honor; men who will not lie; men who can stand before a demagogue and damn his treacherous flatteries without winking! Tall men, sun-crowned, who live above the fog in public duty and in private thinking. For while the rabble, with their thumb-worn creeds, their large professions and their little deeds, mingle in strife, lo! Freedom weeps. Wrong rules the land, and waiting justice sleeps. God give us men! Men who serve not for selfish booty, but real men, courageous, who flinch not at duty; men of dependable character; men of sterling worth. Then wrongs will be redressed, and right will rule the earth. God give us men!''

''Amen.''

''Amen!''

Ritter raised his eyes to Bolan's once again. ''Will you, by your daily life as a Klansman, earnestly endeavor to be a living answer to that prayer?''

"I will."

"It is indeed refreshing to meet face-to-face with a man like you, who, actuated by manly motives, aspires to all things noble for yourself and for humanity. The luster of the holy light of chivalry has lost its former glory and is sadly dimmed by the choking dust of selfish, sordid gain. Pass on."

On cue, the red-robed chaplain took up the ritual where the wizard had left off. "Real fraternity, by shameful neglect, has been starved until, so weak, her voice is lost in the courts of her own castle, and she passes unnoticed by her sworn subjects as she moves along the crowded streets and through the din of the marketplace. Man's valuation of man is by the standard of wealth and not worth; selfishness is the festive queen among humankind, and multitudes forget honor, justice, love, and God and every religious conviction to do homage to her. And yet, with the cruel heart of Jezebel, she slaughters the souls of thousands of her devotees daily. Pass on!"

For the first time, the anonymous black-robed Klansman had something to say. "The unsatiated thirst for gain is dethroning reason and judgment in the citadel of the human soul, and men maddened thereby forget their patriotic, domestic and social obligations and duties and fiendishly fight for a place in the favor of the goddess of glittering gold. They starve their own souls and make sport of spiritual development. Pass on!"

Back to Ritter. "Sir, we congratulate you on your manly decision to forsake the world of selfishness and fraternal alienation and emigrate to the delectable bounds of the invisible empire and become a loyal citizen of the same. The prime purpose of this great order is to develop character, to practice clannishness, to protect the home and the chastity of womanhood and to exemplify a pure patriotism toward our glorious country.

"You, as a citizen of the invisible empire, must be actively patriotic toward our country, and constantly clannish toward Klansmen socially, physically, morally and vocationally. Will you assume this obligation of citizenship?''

"I will."

"You must unflinchingly conform to our requirements, regulations and usages in every detail and prove yourself worthy to have and to hold the honors we bestow. Do you freely and faithfully promise to do this?''

"I do."

"Sir, if you have any doubt as to your ability to qualify, either in body or character, as a citizen of the invisible empire, you now have an opportunity to retire from this place with the goodwill of the Klan to attend you. For I warn you now, if you falter or fail at this time or in the future as a Klansman, you will be banished without fear or favor from citizenship in the invisible empire.

"This is a serious undertaking. We are not here to make sport of you nor indulge in the silly frivolity of circus clowns. Be you well assured that he that puts his hands to the plow and looks back is not fit for the kingdom of heaven or worthy of the high honor of citizenship in the invisible empire or the fervent fellowship of Klansmen. Do not deceive yourself; you cannot deceive us, and we will not be mocked. Do you wish to retire?''

"I do not."

"Sir, have you assumed without mental reservation your oath of allegiance to the invisible empire?''

"I have."

"Mortal man cannot assume a more binding oath. Character and courage alone will enable you to keep it. Always remember that to keep this oath means to you honor, happiness and life; but to violate it means disgrace, dishonor and death. May honor, happiness and life be yours.''

Ritter lifted the pitcher of water from the makeshift altar, holding it at arm's length without a tremor in his hand.

"With this transparent, life-giving, powerful, God-given fluid, more precious and far more significant than all the sacred oils of the ancients, I set you apart from the men of your daily association to the great and honorable task you have voluntarily allotted yourself as a citizen of the Invisible Empire of the Teutonic Knights of the Ku Klux Klan.

"As a Klansman may your character be as transparent, your life's purpose as powerful, your motive in all things as magnanimous and as pure and your clannishness as real and as faithful as the manifold drops herein, and you a vital being as useful to humanity as is pure water to mankind.

"You will kneel upon your right knee."

Bolan did as he was told, head bent before the altar. From the corner of his eye, he watched as Mason Ritter dipped the fingers of his free hand in the water, flinging droplets over Bolan's head and shoulders in a sort of mock baptism.

"Beneath the fiery cross, which by its holy light looks down upon you to bless with its scared traditions of the past, I dedicate you in body, in mind, in spirit and in life to the holy service of our country, our Klan, our homes, one another and humanity. Rise, Klansman, and be recognized!"

Bolan rose as the surrounding Klansmen peeled their masks back and removed their pointed hoods. He recognized the men in white as Bobby Shelton and his shotgun rider. Ritter, in his regal purple robe, appeared to be the man in charge. The others, dressed in red and black, were strangers.

"Welcome to the Knights," said Mason Ritter, wringing Bolan's hand as if to test his strength. "I want to introduce the brothers to you."

Turning to the man in red, whose graying hair and double chins placed him somewhere in his middle forties, Ritter said, "Our kludd—the chaplain, that is—Reverend Jacob Halsey."

"Pleased to meet you, Reverend."

"Likewise, son."

The pastor's grip was firm and dry. Incredibly, despite his garb, despite all that had been said, there appeared to be no meanness in his face.

"And our klaliff—that's equivalent to the vice president," Ritter continued, turning toward the man in black, "is Jerome Freeman, esteemed chairman of the Aryan Vanguard."

"A pleasure, Mr. Bowers."

"Sir, the pleasure's mine."

He did not recognize the blond man, would have sworn that he had never seen the face before, but there was something about the Klansman's hands. So small, so delicate, his fingers like the digits of a child. As if in line with Bolan's train of thought, the klaliff disengaged himself and busied his tiny hands with the mechanics of disrobing. The other Klansmen were doing likewise, stripping down to their street clothes.

"Time to share a toast of celebration, son. This way."

He followed Ritter and the others across the floor of what appeared to be an empty warehouse, through a doorway leading to a narrow corridor with offices on either side. The wizard chose the first door on his left.

Inside, a fair-size conference room had been converted to a smallish dining hall. In the center of the room was a single folding table, and a smaller one stood against the wall, supporting a coffee machine, several mugs and boxes of mixed pastries. A slender dark-haired woman was testing the coffee as they entered, and she turned to greet them with a smile.

"Mike Bowers," the chaplain rumbled, "may I introduce my niece, Lynn Halsey?"

"By all means."

"A pleasure, Mr. Bowers."

"Call me Mike."

A warning flash lit up the pastor's solemn eyes. "We must be going, Lynn," he said. "These gentlemen have business to discuss."

"Of course."

Was there a hint of disappointment in her voice, Bolan wondered, or was he letting his imagination run away with him? Her uncle guided her protectively in the direction of the door. So much for clannishness, he thought as Bobby Shelton dug an elbow in his ribs.

"The reverend is a holy man, but some of us are just a bit more human. Would you like a little something extra in your coffee, Mike?'' As Ritter spoke, he pulled a whiskey bottle from a cupboard overhead.

"I wouldn't turn it down."

"Good man." A liberal shot of whiskey disappeared into Bolan's mug. "We'll have you fitted for a robe and whatnot in a day or two. Right now, we need to talk about your new profession."

"What profession's that?"

"Why, you're a teacher, son. I thought you understood that going in. You're going to teach your brother Klansmen how to kill."

9

Jerome Freeman parked his Lincoln near the entrance to the banking complex, killed the heavy engine, locked it up. His preference ran more toward the Mercedes-Benz, but his position as a mouthpiece for the nativists compelled him to insist upon domestic transportation for himself. It was a stricture he could live with. For the moment.

Through revolving doors, across the air-conditioned lobby. Right turn for the bank, left turn for the loan department. Freeman held his course, proceeding straight ahead until he reached the bank of elevators, found one waiting for him, stepped inside and punched the button marked Exec. The executive offices were on the top floor of the complex, and Freeman had been there only once before. His summons was in striking contrast to the usual routine of covert phone calls taken late at night. An audience with Michael Andrews ranked somewhere just below a meeting with the President.

The several levels of the complex had been named rather than numbered, catering to some small whim of Andrews's, but the Vanguard's leader knew he had reached the thirteenth floor when the pneumatic doors whisked open, offering a view of the resplendent corridor beyond. No effort or expense had been spared in decoration, from the deep shag carpet to the hardwood paneling and the seemingly authentic artworks on the walls. He was impressed; the vision Andrews had created reaffirmed his own desire to live in luxury with servants waiting on him hand and foot. Male servants. Young. Delicious.

Freeman drew his mind back to the present errand, dou
ble-checking that his tie was straight before he reached the
broad desk of the receptionist. She graced him with a daz-
zling smile designed to set his blood on fire. Not her fault,
Freeman thought, that her attempt did not have the desired
affect.

"Good morning, Mr. Freeman. Mr. Andrews is expecting you. I'll let him know you're here."

The sleek receptionist returned, all smiles. "Mr. Andrews will see you now. Please follow me."

"My pleasure, hon."

She almost giggled, caught herself and led the way along
another corridor to reach the inner sanctum of the man who
covered both their salaries. She left him with another
hundred-candlepower smile and stopped just short of
winking at him as she sashayed back along the hall. It was
a pity, all that effort wasted.

"Jerry, glad you could make it. Always good to see you."

That was bullshit, seven ways from Sunday. No one called
him "Jerry" anymore, and there was no way in the world he
could have missed the meeting, even if he'd wanted to. Not
that it had ever crossed his mind.

A face-to-face with Andrews was a rare event. A challenge, testing Freeman's own ability to keep up his facade.
He must not let the banker know his secret had been compromised. Not yet. Above all else, he must preserve his own
small mysteries from prying eyes. If matters got away from
him, it would be serious—no, fatal—and he had no great
desire to die before his time.

"My pleasure, Michael."

They were on a bullshit first-name basis, even though he
recognized that Andrews thought himself superior in every
way. It was ironic, with his thinning hair and his waistline
running recently to blubber. Middle age had not been
merciful to Andrews. Neither, Freeman thought, would he.
When it was time.

"A glass of brandy?" Andrews offered. "A cigar?"

He knew Freeman did not smoke, had known it for more
than a year, and still he offered, every inch the perfect host.

"No, thank you."

"Ah, too early in the day, perhaps? How are you, Jerry?"

"Busy."

"Yes, of course." The blunt reply did not seem to faze him; he was still all plastic smiles. "It's business that I wanted to discuss."

At last, a stab at getting to the point. "What can I do for you?"

"I'm curious about your progress," Andrews said.

"You could have said that on the telephone."

"I sometimes find the element of human contact beneficial in analyzing situations." Same old bullshit, Freeman noticed. "Please speak freely. I assure you that this office is secure."

It should be, Freeman thought. The banker spent a small fortune every year on debugging and antisurveillance equipment, employing technicians with government backgrounds to spot weaknesses, trace them and see to their swift elimination.

"Very well," Freeman began. "As you know, Theo Brown's funeral was held day before yesterday. That portion of our contract is completed."

"And the union?"

"Hanging on, but obviously weakened. Protests are on hold while they select another leader to replace the dear departed."

"Candidates?"

"The front-runner seems to be Brown's father. He's an outsider, new to the union, but he's articulate enough, and he's got the sympathy vote sewed up tight. At the moment, he has no viable opposition."

"Plans?"

"I'd like to wait a while and see what happens. Taking out another organizer now would bring down heat you won't believe."

"That bothers you?"

"Of course it bothers me. The ultimate objective is to crush the farmers' union, not be crushed ourselves. Another hit this soon would draw the FBI like flies to honey.

It might even force the Chatham County locals to wake up and take some action.''

''I'm not interested in the problems. Just results.''

''You should be interested in the problems, Michael. Problems cost you money, and they could cost me a great deal more.''

''Your people are expendable.''

''I'm not. The kind of heat we're risking wouldn't stop with grass-root arrests. The Feds aren't satisfied with trig-germen these days. They want the backers. The capos. The imperial wizards.''

''You're worried about Ritter?''

''Certainly. If he goes down, there's every possibility that he might talk to save himself.''

''A leak can't be that difficult to plug.''

''We're making smoke here. None of this has happened yet, and there's no reason why it should if we use common sense and bide our time.''

''I need results,'' the banker said. ''My backers are impatient.''

Freeman knew about his ''backers''—those he publicly avowed, and those who *really* pulled the strings. If Andrews had been conscious of the way in which he stood exposed, it would have wiped the smug self-satisfaction from his face. Oh, yes, indeed.

''Advise them of the risks involved.''

''I've tried.'' The banker spread his open hands in a helpless gesture. ''They have profit on their minds. It's strictly business.''

''Sometimes business has to wait.''

''Not this time, I believe. The union is already wounded. It would be a foolish error to give them time to lick their wounds and find another charismatic leader.''

''You must realize that every act of violence strengthens their resolve. For every member lost, they find another one to take his place. Short of wholesale annihilation, I can't guarantee a broken union on any sort of timetable.''

"But you have guaranteed it, Jerry. Remember?" The voice was satin-covered steel. "You promised satisfaction."

"If I ran the show *my* way. You can't impose a whole new set of terms and still expect the same results."

"Regrettably, I have no choice. My backers—"

"Have a lot to learn about America."

Oh, God.

"What do you mean by that?"

Too late to snatch back the words, but he still might have a chance to save himself if he was quick and cool enough. "I mean you've all been living in your ivory towers so damned long you don't remember how the little people think, or how they feel." A little bluster wouldn't hurt at this point. "When you slap a farmer down, his instinct is to get back up and kick your ass. My men can't play this game by boardroom rules."

Andrews studied his face for a long moment, finally seemed satisfied with what he found there, reassured that his cover was intact, his secret safe from prying eyes.

"Results," he said at last. "The money's not important."

"While we're on the subject, there's a hardware shipment coming in tonight or late tomorrow, C.O.D. I'll need to cover it."

"Of course."

"I also have another man on salary. A trainer for the troops."

"Is that advisable?"

"I'd say it's mandatory for the kind of plays you have in mind. We won't get anywhere with untrained rednecks."

"I suppose you're right. Is he secure?"

"We ran him through the sheriff's office. He's an ex-con with a history of racial incidents. I'd say he's perfect."

"Fine. I'll leave it in your hands. About Brown's father—what's his name?"

"Wilson."

"I think we should deal with him promptly, don't you?"

"I've explained what I think. It could be a disastrous mistake."

"Even so."

"You insist?"

"If you like."

"Very well."

"Good. It's settled, then."

"I don't suppose you had a special date or place in mind?"

"I wouldn't dream of interfering, Jerry, you know that."

"Of course."

"Some time within the next two weeks should be sufficient."

"And the rest of it?"

"Long-range, I'd say we have six months."

"Six months!"

"Surprised?"

"You could say that."

"You have my sympathy, of course, but circumstances alter cases, as I'm sure you understand."

"We'll need more trainers."

"As you like."

"More money."

"Certainly."

Six months was lunacy, but Freeman saw no gain in pointing out that Andrews was demanding nothing short of suicide. The banker knew that, *had* to know it. He might be many things, but he was not a reckless man; each move was calculated, weighed in terms of energy expenditure and probable results. If he was opting for a deadline that was certain to result in chaos, then he had his reasons.

Fine.

Six months was time enough for Freeman to inflate expense accounts and "order" shipments that would never be received. Acceleration of the schedule meant acceleration of his plans, as well, but there were unexpected benefits. With Andrews pushing for results, a six-month deadline, there would be less opportunity for him to breathe down Freeman's neck, observing every move. If money was no object, he would not be prone to question Freeman's spending, the amounts that disappeared without a trace into the Vanguard leader's numbered Swiss accounts.

He had been counting on a longer time, demanding different strategies, but shorter deadlines would require a change of plan. Instead of wooing Andrews for the money, it would be a case of rape and run...but that could be amusing, too. It could be *damned* amusing with the proper partner.

Later.

Business now, with pleasure in the back seat, waiting for another time, another place. He had too much to deal with as it was, without the complication of a hasty love affair. Still...

"I beg your pardon?"

Andrews frowned at having to repeat himself. "I asked if there was anything else?"

"I don't believe so." Freeman made a show of pondering the question, finally shook his head in an emphatic negative. "No, not offhand."

"Well, then, I know you're busy, as I am...."

Dismissal. Freeman shook the banker's hand and thanked him for his time. "I trust your partners will be satisfied with the results of their suggestions."

There. The dig was irresistible, but it was time to go. He left the banker standing at his desk, a quizzical expression on his face, and closed the door behind him, cutting off the stare. He passed the receptionist's desk, then paused and turned back to face her.

"I wonder if I might just trouble you for one small thing?"

"Of course?"

"Your phone number?"

Freeman noticed that her hand was trembling as she wrote it, folding the piece of paper twice before passing it into his palm.

"I hope you'll use it soon."

"My dear, are you Italian, by any chance?"

"Why, no. What makes you ask?"

"Because I think you made an offer that I can't refuse."

Delighted laughter trailed him to the elevator. Freeman felt pleased with himself, overall. He had outwitted Andrews, or would do so shortly, and had simultaneously found a way to relieve his pent-up tensions. It would take some getting used to, but the girl seemed sympathetic, eager, and he thought that with a bit of raw imagination he would manage nicely.

It would be a memorable new experience.

MICHAEL ANDREWS SPENT a moment staring after Freeman, finally settling back into his leather-upholstered desk chair. The mercenary's arrogance was irksome, but it came with the territory. If Freeman thought himself in charge, so much the better. Let him posture for his troops, for the jackals of the media. While Freeman drew attention to himself, Andrews was free to operate behind the scenes, secure from public scrutiny. And if the heat got back to him at some time in the future...well, there were means of dealing with that problem, as well.

It had been easy so far, manipulating both the Vanguard's chairman and his "partners" in the Southern Bankers' Conference. How foolish all of them would feel if they knew how they had been used. And all the time they thought they were using him.

Suppressing laughter, Andrews crossed the room and poured himself a brandy. Never mind the hour; he had earned a drink, and he would have it. Celebration was in order now, with victory approaching, well within his grasp. There had been times—and recently—when he had lived in fear of failure, dreading contact with his secret sponsors, fearing they would sicken of delays and scrub his mission, laying waste everything he had achieved.

It had taken years for Andrews to achieve his present status. Years of private struggle with support from his clandestine backers, knowing they could snatch the rug from under him at any moment. If his associates could only realize...

At age nineteen, he had arrived in the United States from Canada, a border crossing carried out in darkness by a young man frightened for his life. The documents he had carried were forgeries—the best Dzerzhinsky Square could offer at the time—and they had served him well as he began the journey southward, following the Mississippi River to his destination. He was Michael Andrews, then, and so he would remain. Mikhail Andreivich was dead and gone, his memory entombed in Moscow in the files of KGB.

The concept of a "sleeper" agent was not new, by any means. Throughout the postwar era they had been used to good effect in Europe and America.

Sleepers had succeeded in securing information that a transient operative might have missed. A few had penetrated special targets—even, it was rumored, the inner ranks of Hoover's sacred FBI. Andreivich could not evaluate such rumors, and he did not waste time trying. His employers had decreed a different sort of mission in America for him, and he was anxious to begin his work on behalf of the people's revolution.

Unlike sleepers who were planted with an eye toward the gathering of information, "Michael Andrews" had been trained to serve as a provocateur. His placement in the South in 1955 had been no accident of fate. A short year earlier, the American Supreme Court had struck down the "separate but equal" rule established during the nineteenth century, with *Plessy* v. *Ferguson*. Racial integration was the new law of the land, and Washington commanded that it should begin "with all deliberate speed." In more than a dozen states where segregation was enshrined as God's own law, an angry ruling class responded with defiant shouts of "Never!" Political careers were built on little more than the ability of candidates to bellow "Nigger!" from the back of flatbed trucks, and grass-roots bands of white Americans devoted to "patriotic resistance" sprang up in abundance like noxious weeds across the fertile countryside.

In all, it was a situation made for propaganda, and the KGB was not naive enough to let the chance slip through its fingers. Michael Andrews was among their best, and he had

been assigned to penetrate the South, achieve financial
prominence, acquire respectability, present himself to one
and all as a staid pillar of society. In that pursuit, the cof-
fers of the Comintern were opened wide; what Andrews
needed he received, and in a decade he had risen from a
lowly teller to the presidency of Razorback Savings and
Loan. From there, investments had paved the way for cor-
porate expansion and proliferation, dollars breeding dollars, and in time, he hardly ever called upon his backers for
support. He had arrived.

In the beginning Andrews reported faithfully to his control, a minor politician, formerly a lawyer noted for resisting integration suits—and losing every time. Another
sleeper, the control had done so well at taking on the attri-
butes of an American that he had gradually drifted out of
Moscow's confidence. Members of the KGB had suspected
him of "going over" to the enemy, in mind if not in fact, of
becoming "too American" to be of further use. Upon
command, Mikhail Andreivich had killed his sympathetic
contact, staging the event to pass for accidental death, the
result of too much alcohol behind the steering wheel. At
twenty-seven, he had suddenly been in business for himself . . . and business was good.

Along the way from a subsistence wage to comfort and
from there to opulence, he had contributed his time and
money to a wide variety of racist groups. A dozen different
factions of the Ku Klux Klan had welcomed his largesse, as
had the White Citizens' Council, the American Nazi Party
and the National Association for the Advancement of White
People. When disgruntled Klansmen found the KKK too
tame and organized their own mobile demolition team,
dubbed Nacirema—American spelled backward—Andrews was among the contributors who helped finance their
hobby. Wherever racial violence seemed a possibility, the
rising banker did his secret best to make it a reality, the word
made flesh and blood. Especially blood.

To prove himself nonpartisan, he funneled cash to other
groups as well. At one time or another, Andrews had pa-
tronized the Black Panthers, the Black Liberation Army, the

Republic of New Africa and the Revolutionary Communist Party, which had no more connection with the KGB or Moscow than it did with Ronald Reagan's own Department of Defense. It pleased him to amuse himself by playing both ends off against the middle. How much more exciting if the blacks were armed and ready—even eager—to fight back.

When Andrews thought about it, which was seldom now, he realized the FBI was likely to maintain a file on his activities. Their infiltration of the KKK and of black militant societies was well established in the press, and it would be pure luck if he had managed to escape their scrutiny for more than thirty years. In fact, he had no reason to believe that he had been so lucky, no desire for them to overlook his numble efforts.

If the Bureau had a file on Michael Andrews, why, so much the better. From the outset of his mission, he had been aware of every risk involved, the possibility of his indictment and conviction on assorted charges of conspiracy. Donations to the Klan and allied groups was not a crime per se, but Andrews had been instrumental in supplying weapons, ammunition and explosives to the groups he favored with his generosity. How many churches, schools and private dwellings had been leveled with the dynamite he had purchased through the years? How many victims had been killed or wounded by the weapons he had supplied to Klansmen, Nazis and warriors of "black liberation"?

On a personal level, he had murdered only the once, but it had been exhilarating, an experience beyond compare. The tension mounting as he waited for a visit from authorities; the sweet relief—almost orgasmic—that he felt on realizing that his plan was foolproof, that he would not be identified. From time to time he dusted off the memories, examined them with loving care. A cherished moment in his life . . . and one he would gladly duplicate, provided any decent opportunity.

He thought of Freeman, and the man's remark about his backers having much to learn about America. A mere coincidence? What else? Freeman was a clever man, within his limitations, but it was preposterous to think he could have pierced the veil that Andrews had constructed over thirty years and more. Preposterous, and yet . . .

It would be desirable to eliminate the risk before it went too far. If there was any chance at all of ultimate exposure, he might be required to use his own initiative, eliminate the threat through drastic action. It was acceptable for an American financial wizard to be tried on charges of supporting racist lunatics—the KGB would love it, benefiting greatly from the propaganda that a trial would generate— but it was something else entirely for a Russian sleeper to be dragged before the bar. Exposure of his mission in America would be disaster, pure and simple. It would set the cause back years, perhaps decades. And it would all be his fault in the end.

At the moment he needed Freeman, but in time the mercenary would exhaust his usefulness. Expendable already, he would soon become a detriment to Andrews and the master plan. At that point, it would be the pleasure of Mikhail Andreivich to play another game of hide-and-seek with the authorities, observe them as they launched an investigation of another timely "accident." Too long since he had felt the heady rush of danger and excitement. Much too long.

He hoped that Freeman would be swift about his business, putting everything in readiness. The mercenary was a perfect object for the game that Andrews had in mind, and he was looking forward to it now. Entertaining, yes. It could be all of that and more.

The banker's smile was hungry, scarcely human. He felt tremendous.

After all these years, the sleeper was awake.

10

Perched above the game trail on a stout oak limb, Mack Bolan waited for his prey. His face and hands were daubed with camouflage cosmetics, and his tiger-stripe fatigues merged perfectly with the surrounding foliage. In his hand, the heavy pistol pointed earthward, covering the trail. He had been waiting for almost fifteen minutes, but his targets were approaching now. Two of them, judging by the sounds.

It was his first day on the job as drill instructor for the troopers of the Vanguard and the Klan. The night before, with some help from Mason Ritter, he had acquired a tiny apartment in Parrish, settling his few belongings in and making the place secure before he went to sleep. At dawn he had rendezvoused with Ritter for the short drive west of town to Camp Nordland, a compound including barracks, towers and a dining hall, constructed in the middle of the woods on land belonging to the Vanguard. According to the wizard, seven hundred acres were available to "patriots" for training and maneuvers. It would be "Bowers's" job to prepare the latest class for combat and to refine the drill in order to accommodate larger, more frequent groups.

Twelve men had fallen out on Bolan's order, garbed in camouflage or olive drab, three of them sporting stringy hair below their collars, six in need of shaves. Their weapons were a motley assortment, including several shotguns, AR-15s, Ruger Mini-14s, a Kalashnikov reworked for semiauto fire to make it legal in the States. Most of them also carried handguns, and they seemed partial to huge "survival knives," more noted for their weight than for their practicality.

Bolan stood before them, withering the would-be soldiers with his stare.

"How many of you men believe you're fit to call yourselves soldiers? Right now, let's see your hands!"

A dozen hands went up, a few more hesitantly than the rest. One of the rumpled soldiers snickered to himself, amused by something that was not apparent to the others present.

"Fine. I like to see a group of men with confidence." He moved along the ragtag column, studying each face in turn. "Let's make a deal here, shall we? Let's forget about the training for today and play a little game of hide-and-seek. I'm it. Whoever tags me graduates today. If I tag anyone, that person gets a decent haircut, shaves his scraggly face and comes back here tomorrow morning *looking* like a soldier, ready to begin from scratch. Who wants to play?"

Again the dozen hands went up, a few more hesitating this time at the prospect of some work involved.

When all the hands were raised, Bolan said, "You'll need to check your weapons. That includes the pistols. Keep the knives, if they make you feel better." Stooping, he opened a footlocker, revealing the air guns and extra loads of paint pellets within. "We'll be using these today. A hit between the hairline and the knees is fatal. Dead men show up in the morning clean and early to begin their training. Any questions?"

"Can we hunt in teams?"

"Hunt any way you like. It won't make any difference."

The mock commandos muttered over that among themselves, and Bolan let them gripe a while before demanding their attention once again. He used the time to choose an air gun, loading up and filling the pockets of his camouflage fatigues with extra tubes of paint balls.

"Pick your weapons," Bolan ordered. "Then you shag ass back inside the dining hall and give me ten. I'll start off heading north. From that point on, it's up to you "

Despite the Klansman's question about hunting in teams, most of the troopers had preferred to run singly, pursuing their quarry with all the panache of a bull in a china shop. Bolan had taken the first as he thrashed in a clump of wild roses, ensnared by the long, wicked thorns. Number one had attempted to fire, but the thorns had snagged his sleeve and prevented the weapon from locking on target. He took the paint square in his chest, a bright splash of crimson denoting a heart shot.

"Goddamn it!"

"You're dead. Back to camp."

"Jesus Christ!"

Bolan left him to pull himself free and moved on. Number two had been tapping a kidney as Bolan approached from his blind side, contentedly hosing the flora and using his free hand to wave off the flies. Bolan wasted no time with the pisser; a shot to the back of the head brought him leaping around in surprise, urine sprinkling his shoes.

"That ain't fair!"

"Zip it up. Back to camp."

Now he waited for two who had chosen to hunt as a team. Teamwork was wise, if you did it correctly, but these two were buddies enjoying a game, communicating in raspy stage whispering, imitating Rambo as they blundered from one tree to another, telegraphing every move with excess noise.

"I'm telling you, he won't be on the trail."

"Shut up! He could be anywhere."

"My ass."

"No, thanks, I've got a girlfriend."

"Shithead."

Helpless laughter from the Klan comedian as he came out into the open. Close behind him, his disgruntled partner dragged his feet and held his air gun carelessly, its muzzle pointed toward the earth. Bolan let them close the gap, moving with less caution now, speaking in normal tones as they bantered back and forth. Their jokes revolved around the antics of priests and rabbis, who were constantly begging for donations, getting laid or both. The pair was no more than thirty feet away from Bolan's perch.

"And so the mother superior says, 'Two dollars, Father, the same as in town!'"

The taller Klansman stood with head thrown back in laughter, loving it, his oval lips a perfect bull's-eye. Bolan saw no reason to resist. He sighted quickly, squeezed the air gun's trigger and watched his target stagger, spitting crimson paint and sputtering surprise.

The joker watched his sidekick for a heartbeat, trying to decide if he was sick or merely clowning, but he never had the chance to work it out. A second paint ball burst against his cheek, bright rivulets describing abstract patterns in his scraggly beard and across the blouse of his fatigues.

"A lousy, frigging ambush!"

Bolan dropped, catlike, to stand before them. "What were you expecting, soldier? Hearts and flowers?"

"You could give a man a chance!"

"You had one, and you blew it. Back to camp."

He watched them disappear around the bend, then struck off through the trees, avoiding vines and creepers that reached out to snare him, bring him down. It was a challenge, moving silently through so much tangled undergrowth, but Bolan managed. Years of field experience had taught him every trick imaginable, and he used them now to good effect. The hunters, meanwhile, seemed to thrash about with greater noise than ever, setting birds and animals to flight before them, keeping Bolan constantly apprised of their locations.

And the Executioner began to take them. One by one.

He crossed the trail of number five a short ten minutes after "killing" three and four. The guy was blundering along without a backward glance, cutting a swath through the ferns and saplings, using his air gun like a blunt machete to beat down the brush. Bolan fell in behind him, taking advantage of the incompetent tracker's noise, closing rapidly to point-blank range. Up close, he could hear the Klansman talking to himself, bemoaning his discomfort.

"Fucking trees. Can't see a goddamn thing."

"You're history."

The soft voice brought his target spinning around, and Bolan shot him in the chin, the red paint dribbling down his neck and shirt as if he had been interrupted in the middle of eating a cherry pie. The Klansman stared at Bolan, dumbstruck.

"Back to camp."

Number six was thirsty, had already drained his canteen. Bolan found him kneeling beside a forest stream, glancing nervously around as he refilled the water bottle, his air gun resting on a bed of leaves beside him. He bent to wash his sweaty face, presenting Bolan with a target he could not resist. The pellet stung the barracks trooper's buttocks, and he reached around reluctantly to test the damage, fingers bright and sticky as they came away from the seat of his pants.

"A hole in one. Head back to camp."

Number seven took a page from Bolan's book and found himself a high-side vantage point. Unfortunately, scuff marks on the tree trunk from his boots betrayed him, and his skill at camouflage left much to be desired. In spite of tiger-stripe fatigues, he stood out from the foliage rather than becoming part of it, and while he might have foxed his comrades in the hunt, the Executioner was not deceived.

It was a tricky shot for all of that. The gunner had a clear view of his chosen game trail either way, and blind-side access gave him perfect cover from the tree's trunk. Bolan finally had to backtrack fifty yards and cross the trail beyond his target's line of sight, returning on the far side, keeping to the trees, until he stood directly opposite his mark.

No problem then. Thirty feet away, the target perched above the deer track like a giant Cheshire cat, all smiles and smug self-satisfaction. Bolan wiped the smile off with a pellet to the forehead, bright paint mingling with the camouflage disguise.

"You're finished. Hang it up."

"Hey, damn it, where'd you come from?"

"From your nightmares. Back to camp."

Number eight was stalking number nine when Bolan overtook him, and the warrior left him to it, watching from a cautious distance as the Klansman flanked his comrade, unaware of what he was about to do. Anxiety or zeal betrayed the tracker at the final instant and he let loose a rebel yell, alerting his intended prey. The amateur commandos opened fire together, peppering each other with a spray of paint at point-blank range.

"Great work," the Executioner announced, emerging from the forest shadows. "You'll make it easy on the enemy."

"Goddamn you, Vern, you horse's ass!"

"Don't try'n blame this mess on me, you stupid bastard!"

"Why don't you kiss my ass?"

"Why don't you both go back to camp?"

The last three almost took Bolan, working in conjunction, and the soldier later blamed himself for growing overconfident, complacent, as he stalked the stragglers. Using one as bait, the other two had staked their partner out like big-game hunters with a tethered goat. It nearly worked—but not as they had planned.

Approaching in silence from the south, Bolan saw the decoy first and froze. He scanned the undergrowth, the overhanging trees, and found the nearest gunner, offering a mute congratulation to the stalkers for originality. He meant to take the sniper first, deflating ego with surprise. In doing so, he overlooked the second gunner waiting in the shrubbery a dozen yards away.

The sniper he had spotted was a portly mechanic in his mid-twenties who carried the smell of the lube rack with him everywhere he went. His face was grimed and dark without the use of camouflage cosmetics, his oily hair concealed beneath a rumpled bush hat. Bolan was surprised to find him in a tree at all, decided there had to be muscle somewhere underneath the flab.

The sniper's chosen limb was large, but he was still precariously balanced, stretched out lengthwise for maximum support. A simple nudge would do the job, Bolan thought, out he could not climb the tree and take his quarry by surprise. A shot would have to do instead.

He held the air gun in a classic dueling stance and sighted down the barrel at a point behind the gunner's ear. It was an easy pop, and he would follow through by dropping forty-five degrees to pin the Judas goat before he could react.

He fired and saw the pellet find its mark, a ruby blossom opening its petals on the Klansman's neck. Unhurt but startled, Bolan's target lost his purchase on the limb, made one attempt to catch himself before he fell, all arms and legs and bleating cries, immediately silenced by his jarring impact with the ground.

The gunner's cry of warning was enough to spook his partner, and the human bait was on the move as Bolan dropped his aim to bring the second Klansman under fire. He was already squeezing off, afraid he had been too slow, when he was startled by a sudden crashing in the undergrowth no more than twenty feet away.

Another hostile, closing fast and firing as he ran. A pellet grazed the tree trunk next to Bolan's shoulder, spattered harmlessly on bark and leaves. The soldier pivoted and hit a combat crouch, his air gun tracking, seeking a substantial target. Bolan knew that he had blown it, thrown the game away. It would take a miracle to save him now.

A miracle, or simple clumsiness by his opponent.

The grinning Klansman snapped a second shot at Bolan, missing him by inches, charging headlong through the trees. He didn't see the hidden root that snared him, pitched him headlong to the ground, his air gun jarred from startled fingers. Cursing, he dragged himself forward on knees and elbows, stretching to retrieve the weapon in the fraction of a second left to him. Bolan seized the moment, planting one between his eyes.

The Klansman groaned in disgust and slammed his fist into the drift of leaves, rewarded by a painful *thunk* as knuckles met another hidden root at high velocity.

"Goddamn it!"

Bolan was already searching for the decoy when the last man showed himself, his weapon braced in both hands, sighting for the kill. He fired as Bolan hit a flying shoulder roll, wasting his pellet on a bank of ferns.

The Executioner came up firing. Once. Twice. Three times, all in rapid-fire. His pellets etched a bloody pattern on the gunner's chest and left him staring mournfully at camouflage fatigues turned crimson in the mottled light of early afternoon.

"All done. Let's take it back to camp."

It was a different group of men that stood before him in the shadow of the mess hall, daubed with paint and wearing faces molded out of anger and humiliation. Staring at them, Bolan wondered which of them—if any—had been present at the death of Theo Brown. Which of them held the answers to a dozen different crimes of violence that had terrorized the county during recent months?

"How many of you think you qualify as fighting men?" he asked again. This time no hands were raised. "All right. Before you hit the showers, carry this thought with you: in a real-life combat situation, each and every one of you would now be dead! Not wounded, not arrested or indicted. Dead. You're no damn good to anyone as corpses. Do you read me?"

"Yeah, all right."

"We get the message."

"Do you? Well, I hope so. I've been asked to let you have the benefit of my experience and training, in an effort to prepare you for survival in a real-life, down-and-dirty combat situation. Someone told me you were soldiers, but you'll have to prove it after what I've seen today."

He let them simmer in their anger for a moment as he moved along the line, examining their sweaty, paint-streaked faces. So what if they hated him. In the last analysis, it would not matter either way.

"Tomorrow, when you fall in here at eight o'clock, I want you clean and shaved, with military haircuts. Bring whatever weapons you have for openers; we'll fit you out with decent hardware as the opportunities arrive. Above all else, I want you here prepared to work your butts off. Anyone allergic to hard labor might as well stay home. Fall out!"

He turned to find Lynn Halsey watching from the shaded doorway of the dining hall, and caught her as she tried to hide a smile.

"You're pretty tough," she said.

"Sometimes."

"It's all that time in uniform, I guess."

"I guess. What brings you to the woods?"

"My uncle. Actually, he's not here, but I came out to pick up some things for him."

"Reverend Halsey goes to camp?"

"He doesn't train with them, but they have meetings here sometimes, and he officiates. As chaplain."

"Ah."

"What's your job here?"

"You saw it. I'm the new DI."

"DI?"

"The drill instructor. Ritter thinks his troopers need a little spit and polish."

"They could use the polish, true enough. I wouldn't know about the other."

"You don't like them much."

"They can be so vulgar sometimes. For a group of 'Christian soldiers,' they come off a good deal more like heathens."

Bolan smiled. "Maybe that's why they need the spit and polish."

"I don't think you're here to change their life-styles."

"Oh? Why *do* you think I'm here?"

"To make them better fighters. Better killers."

"Better *soldiers*."

"It's the same thing, isn't it?"

"You don't approve?"

"Let's say I've seen enough death as it is."

"Might be you need to see some life."

There was a hint of mockery in her smile. "I wondered when you'd get around to that."

"Around to what?"

"The line."

"I guess you've heard them all."

"Enough to recognize the opener."

"Okay."

"Okay? You're giving up?"

"I've got no taste for failure."

"Lord, a modest man."

"Just cautious."

"You surprise me."

"Why?"

"I didn't have you figured as a quitter."

Bolan smiled, adjusting to the rhythm of the game. "Well, if you're free tomorrow night..."

"I'm not."

"Perhaps another time."

"I'm free tonight."

It was the soldier's turn to be surprised. "Tonight?"

"Let's call it seven, shall we?"

"Seven."

"Don't be late."

"Don't be late where?"

She rattled off a Little Rock address, and Bolan logged it in his memory.

"Seven."

"Seven. You can tell me why a soldier comes to Arkansas and joins the Klan."

"I might," he said, "if you'll return the favor."

"How?"

"Oh, you could tell me why a clergyman wears the robe, and why his niece helps out around a training camp for private soldiers."

"I just might at that."

"I'm looking forward to it."

Bolan swiveled on his heel and struck off toward the shower block. He felt Lynn's eyes upon him, boring between his shoulder blades like gun sights. One more mystery; it might have little bearing on his mission of the moment, but even so, he thought it would be worth a closer look.

He wondered briefly how the lady's uncle might react to news that she was stepping out with a supposed ex-con. Immediately he was troubled by another thought. Suppose her uncle was behind the bold, unexpected approach? Or Mason Ritter? Even Freeman? Was it possible that someone in the hierarchy of the Vanguard or the Teutonic Knights was using Lynn to pick his brain or test his loyalty?

Anything was possible, of course, and he would have to be on guard, at least until he had a chance to study Lynn up close and find out for himself what might be going on inside her mind.

There were worse duties, he decided. Yes, indeed.

If Bolan was not careful, there was every chance he might enjoy himself tonight.

11

The restaurant aspired to intimacy in its lighting and design, with numerous partitions forming semiprivate cubicles, and simulated candles mounted on the walls providing dim illumination. Lynn had picked the place, and Bolan was surprised by her selection. He had been expecting something with a more distinctive Southern flavor, open booths and plenty of exposure.

"I hope this isn't too expensive for you."

"I'm a working man, remember?"

"That's what we were going to discuss."

"That's *one* thing."

"Right. So tell me: why the Klan?"

"Why not?" he countered. "If it's good enough for Uncle..."

"That's another story."

"Everyone's another story, Lynn."

"So tell me yours."

"It's not the perfect dinner conversation."

"Try me."

They were interrupted by the waiter. Bolan ordered steak; the lady went for lamb with mint sauce. They agreed to start off the meal with a glass of wine.

"As you were saying?"

Bolan sipped his wine and shrugged. "I joined the Army out of high school, tested for the Special Forces, got accepted. No big deal. I did my bit in Vietnam and signed up for a second tour of duty."

"Was it terrible? I mean, as bad as people say?"

"Depends upon the people, I suppose. There's no such thing as pretty war, but on the other hand, it wasn't Auschwitz, either."

"You don't like to talk about it?"

"I don't mind. There never seemed to be much point."

"What *was* it like?"

His smile was slow and cool. "You mean the killing?"

"Well . . ."

"Don't be embarrassed. Everybody wants to know, unless they've been there for themselves." He let the waiter serve their salads, sampled his before continuing and found it excellent. "It's like a job, that's all. You draw assignments—take this hill, clean out that village—and you carry out your orders. Anyone who tries to kill you in the process is the enemy, and you respond accordingly. It's strange the first few times, I guess. But you get used to it."

"I wouldn't."

"Well, you never know until you try."

"I know. What happened?"

"Where?"

"In Vietnam. I do some filing for the Knights," she told him, blushing prettily. "I know you had some trouble with the Army."

"Not the Army, just one officer. He liked to run patrols at night and try to ambush Charlie."

"Charlie?"

"Vietcong. VC. In military double-talk, that's Victor Charles, which gives you Charlie."

"Oh."

"We ran a few patrols without much problem, but it started sinking in that this lieutenant always sent the same men out. At least, he always sent out the same *kind* of men."

"Meaning white?"

"Bingo."

"May I assume this lieutenant was black?"

"As a coal bin at midnight."

"Go on."

"We got zapped pretty bad two nights running. There wasn't much left of the squad either time. When he called up a third night patrol for the same week, I thought an objection was called for."

"You hit him?"

"A few times. The details are hazy. Review boards got into it, he got a transfer, and I got a general discharge."

"That's bad?"

"It's limbo. Not dishonorable—that's the worst—but still, it follows you."

"And since the Army?"

"I've been here and there, done this and that. You couldn't say I've been immune to trouble."

"Mike, I know you've been in jail."

"In prison. There's a difference."

"I understand."

"Don't bother. I was guilty, and I did my time. I'm out now."

"For how long?"

He smiled. "I gave up telling fortunes, Lynn."

"I'm serious. The Vanguard and the Knights are like a magnet, drawing trouble. I can feel it coming."

"But you stick around."

"My Uncle Jacob's all the family I have left."

"Which brings us back to my turn," Bolan said. "What draws a minister to the Klan?"

"You'd be surprised how many clergymen belong, or have belonged. Do you know anything about Klan history?"

"Not really." Bolan knew a fair amount, in fact, but he was interested in the lady's version, anything at all that might provide him with a closer look inside her mind.

"The Klan has been around for something like 120 years," she told him, slowly warming to her subject. "It was strongest in the twenties and the early thirties, with about four million members coast to coast. The organizers canvassed every state, and never came up empty. Most people don't realize that eighty to ninety percent of those organizers and recruiters were ministers, fundamentalists like my uncle. For them, the Klan became a new religion...or, I should say, an extension of their own."

"How so?"

She shrugged. "You took the oath. It's nothing but a sermonette about the Klan's devotion to the church, the U.S.A. and womanhood. Of course, it doesn't always work that way in practice, but the Knights, as stated in their constitution, see themselves as soldiers of the cross, a militant arm of the Christian church."

"And where does the Vanguard fit in?"

"Like a hand in a glove," she replied. "While the Klan concentrates on religion and morals, the Aryan Vanguard takes care of the business and politics."

"Ritter's in charge?"

"He may *think* so," she said, and he noted a strong trace of scorn in her voice. "Freeman gave him the Klan, so to speak, but the Vanguard has three times the membership, most of the money—you name it. Mason rubber-stamps Freeman's decisions, but it's a charade."

"Getting back to your uncle..."

"My father," she said, taking Bolan off guard, "was a farmer. He got into debt, and it broke him, over time. I was away at college when it happened. There were payments to be made, he couldn't raise the money and the bank foreclosed. They set a date to auction off the furniture, machinery...everything. The night before the auction, Dad cracked. He shot Mom, then he set the house on fire and just sat there. I was driving home to see if I could help. I made it for the funeral."

She told the story in a monotone, but her eyes were glistening with tears as the waiter arrived with their food. Bolan waited for the guy to leave before he spoke.

"I'm sorry."

There seemed nothing more to say. Her memories had touched responsive chords in Bolan's past, recalling visions of his father, mother, sister—all cut down in an irrational explosion sparked by outside forces.

"Don't be. Really. It all seems so long ago." She tried the lamb and forced a smile. "My uncle couldn't understand, of course. I think what happened put him through a kind of crisis, making him question his faith in God, the country, all of that. Around that time, the Vanguard and the Knights were looking for a few good men, recruiting pastors wherever they could. The movement offered Uncle Jake a chance to even up the score. No, that's too much; let's say it offered him an opportunity to try and help somebody else. I honestly believe he thinks he failed my father. He's atoning for his failure.''

"What about yourself?''

"I went to stay with Uncle Jake after...everything. School didn't seem to make much sense, and when he moved down here to take a job with Ritter, I just sort of tagged along.''

"I gather you don't buy the Vanguard's line.''

"It was persuasive for a while, I guess. The things they said about the farmers being beaten down and trampled on. But things have changed along the way. These days it's 'nigger' this and 'Jew-boy' that. The farmers still get lots of sympathy from Freeman and his crew, but that's about the size of it. If anyone has actually been helped by anything he's done, I must have blinked and missed it.''

"Still, you work for Ritter.''

"We can always use the extra money. I play secretary, type my uncle's sermons, things like that. I don't go to meetings, I don't read the literature if I can avoid it. It's a living.''

She hesitated, putting on a mischievous smile. "I really shouldn't be telling you this. You might report me to the wizard.''

"Not my business,'' Bolan answered. "Everybody's got their reasons for the things they do. I've always thought money was as good as any other.''

"That makes you a mercenary, doesn't it?''

"Maybe. I have a marketable skill, and Ritter's buying. If we happen to agree on certain points of politics, so much the better.''

"You don't fit the mold.''

"How's that?''

"The average member of the Vanguard or the Knights is long on talk and short on action. Lots of them are short on brains, from what I've seen. You saw that group today."

"I didn't notice any rocket scientists."

"My point exactly. You seem ... different."

"Flattery will get you anywhere."

"How much is Ritter paying you?"

"Enough."

"To risk another prison term?"

"No law against rehearsals, if you watch your p's and q's."

"And what about the main performance? You don't really think those men are training to protect their homes and families?"

"It's not for me to say."

"The hell it's not." Her cheeks were flushed, the added color making her that much more desirable. Bolan brought his mind back to business as she continued. "They're practicing for war, and anyone who thinks they've got a chance to win should have his head examined."

"Preparation never hurts."

"And what about assassination? Bombings? Arson? Do you know what's happened in this state the past few months?"

"I'm new in town," he told her, playing out the line, intent on seeing how far she would run with it.

"Less than a week ago, a man was murdered. He was black, a union organizer. And he's not the first."

"You think the Vanguard was responsible?"

"The Knights, the Vanguard, someone on their payroll. If they didn't pull the trigger, they certainly loaded the gun."

"Where's your evidence?"

"I know what I know."

"You should tell the police."

"No. I can't."

She was frightened, he sensed, but not for herself.

"Was your uncle involved?"

"No!" Her answer seemed to Bolan too abrupt, too emphatic. "He wouldn't condone such a thing. Never."

"Well, then..."

"I just can't be sure." It was almost a whisper, and Bolan was forced to strain to hear the words.

"Have you asked him?"

Lynn shook her head. "If he's not involved, I'd only hurt his feelings needlessly. And if he *is* ... well, I'm not sure I want to know."

If she was acting, Bolan was prepared to nominate the lady for an Oscar. He wondered at her openness with him, a Klansman, on such short acquaintance. Was she an uncanny judge of character? Or was there something more behind her revelations, some elaborate snare that he could not detect? With no alternative, the Executioner decided to trust his instincts.

"If there's some way I could help..."

"You have," she said, "by listening. There aren't that many people I can talk to."

Bolan thought that that was probably the understatement of the year.

"Why don't you leave? Go back to school?"

"I've thought about it, but I can't. Not now. I let my parents down; I can't run out on Uncle Jake when he's in trouble."

"If he is in trouble."

"Either way, it's coming. If he's not involved now, he will be sooner or later. It's unavoidable."

"Maybe not."

"What do you mean?"

Bolan caught himself, resisting the urge to offer reassurances. For all her attractiveness, her apparent sincerity, Lynn was still on Ritter's payroll, a potential enemy. He settled for a shrug and said, "You never know how things may go."

"Philosophy?"

"Experience. Whenever I begin to count on something, then I know it's time to guess again."

"It sounds like you've been disappointed once too often."

"No, I just expect the unexpected."

Lynn declined dessert, and Bolan paid the waiter, tacking on an appropriate tip. Both were quiet on the slow ride back to the suburban house where she resided with her widowed uncle.

"I appreciate the sympathetic ear," she said when they were parked outside her home.

"I've got another one just like it, if you ever feel the need."

Her smile was teasing. "Next time, maybe we should try a different topic of discussion."

"Next time?"

She pretended to be hurt. "Forgive me. I assumed—"

"Correctly," Bolan finished for her. "Next time."

"Call me?"

"Absolutely."

Leaning forward quickly, unexpectedly, she kissed him lightly on the lips.

"Be careful. Please."

"I always am," he lied.

"Good night."

He watched her disappear inside after a parting wave, and then he dropped the rental into gear, the engine purring as he pulled away. Behind the graveyard eyes, his mind was racing, tackling the questions Lynn had dumped unceremoniously in his lap.

Was she as disaffected with the Klan and the Vanguard as she seemed? How deeply was the Reverend Halsey involved in the violence that had shaken Chatham County? If the man was implicated, could he possibly be salvaged? Or was the pastor simply one more target for the Executioner?

He did not want to think about that now. Aware that Lynn had moved him, Bolan set about the task of separating personal desire from professional duty, ruthlessly stamping out feelings that might slow his hand at crucial moments. Anything that might endanger him, his mission, would be set aside for now, perhaps forever. Soldiers on the firing line had enough to do without subordinating duty to emotion.

He had not survived the living hell of Vietnam, his ever-lasting private war with terrorists and mafiosi, by surrendering to each hormonal urge that came along. If it was possible to do his job without inflicting further harm on Lynn or her family, then he would do his best. But if the lady or her uncle betrayed him, if a human sacrifice was necessary for the general good, he would have to face that moment when it came.

Unsmiling, Bolan turned the rental back toward Chatham County, thankful for the drive ahead. It would allow him to try to relax, unwind. But he doubted he would succeed. Unless he missed his guess, he would get little sleep tonight.

"I'M GLAD YOU'RE HOME."

Lynn nearly jumped. Then, embarrassed by her reaction to her uncle's voice, she said, "I thought you'd be in bed by now."

"I had some notes to work on for the Sunday message."

"How's it coming?"

"I'll be ready." Jacob Halsey took her hand in both of his. Lynn saw the worry in his sunken eyes. "Are you all right?" he asked.

"Of course. What's wrong?"

"You must be careful, Lynn. I've told you that before."

"A simple dinner." She knew what was bothering him now. "That's all. You see, I'm here."

"He didn't try to...take advantage?"

"Uncle Jake, he was a perfect gentleman."

"Some of these men are rugged souls," he cautioned her. "They lack your innocence."

"I'm not that innocent."

"You'll always be that innocent to me."

"I love you, Uncle Jake."

"It has occurred to me that you've postponed your education long enough. Do you ever think about finishing college?"

"We can't afford that now."

"I've made a few investments recently. We're not on easy street, by any means, but college shouldn't be a problem."

"What investments?"

"Business deals. With Mason and Mr. Freeman."

"Uncle..."

"Never mind. You were so close to graduation, Lynn. I want you to consider going back. For my sake, if no other reason."

"I'll consider it."

"All right." He hesitated, searching for the words. "About this new man, Bowers..."

"Please don't worry."

"Someone has to."

"I'm a big girl, Uncle Jake."

"Precisely. That's the problem."

"I can take care of myself."

"Your father thought so, too."

"I'm stronger."

Halsey searched her eyes a moment, finally nodding. "I believe you are, at that."

"If I go back to school, will you come with me?"

His smile was infectious. "I believe I'm just a bit old for the freshman class."

"I mean it. There are lots of things that you could do. I'll bet that you could find yourself a church, no problem."

"Lynn, my work is here."

"What work? Mason Ritter's? Freeman's?"

"I have duties here. I swore an oath."

"You swore a higher oath when you became a minister."

"I know it's difficult for you to understand—"

"I understand, all right. What hold does Ritter have on you?"

"I'm not a hostage, Lynn. And I am not a child. A crisis is upon this nation, and our leaders have no strength or will to see us through. That task may fall on other shoulders, mine among them."

"Uncle Jake—"

"A change is coming, Lynn. You may not see it now, but I assure you, it *is* coming. I mean to see it and do everything I can to help that change along."

"What are you saying?"

"I have personal commitments here. I have a duty to perform."

"I thought your duty lay within the church."

"The church is everywhere, in every man."

He spoke with grim determination, but Lynn caught a hint of doubt behind his eyes. She sensed an insecurity within him, something she had never seen or felt before.

"We wouldn't have to tell Mason we were leaving, Uncle Jake. He'd never find us."

"Would you have me creep away like Judas in the middle of the night?"

"You don't owe Ritter anything. You certainly don't owe your life to Freeman."

"I can take care of myself."

"Like Daddy?"

Trapped, his own words turned against him, the pastor found himself unable to respond. Instead, he turned away from Lynn. "You'd better get some sleep."

She started for the stairs, arrested by his voice before she got there.

"Please be careful with these Klansmen."

"*You're* a Klansman, Uncle Jake."

As Lynn undressed for bed, she replayed in her mind the conversation with her uncle.

His evident concern for her was touching, but it raised more questions than it answered. He was obviously fearful of the escalating violence in Chatham County and around the state, afraid that it would touch her more directly than it had. She thought he might be frightened for himself, as well, but he was stubborn—like her father, damn it—and he would not run away from what he thought to be his duty.

Bowers was another problem. He was not the man she had anticipated, though he carried danger with him like the scent of musk. He would be capable of fearsome violence, but beneath the gruff facade she recognized a tenderness, as well.

What did she feel for him exactly? Was she simply falling prey at last to eighteen months of celibacy, weakening before a handsome face and a masculine physique? There had been other offers—many of them, often crudely phrased—and Bowers had not even made an offer. Yet.

He would, though. That was certain.

If he didn't, for whatever unimaginable reason, Lynn thought she might take the initiative for herself. Before it came to that, however, she would need to know the man much better. She would need to have her first impressions verified, confirmed by personal experience and contact.

Contact.

It was something to anticipate with pleasure, and she was smiling as she drifted off to sleep.

12

Bolan stood before his wilted "troops" and watched them sweat. Shaves and haircuts had done something for their appearance, but they were still a ragtag bunch of amateurs, and they were none too happy with him at the moment.

A forty-minute round of calisthenics followed by six hours in the woods and on Camp Nordland's tough assault course had removed their starch and left them sagging in their sweat-soaked uniforms.

"Tomorrow," he told them, savoring the impact of his words, "we do it all again. Some of you still can't cut the woodland run, and frankly, gentlemen, your time on the assault course sucks!"

One of the Klansmen—Jeeter, according to his name tag—raised a grimy hand.

"What is it?"

"Guns," the trooper croaked. "When do we get to shoot 'em?"

"When you're ready. Fitness is the combat soldier's first priority. An eighty-year-old woman in a wheelchair can be taught to fire a rifle and never miss, but I wouldn't want her covering my ass in battle. Any other questions?"

One more hand went up. The tag identified its owner as Martello.

"Yes?"

"Will we be learning any unarmed combat? Hand-to-hand, that kind of thing?"

"You will if you survive the basics. Anybody else?"

No hands. Bolan sent them to the showers with a reminder to return at eight the next morning. He was walking back across the compound toward the hut that held his dressing room and private shower when he noticed Bobby Shelton standing on the sidelines, smiling like a well-fed cat.

"Looks like you mean to work their asses off," Shelton commented.

"Most of them have a couple extra pounds of ass to spare."

"I'd say you're right. You all played out, or would you care to try a little action on for size tonight?"

"What kind of action?"

"Well, that hadn't rightly been decided yet. Let's say a couple of the Ku Klux feel a need to cluck."

"And I'm invited?"

"If you want. Of course, if you've got something more important going—"

"No, tonight's wide open. Count me in."

"You got it, Mike. Why don't you swing on by the meeting hall, say nine o'clock. You can leave your car there, and we'll take the battlewagon."

"Battlewagon?"

"Just wait and see. You'll love it. See you later?"

"I'll be there."

Bolan took his time in the shower, adjusting the water from steamy hot to ice-cold and back again, rinsing away the forest dirt and giving himself time to think. The invitation to participate in a nocturnal action by the Klan had come as a surprise. Traditionally, Bolan knew, rookies were not chosen as night riders, for security reasons if nothing else. The exception in his case might mean the local Klan was short of talent, though an estimated membership of seven hundred should have yielded enough volunteers for a bit of "clucking." Bolan was inclined to view the invitation as a test—of his abilities, of his loyalty to the movement— and he could not afford to let it pass. There might not be another opportunity for him to get inside the Klan's hard-core commando group, and after all, that had been the point of his mission.

It bothered Bolan that he knew no details about the night raid. If it was aimed at members of the farmers' union, he had no way of warning them beforehand. If the Klansmen meant to target blacks or other citizens selected off the streets at random, he would not have time to contact the authorities. There was a possibility, of course, that he could intervene with force, prevent the raiders from committing some atrocious crime. But doing so would sacrifice his cover, blowing any chance he had to get closer to the Klan and Vanguard leader.

Toweling off, the soldier made up his mind to preserve his cover if he could. With no indication of the chosen target, their itinerary for the night to come, he would be forced to play the lethal game by ear. There might not even be a target yet; he knew it was fairly common in some parts of Dixie for the Klan to launch "patrols," relying on the team leader to choose his mark and handle all the details on the spot.

He would keep his date with Bobby Shelton and attempt to be prepared for anything. If there was murder to be done, or other bloody work, he would evaluate the situation as it came. In the meantime, he could take a few precautions, warn a few people.

When he got back to his apartment, Bolan's first call went to Wilson Brown. He would have to take the chance that no one in the Klan or the Vanguard had expertise enough to tap his phone. He reached the former lineman at his motel room in Parrish.

"Lucky thing you caught me. I'll be moving out tonight."

"You're leaving?"

"No such luck. The union's found a place for me to stay awhile. I'll save some money, and it puts me closer to the union hall."

"I guess that answers my next question."

"Yeah, I'm in. For Theo, mostly. Anyhow, it started out that way. I've got to tell you, though, it kind of grows on you, this standing up for what you think is right."

"I've heard that."

"So what's shaking?"

"That's the problem; I'm not sure. A few of Ritter's Kluxers want to cluck, and I'm invited, but they wouldn't tell me anything about the program."

"When?"

"Tonight."

"I'll pass the word. Our people mostly travel armed these days . . . since Theo. If you try to take a union man, you'll need to watch yourself."

"I'm hoping it won't come to that."

"Tonight, next week, it's coming, man. You know that, well as I do."

"I'll see what I can do to head it off."

"Don't blow it, Sarge."

"Stay frosty."

"All the time."

The Executioner was not surprised to learn that Wilson Brown was staying to continue the battle his son had started. Pride and family honor were at stake, along with all the other lives Theo Brown had touched before his own was savagely cut short. The ex-lieutenant might have lost a foot in Vietnam, but his sense of justice was intact, and he could no more turn away from Theo's mission than he could decide to give up breathing for a day.

Bolan's second call, long-distance, went to Leo Turrin.

"Justice here."

"That's what I need."

"Hey, Striker, what's the rumble?"

"I'm invited to a hayride, courtesy of the Teutonic Knights."

"So soon? You're coming up in the world."

"Feels like down."

"Any word on the target?"

"They're playing it close to the sheet," Bolan told him. "The truth is, I'm hoping the Bureau has someone inside who can find out before things get heavy."

"No sale. They've been trying, but Ritter and Freeman are cagey. When one of their clique gets cold feet, you can bet he'll be having an accident soon."

"No defectors?"

"A few from the fringes, but none from the core. They recruit on two levels, you know. Rank and file go to meetings, dress up, scream and shout, all that hoopla. The hard core hangs tough; once you're *in*, there's no *out* but the boneyard."

"And so far they're solid."

"Like steel. Rumor has it the Bureau would cough up six figures for someone who fingers a cyclops or better. No takers so far."

"That's unusual."

"Very. Most Klansmen would rather turn fink on a brother for money than shout hallelujah in Sunday school. Freeman and Ritter must have some kind of discipline going."

"I'd say. Does the Bureau's Little Rock field office keep up surveillance?"

"Whenever they can. They're spread pretty thin. So what else is new?"

"Yeah. Have them do what they can, will you? I don't know who we'll be hitting or where; I just know it's tonight. If there's some way to minimize damage..."

"You've got to play straight with these guys while you're building a cover. If Ritter or Freeman sniff out what you're doing, you're dead."

"I can't promise you anything, Sticker."

"You've done this before. Different players, same game."

"Not exactly. Before, if I had to audition, the mark was some guy I'd have probably iced later anyway. This time, who knows?"

"I don't envy you, guy."

Bolan shrugged off the little Fed's sympathy. "Once I'm inside the hard core—if I make it that far—I'll be looking to tag Freeman's backers. I'll need any background you have."

"I can pull it together this evening. Watch out for Mike Andrews, okay? He's not only big money; he's *cold*. Over twenty-odd years, he's been playing both sides of the fence, funding hate groups regardless of race, creed or color."

"That's weird."

"Justice thinks so. A banker from Dixie who slips a few bucks to the Klan on the sly isn't all that unusual, sorry to say. But a banker in Dixie who *also* pays rent for the Panthers and Muslims is one of a kind."

"What's his angle?"

"Who knows? If he's crazy, he's been damned selective about his donations. If not . . . well, your guess may be better than mine."

"I'll look into it."

"Thought you might. Listen, I know I'm wasting my breath, but—"

"Be careful?"

"Okay, so you're reading minds now."

"Later."

"Sure," Leo muttered. "I hope so."

Bolan hung up the phone, little wiser than before, then headed down the street to get something to eat at the little café a stone's throw from his rented quarters.

Back in his room an hour later, he considered his weaponry for the night's excursion. He went with the Browning again, and the Colt in its ankle rig, slipping some spare magazines in his pockets before he went out to the car.

At midnight on the dot, Bolan pulled up in front of the warehouse-cum-meeting hall used by the Teutonic Knights. Bobby Shelton was waiting outside with three men Bolan recognized as cellmates from the Blackboard incident: McCullough, Jackson, Thorndyke.

Shelton introduced the "brothers" briefly, adding first names: Skeeter, Amos and Barry. Bolan shook hands all around, then climbed into the back seat of the waiting car with Thorndyke and McCullough wedged in tight on either side.

"You packing?" Shelton asked when he was settled in the shotgun seat with Jackson at the wheel.

"I always come prepared."

"Good deal. We shouldn't need the hardware, but you never know. I'd rather be judged by twelve—"

"Than carried by six. Yeah, we know," Jackson finished, and everyone laughed at the seemingly well-known routine. "First time out?"

"First of many, I hope," Bolan responded, and caught Shelton's grin in return.

"That's my boy. Like the car?"

"It's okay."

Shelton snickered. "Okay? Boy, she's one of a kind. Got your reinforced bumpers for ramming, a supercharged engine for speed and enough hidey-holes for a decent-size arsenal."

"Yeah?"

"Show him, Skeeter."

McCullough reached forward and depressed a catch on the side of the driver's seat, dropping the back of the seat in their laps like the door to a large glove compartment. Inside, held in place by elastic and Velcro, two shotguns surmounted a tommy gun fitted with a 30-round box magazine.

"You're sitting on some more," McCullough said, "and we got other stuff in back."

"I take it this is the battlewagon."

"Son, you take it right."

"So what's the action?"

"This evening we're into remodeling," Thorndyke advised him. "Like urban renewal, you know?"

"There's a preacher in town who's been getting a little bit uppity," Shelton explained. "Telling niggers they ought to go big for the union, and all kinds of bullshit like that. We're obliged to remind him what color he is and advise him to stay in his place."

Alarm bells went off in Bolan's skull, but he kept a straight face. Shelton had said they shouldn't need their guns. From the sound of it, they were intent on destruction of property rather than lives.

"Time to time, niggers need a refresher. You know what I mean?"

Bolan nodded, said nothing, intent on the street signs and landmarks they passed in the darkness. Too late now for a phone call to warn Turrin or Brown. He would keep his fingers crossed, praying that Shelton and company would be content with a building for now. If their hatred spilled over, endangering lives, he would be forced to act, to blow his cover in lieu of being a witness to murder.

He thought he could take them all down if it came to that. They were armed and presumably competent with their weapons, but he was a "brother" and, as such, above their suspicion. With timing, surprise on his side, he might just pull it off.

And he might ruin everything else in the process.

Again, Leo's warning came back to him. *Don't blow it, Sarge.* There was far more at stake than some property damage, he knew, but a life in the balance would change things. For all the blood on his hands, all the scars on his soul, he could not sit back idly and watch while the Klan killed an innocent man.

"Here we go," Shelton said to no one in particular. Jackson turned left down an alleyway running behind seedy shops, a small market, a restaurant. Killing the headlights, he finished the last thirty yards with some help from the moon.

"There she is."

On the opposite corner, a church thrust its steeple toward heaven, its bell silent now, windows darkened and blind. A sign out front identified the church as Bethany AME.

"Let's take her," Jackson growled. He sounded hungry and eager.

They scrambled from the car, and Bolan followed as they gathered around the trunk expectantly.

"Get to it, Amos."

Jackson raised the lid, revealing rifles, shotguns, lengths of chain and metal pipe cut down for use as clubs and flails. Wedged in beside the spare, a cardboard shoe box had been cushioned by a folded bedspread to keep it from jarring out of place.

"Let's go!"

"I've got it. Keep your pants on, will you?"

Jackson lifted out the box and handed it to Bobby Shelton, treating it with something close to reverence. Shelton, in his turn, faced Bolan, offering the shoe box with a crooked smile.

"All yours," he said.

"What's this?"

"A little contribution to the reverend's building fund. Just think of it as Christmas coming early." Dipping in a pocket of his leather jacket, Shelton came out with a squarish object the size of a cigarette pack that Bolan instantly identified as a detonator. "Radio controled," the Klansman told him, beaming. "Foolproof."

"Sure, unless a taxi or police car happens by, or maybe some clown playing with his new CB."

"Don't worry, son. This isn't what you'd call an electronically enlightened neighborhood." The others laughed at that, and Bolan took the shoe box, grimacing. "We'll cover you from here."

"Oh, good. I feel much better now."

"Get on with it," McCullough growled. "We haven't got all night."

"Don't bust a gut. I'm going."

Pausing in the alley's mouth just long enough to scan the sidewalks, Bolan crossed the street without encountering pedestrians or motorists. From all appearances, the neighborhood was dead, abandoned, its inhabitants evacuated for the evening. He hoped that was true of Bethany AME, wishing he could see the parking lot on the other side of the building. There might be a watchman or a janitor at work inside the church, oblivious to sudden death approaching through the darkness. If the church was not deserted . . .

Suddenly he had another thought. Suppose his cover had been faulty, flawed in some way that had revealed him to the Klansmen as a plant. Would they have put him through the ceremony of initiation, let him work at their camp for two days, only to eliminate him now by the premature explosion of the bomb? He pictured Shelton's finger on the button, silent death pursuing him to strike a spark inside the shoe box, scattering his limbs and viscera across two lanes to greet early-morning drivers on their way to work.

Would Ritter and his people go to all that trouble when they could have slaughtered him half a dozen times already, free from any threat of possible discovery? It seemed unlikely, but stranger things had happened. He would not let himself relax until the shoe box left his hands and he was safe outside its killing radius.

From weight alone, he judged the bomb to be of ample power for the intended job. Dynamite would pack less wallop than plastique, but either way he had a lethal package on his hands. Where to place it had apparently been left to him, and as he reached the sidewalk, merging swiftly with the shadows there, Bolan scanned the visible perimeter of Bethany AME.

He found a service entrance on the side with three steps leading up, and beside the concrete steps a basement window. Bolan wedged his parcel against the stoop, next to the wall of cinder blocks, remembering to check for line-of-sight alignment with his backup waiting in the alley opposite. When he was satisfied that he had done his job, the Executioner retraced his steps across the silent street, relieved to reach the cover of the alleyway intact.

"Pile in."

On Shelton's order, everyone got back in the battle-wagon. Jackson turned the engine over, edging forward several feet to give the detonator ample clearance.

"Show time."

Shelton aimed the telescope antenna of his detonator at the steepled structure, pressed the button with his thumb—and hell erupted in the house of God. The shock wave shattered windowpanes on both sides of the street as Bethany AME met her fiery end. The southern wall imploded, oily flame erupting in the breach. A flash fire swept the basement and the sacristy at once, igniting secondary blazes in the sanctuary, blowing off the tall front doors. The ancient building seemed to sag, its spirit broken, rafters swinging free like pendulums of fire.

"I've seen enough."

With screeching tires, the battlewagon's driver took them out of there. Behind them, in the darkness, Bethany AME was consumed by flames, a Gothic funeral pyre.

"You did it, man."

"Nice job."

"I told you this one was a pro."

All smiles, Bob Shelton turned around to place a hand on Bolan's knee. "You earned your wings tonight, son. Welcome to the wrecking crew."

13

Wilson Brown walked slowly through the smoking rubble of the church. His clothes were grimed with soot, the smell of charcoal in his nostrils calling up memories of bygone wars. Remembering the afternoon of Theo's funeral in this church, he tried to make some sense of the confusion, resurrect some memory to make the structure whole again, but it was all in vain. He recognized the blackened outline of the pulpit, found the wooden pews reduced to ashes, walls consumed by fire or shattered by the force of the explosion.

His foot scuffed something on the floor, and Brown stooped to lift a hymnal, its cover black and blistered from the heat. Incredibly, a number of inner pages had been spared, though they were scorched around the edges, brittle now. With cautious reverence, he started leafing through the book, reading off the song titles to himself. "Onward Christian Soldiers." "What a Friend We Have in Jesus." "Throw out the Lifeline" "On Christ the Solid Rock I Stand."

Consumed by sudden rage, he hurled the hymn book across the room—but there *was* no room, and it sailed on beyond the point where solid walls would once have stopped it cold. He watched the book flutter like a dying bird in flight before it fell to earth.

"Goddamn it! *Goddamn it!*"

"Wilson?"

Reverend Cletus Little stood beside his withered pulpit, a dazed expression on his face. The tracks of tears were shiny on his cheeks.

"I'm sorry, Reverend."

"Who could have done this thing?"

"You know who did it."

"So much malice in a human heart."

"I wouldn't positively call them human, Reverend."

"God's children."

"Every family has some bastards in it."

"The Bible tells us we should love our enemies."

"I'll love them to death."

"We must not be discouraged."

Despite his brave words, the minister's voice broke. Brown looked away in embarrassment, sparing the man what he could in the way of dignity. From the direction of the street, a murmur of angry voices reached his ears, and Wilson turned to find a crowd collecting on the sidewalk, spilling over onto lawns and across the lanes of traffic. Several motorists had left their vehicles in the middle of the street with their engines running, to join the crowd and gawk at what was left of the church. Uniformed patrolmen were outnumbered as they tried to hold people back with warnings and riot sticks. One of them was on a walkie-talkie, urgently requesting backup

"Reverend?"

"Yes?"

"We're needed on the street."

He waited while the pastor pulled himself together, joined him in the ruins of the sanctuary's central aisle. Together, side by side, they left the ruins, gingerly descending concrete steps still slick with water used in the futile effort to control the blaze. At one point, Reverend Little lost his footing, nearly fell, but Brown was quick enough to slip a hand beneath his arm and steady him on his feet.

The deputies looked apprehensive as the minister and Brown drew near, for their presence stirred visible reactions in the angry crowd. The muttering became a snarl, and fists were being shaken at the badges now, the front ranks surging more insistently against the flimsy human barrier.

Cletus Little tried to speak but could not find his voice; he spread his hands in a mute appeal and shook his head.

Impulsively Brown took a long step forward, raised his arms to silence the crowd.

"Be quiet, please. *Be quiet!*"

The murmurs gradually died away. One hundred pairs of eyes were fixed expectantly on Brown.

"I recognize a few of you," he said, "and most of you know who I am. You know how much I've lost already here in Parrish.

"Now, some of you have suffered loss. The Reverend Little here has had his church destroyed by men who think that they can purge the truth with fire.

"I know exactly how you feel," he told the sullen faces, and he meant it. "You want to find the men who did this, and you want them *punished*!"

"Right on!"

"But I'm here to tell you there's a right way and a wrong way to achieve your goals. You won't gain anything by turning on these officers or punching out the first white folks you see today. That's wrong, because it makes no sense."

The crowd was silent now. He had them, but he knew his grip was tenuous at best.

"When I got word my son was dead—that he was *killed*— I want to tell you, I had murder in my heart. I still have murder in my heart. If I could stand before the triggerman today, I don't know what I'd do. But I know what I hope I'd do. I hope that I would let the sheriff and the FBI go on and do their job. Because if I go out and seek revenge I'll find myself in jail. And then the men who killed my son will know they've taken out *two* niggers for the price of *one*."

A whisper of astonishment spread through the throng like ripples in a pond.

"You cannot reach the men who did this evil thing by going out from here and punishing the innocent at random. It's ridiculous. It's senseless. In fact, disorganized revenge is worse than useless; it's destructive. Stop and think about what happens in a riot. Who gets killed? Whose shops and homes get burned? Is it the Klan that suffers?"

"No." They were warming to him, slow but sure.

"I look around, and I'll be damned if I can see a Klansman anywhere. How many of you want to trash this neighborhood and make the *whole* place look like this?" He stabbed an angry finger toward the ruins of the church. "How many of you want to help the bombers finish what they started here last night?"

"We can't just *take* it!"

"Men have got to stand!"

"That's right!" he answered, moving closer to the crowd, aware that it could still go either way. "But men stand up in self-defense. They guard their homes, their families, the ones they love. No *man* did this. I want a show of hands. Who wants to go to jail for whipping on a lousy two-bit yellow dog?"

Another angry murmur in the crowd. No hands were raised.

"Who wants to leave his family and go to prison for the fun of taking out a rotten, spineless coward?"

And again, no hands.

"These officers have got a job to do," he said. "You pay their salaries, and their job is to stop you if you try and do more damage here today. The longer you make noise down here, the less time these police have to find the trash who lit this fire. You want to help the Klan? You want to help the Vanguard? Go ahead! Go on! Get to it! Finish what they started! Burn down your own damned stores and houses!"

"No, sir!"

"That ain't the way."

Behind the mob, a line of black-and-white patrol cars coasted to a halt, their colored lights revolving, their engines idling. The doors sprang open, spilling uniforms and nightsticks, boots and helmets, mirrored shades. From where he stood, Brown saw the Chatham County sheriff circling the angry crowd.

"Here are more officers arriving now," he told his audience. "They're here to do a job for you, and they can't do it right unless you let them be. They can't be tracking down the bombers if they're busy fighting you. Go home, now. Go to work. Go on about your business. And for God's sake let the officers get on with theirs. Bethany Church *shall* be rebuilt. The men who did this *shall* be punished. But you cannot do it as a mob, no better than your enemies.''

Reluctantly the crowd dispersed. Brown watched pedestrians drift away and saw the traffic jam untangled with assistance from a couple of the deputies. The sheriff glowered as he crossed the narrow strip of lawn, approaching Brown and Reverend Little.

''My men would've handled this,'' he growled by way of introduction.

''They were losing it. You might have had a riot on your hands.''

''My men can handle rioters.''

''I'm glad to hear it, Sheriff. Can they handle bombers? How are they with murderers?''

''You know I've got detectives working overtime to find who killed your boy.''

''I'm not concerned about the hours, Sheriff. I've been looking for results, and so far I've seen zip.''

''We can't just pull a suspect from a hat, you know.''

''You might try looking underneath a hood or two.'

''Those boys have airtight alibis.''

''Well, that solves everything.''

''I hope you're not insinuating anything.''

''You can always hope, Sheriff.''

The lawman cast a sour eye in the direction of the burned-out church. ''I don't take kindly to this kind of shit inside my jurisdiction. 'Scuse the language, Pastor. You may not believe it, Mr. Brown, but I'm as interested in taking down these boys as you are.''

''And suppose the trail leads back to certain civic leaders. Will you still be interested?''

''I don't deal in speculation. Show me evidence.''

''It's not my job to show you anything. If your detectives can't collect the evidence they need, then hire someone who can.''

The sheriff bristled. ''Don't tell me how to do my job.''

"Sir, I wouldn't dream of it. I *will* tell you to *ao* your job, no matter what it takes. Next time I may not be around to talk the people out of kicking ass."

"What makes you think there'll be a next time?"

"Common sense," Brown answered. "Terrorists don't stop until they're forced to. Lock them up or kill them—either way, you have to take back the initiative. Right now, the rabble is in charge."

The sheriff softened slightly. "I don't like this situation any better than you do," he grumbled, "but until I have enough hard evidence to let the D.A. run with, my hands are tied. I can't build cases out of hearsay speculation."

"I think you're running out of time."

"Is that a threat?"

"An observation, Sheriff. People hereabouts don't have the patience that they had six months ago. They've seen too much. They've suffered too much, and they're tired of going unavenged."

"I won't have any vigilante action in my county."

"You already have it. Now the only question's whether it can cut both ways."

"I hope you're not about to test me, Mr. Brown."

"Not me." He repeated it for emphasis, forcing a smile. "Not me." He turned away and headed for his boarding house, a few short blocks down the street.

The blast that had shattered half of Bethany AME had wakened him like thunder in the night, and he had dressed in hurried, careless fashion, jogging to the scene as quickly as his artificial foot would allow. He had been on the scene before the fire trucks with their ladders, lights and hoses, the men in rubber overcoats and outsize helmets doing what they could to save a hopeless situation. He had been there when the minister had arrived to find his world in flames. And he had been there, waiting, when the angry crowd had begun to gather at the curb, their solemn faces bathed in firelight.

Wilson Brown was tired of being on the scene too late to help and make things right. Too late for Theo. Too late for the church. It was the story of his life, and it was getting old.

His landlady, a shriveled prune of a woman, was waiting as he entered, her eyes alight with morbid curiosity. "I heard it was the church," she said.

"You heard correctly, ma'am."

"Was anybody hurt?"

"Not this time."

"Praise the Lord."

Her offering of thanks rang hollow, and Brown was convinced it would have made her day if someone had been fried or blown to bits. He walked around her, started up the narrow flight of stairs and made it halfway to the top before she stopped him.

"Mr. Brown?"

"Yes, ma'am?"

"You had a phone call a little while ago, when you were out."

"Who was it?"

"Didn't leave his name. I asked him, but he wouldn't say. No message, neither. Said he'd call you by and by."

"I see. Well, thank you, anyway."

"I asked him for his name. He wouldn't say."

"Yes, ma'am."

His room was tiny but immaculate. A cleaning woman in the prune's employ came by every afternoon to dust and vacuum, changing the linen twice a week. He stretched out on the rumpled bed, ignoring how the wrinkled sheet made little knots along his spine. Closing his eyes against the light, he tried to think of anything except his son and a burned-out church.

He was roused from a troubled doze by the insistent shrilling of the telephone downstairs. The shadows on his wall had scarcely changed position, and he guessed he had been asleep no more than half an hour. It seemed to take forever for his landlady to answer the phone.

"Mr. Brown?" Her voice was lilting, almost girlish, as she summoned him. He matched it in his mind with her wrinkled face and broke up, laughing in spite of his discouraged mood.

"It's him," she whispered hoarsely as he reached the bottom of the stairs. "He still won't give his name."

"I've got it, thanks."

Reluctantly she turned away and shuffled toward her room.

"Hello?"

"I'm sorry, Wils."

A little chill raced down his spine as he recognized the big man's voice. "Not your fault, man. You told me all you could."

"It wasn't good enough."

"So what's the story? Are you in or what?"

"I'm on the wrecking crew."

"All right. Now we can start to whip some ass."

"Not *we*, Lieutenant."

"Say again?"

"These boys are on the razor's edge right now. There's nothing they'd like better than to take you down."

"There's nothing I'd like better than to have them try."

"I wouldn't recommend it."

"Didn't ask you, did I?"

"Wils, have you considered backing off on this one?"

"Oh, hell, yes. It took me all the best part of a second to decide. I'm staying."

"Then be aware. They've got a list, and your name's at the top."

"I wouldn't want it any other way."

"I figured. Listen, just because I'm on the team, it doesn't mean they trust me absolutely. There's no guarantee I'll have a chance to tip you when they make their move."

"I understand."

"You'll have to watch yourself."

"I always do."

It seemed to Wilson Brown that Bolan was approaching some sore topic indirectly, stalking it as if it might escape or turn and bite him like a cottonmouth.

"About the church..."

"No need to tell me any more."

"I think there is." He paused to take a breath, then dragged the dirty linen out. "I set the charge."

"Okay."

"I thought you had a right to know."

"I would have done the same thing in your place." Brown spoke around the new obstruction in his throat. "The only problem is, I wouldn't pass the entrance test."

"There's something in the mail. A package. Give it to the pastor, will you?"

"Sure. I guess I shouldn't ask."

"A little something for the building fund. We'll let it be anonymous."

"I think that's best."

"I'll try to keep in touch."

"You do that." Wilson hesitated, finally thought of something else that needed to be said. "Hey, Sarge?"

But he was talking to dead air, the dial tone humming in his ear.

"Goddamn it!"

"Not bad news, I hope?"

He cradled the receiver, putting on a plastic smile before he turned to face the lady of the house.

"No, ma'am, I wouldn't say that."

"Oh." Her face and tone were weighted down with disappointment. Clearly she had been anticipating tragedy—and looking forward to it.

Back inside his room once more, Brown thought of Bolan, trying to imagine what the soldier must have gone through when he drew his orders for the bombing of the church. The guy was hurting, he could tell that much, and all the conscience money in the world would not relieve him of the guilty burden he bore.

It was ironic. Bolan's life was on the line; he had been forced to make an agonizing choice, to preserve his cover in the interests of the mission, yet the demolition of an empty building weighed upon him more than all the lives he had taken on the field of combat through the years of everlasting war.

It was a measure of the man, Brown thought, that such feelings still remained inside him. Other warriors would long since have fallen prey to burnout, running on their instincts, killing out of habit, settling for survival in a dog-eat-dog world. The Executioner was living proof of an alternative approach, and he was *living* in the true sense of the word. The guy was still alive in spite of all that he had witnessed, all that he had done and suffered.

Sergeant Mercy.

They had called him that in Vietnam because he had been known to risk his life retrieving wounded soldiers and civilians—even those of the enemy—without regard for danger. Such had been the flip side of the Executioner, and it was good to know that both sides were still around.

Still fighting.

When the package came he would deliver it to Reverend Little, and the Bethany African Methodist Episcopal Church would rise again, a monument to man's humanity. It was a pity that the pastor and his flock would never know their benefactor's name, his color. If they did . . .

Brown closed his eyes again and concentrated on an image of his son in younger, brighter days. He thought Theo would have understood the Executioner's dilemma and would have been forgiving.

Somewhere down the line, forgiveness had to break the cycle of aggression and reaction. Somewhere, sometime, people had to lay their pain aside.

But not today. Not here. The pain of loss was still too fresh, his anger still a living thing that gnawed his vitals. He was not prepared to let it rest.

Not yet.

Not while his enemies were still alive.

14

"The key to unarmed self-defense is timing," Bolan told his ragged troops. "The second most important thing is leverage. If you can use an enemy's momentum and his weight against him, you've got half the battle won before you start."

"Seems like it's easier to pop the bastard with a sucker punch," Jeeter drawled, smiling as his comrades snickered their agreement.

"Let's find out."

"How's that?"

"Let's test your theory." Bolan snapped his fingers at the Klansman, who seemed suddenly reluctant. "On your feet. Get over here."

"Go on, Lem!"

"Show him."

"Give him one for all of us."

The porky trooper scrambled to his feet and circled Bolan warily. "What is it I'm supposed to do?"

"Whatever suits your mood. A sucker punch, I think you said?"

"Well, shoot, you're ready for it now."

"Is that a problem for you? Fine." He turned his back on Jeeter, closed his eyes. "Just take your time. I'll be here when you're ready."

"Lem, for Christ's sake, do it!"

"Kick his ass!"

Bolan heard the Klansman coming, lumbering across the open ground like an arthritic dinosaur, and he marveled at the thought of any human being with such total lack of stealth. And he had twelve of them to deal with.

Timing was the key, as he had told the class. He estimated Jeeter's distance by the sounds he made, was waiting when the Klansman launched his hard right hand. A side step, pivoting to meet the blow as it sliced empty air, and Bolan seized his adversary's wrist, continuing the move and letting Jeeter's own momentum do the rest. The chunky form described an awkward somersault, and Jeeter landed on his back, lungs emptied by the impact, gasping to regain his breath.

"That's one. Who's next?"

No hands, so Bolan chose a conscript from the ranks. According to the name tag on his camou shirt, the Klansman's name was Martin. Sandy hair and ruddy skin with countless freckles gave the man a dusty, unwashed look. As Martin took his place he passed downwind of Bolan, and the Executioner noted that appearances were sometimes accurate.

"We've seen what you can do against an unarmed man who tries to jump you from behind. But what about the fellow with the knife who'd just as soon take home your nuts for souvenirs?"

He waited for an answer from the class, aware that there would probably be none. After a moment of silence he turned back to Martin, pointing to the twelve-inch bowie knife the Klansman carried on his hip.

"You any good with that?"

"I hold my own."

"Let's see."

A crooked grin broke through the freckles. "Are you serious?"

"Completely."

"Do it, Tommy!"

"Hell, it's your funeral, man."

The bowie's heavy blade caught the sunlight as he drew it from its leather sheath. The Klansman made a couple of exploratory passes through the air, then started circling, knees flexed, the knife held out in front of him, its tip aimed straight at Bolan's midriff.

It was going to be simpler than he had anticipated.

He waited for his adversary, moving only as was necessary to keep Martin in front of him. The Klansman made a full circle around Bolan and was halfway through a second round before he made his move. The lunge was telegraphed by his expression, slack lips tightened across his teeth, eyes narrowing to beady slits before he charged.

Bolan stepped inside the thrust and fastened on his adversary's wrist with fingers like steel talons, twisting, wringing out a cry of pain before a back-kick cut the Klansman's legs from under him. Martin fell heavily, and Bolan followed him down, kneeling on the freckled youngster's chest, wrenching his right arm painfully around until the bowie's blade was kissing Martin's throat. A bit more pressure, any weight at all upon the blade, would loose a geyser of the skinny racist's blood.

"Momentum. Timing. Use them to your best advantage and you'll come out points ahead." He rose and turned away from Martin, studying the class. He checked his watch and found that it was pushing three o'clock. "Let's knock off there and start in fresh tomorrow."

From the corner of his eye he recognized Bob Shelton. Watching. Moving closer as the class dispersed.

"You free tonight?"

"I could be. What's the deal?"

"We've got unfinished business from the other night."

"You mean a couple of walls are standing?"

Shelton frowned and shook his head. "Seems like the preacher just can't take a hint. No matter that he lost his church, the stupid bastard keeps on giving speeches for the union. Now he lets them use his house, if you can feature that."

"Sounds like a stubborn man. Who is he?"

"Reverend Cletus Little." Shelton cracked a wicked grin at that. "I'll bet you that he's *feeling* little when we finish with him. If he's feeling anything at all."

"Another bomb?"

The Klansman shook his head. "Too noisy. Mason thinks it's time the reverend did a disappearing act."

"I'm in," he said. "When should I meet you?"

"Same as last time. We'll be taking on a few more hands for this one. Two cars, maybe three."

"I'll be there."

"See you then."

It would have been too much, he thought, to ask the target's address. With a name in hand he should be able to alert authorities or pass a warning on through Wilson Brown if all else failed. It stood to reason Brown would know the minister—know *of* him, anyway—and he would be the man to contact if the Bureau could not move in time.

When he got back to his apartment, Bolan made two calls. The first, to Leo Turrin, was brief. He gave his friend in Wonderland the name of the intended victim and the time the Klansmen were meeting.

"I don't have an address, but he should be in the book."

"No problem," Turrin said. "I'll put the local office on it. They've been looking for a decent handle on the Knights. This should be perfect."

"Count on two cars, minimum."

"The Bureau always comes prepared. You're in this one, are you?"

"All the way."

"You know, I can't exactly tip the locals off to let you slide."

"I've got it covered."

"Watch yourself."

"Will do."

He severed the connection, dialed Lynn Halsey's number, waited through four rings before she answered.

"Lynn."

"You caught me in the shower. Can I call you back?"

"I'm sorry, there's no time. I have to take a rain check on tonight."

He felt her frowning through the line. "What's wrong?"

"I've got some business to take care of."

"With the Klan?"

"Just business."

She was silent for a moment. "Will you call me when you're finished?"

"I'll be late."

"It doesn't matter. Call me. Promise?"

"Yes."

"About this rain check . . ."

"I was thinking of tomorrow night, unless you have other plans."

"I'll have to check my social calendar."

"Well, if you'd rather not . . ."

"Tomorrow night's fine."

"Okay."

"Be careful. Please?"

"I'll call you."

Bolan stripped the Browning, checked its load and action, then repeated the procedure with the hideout Colt. He emptied extra magazines, refilled them, more to occupy his time then from necessity. His mind, meanwhile, was grappling with the problems and risks presented by his new assignment with the Knights.

The law enforcement end was Leo's headache. After consultation with the FBI in Little Rock, he might—or might not—choose to notify the sheriff's office. If the local force was infiltrated, any leak would jeopardize the mission, blow the ambush in advance. It might be safer all round to keep the action under wraps and let the sheriff know about it when the smoke began to clear.

Security for Reverend Little would be in the Bureau's hands, and Bolan put that problem out of mind immediately. There was nothing he could do about it from his end, in any case, and he would have to trust the G-men, knowing they were experts at their job. The FBI had waged an unrelenting war against the KKK for more than half a century, and they would know what to expect from Ritter's wrecking crew.

His own role in the raid was something else entirely. Bolan would not fire upon the FBI under any circumstances. He might even be forced to intervene on their behalf if

Shelton's crew appeared to have the upper hand. It would be risky playing both sides of the fence at once, and if the Executioner was forced to show his hand before his "brother Klansmen," he would have to kill them all in self-defense. No word of his duplicity would find its way to Mason Ritter or to Freeman before he was prepared to make his final play.

He thought of Lynn and felt a sudden pang of guilt at using her to gain more information on the Klan. He told himself that it was necessary, that her own antipathy toward Ritter and the others would have made her understand. She had not been betrayed, precisely, and he would not harm her if he could avoid it. On the question of her uncle, if it became imperative to take him down . . . well, she would have to take her chances. Bolan's mission took priority over personal feelings, and he would not let his sympathy for Lynn—or any of the other feelings he undeniably experienced in her presence—undermine his sense of duty.

He had come to Arkansas to break the Klan and crush the Aryan Vanguard. He would be satisfied with nothing less than victory.

With time to kill, the soldier settled down to wait.

REVEREND CLETUS LITTLE NEVER THOUGHT about himself in terms of activism. When he thought about himself at all, he wondered at the nature of his predicament. A man of God who tried to set himself above the petty problems of the world, he had been dragged somehow into the middle of a worldly conflict that now threatened to destroy him. Already he had lost his church, and while the Lord might know how it would be restored, Cletus Little did not have a clue.

He had been satisfied with life the way it was until Theo Brown had approached him with the proposal to enlist Bethany AME as the unofficial chapel of his fledgling farmers' union. The minister had been skeptical at first, but Brown had been compelling, charismatic, making light of Little's private fears and couching his request in scriptural terms.

In the end, there had seemed to be no choice. A movement had arisen in the people's hour of need, and who was Cletus Little to say no when lives and souls were hanging in the balance?

From donating the church as a meeting hall it had been a short and easy step to mentioning the union in his Sunday sermons. Nothing radical, of course. A sympathetic reference here and there to working men in danger of eviction from their homes, of losing the land on which their fathers and their fathers' fathers had raised crops to feed the nation. Reverend Little still would not have called himself an activist. Not yet.

And when they had murdered Theo, riddled him with bullets in the middle of the night, it had been a pastor's duty to preside at his funeral services. He had spoken the words that had come to mind, and had meant them with all his heart. Now, in retrospect, he wondered if he would have chosen other words had he been favored with the gift of prophecy.

The pastor would not call himself an activist, but *someone* did. In Parrish—and in Little Rock, as well—were men who hated him for what he was, for what he said in public, for the dreams he cherished in his heart. The burning of his church had been a warning to desist, expressed in terms any man might understand. It was a warning he could not ignore.

But Reverend Little had refused to run and hide. Against his better judgment, he had gone before a meeting of the farmers' union just last night, and he had pledged them his continuing support. Almost before he realized what he was saying, he had offered members of the union space to gather in his home if they were short of room. He heard himself declare that he was not afraid of any man alive, and knew it was a lie.

In fact, he lived with mortal terror every day. The product of a home where Booker T. Washington had been more revered than Martin Luther King or Malcolm X, he had been taught to "know his place" from childhood, to avoid antagonizing whites whenever possible. In spite of federal laws, Supreme Court rulings, all the rest of it, there was a strain of bigotry and violence still alive and well in Dixie. Blacks had made substantial progress through the years, out there were regions where they trespassed at their peril even now. In Chatham County, unions were considered "white man's business" and were viewed with general disfavor even when their membership was entirely Caucasian. The specter of an interracial union organizing hardscrabble farmers to resist the rulers of the county and the state had called for swift retaliation from the power structure. After economic pressure had failed, when members of the union had started fighting back with strikes and boycotts, men in suits and ties had called on others dressed in sheets and neo-Nazi uniforms to teach the blacks and the radicals a lesson in reality.

Somehow, without intending to, the Reverend Cletus Little had been dragged into the middle of it all. Respected in the black community for his position as spiritual leader—and by certain whites for his conservatism—he had suddenly become a figurehead of sorts for peaceful revolution. Fool that he was, the pastor had believed a social revolution could be peaceful, carried on without the bloody stain of violence.

He knew better now, and still he was not wise enough to turn his back and run. As frightened as he was, he could not bring himself to be a coward now.

Outside, a car door slammed. Then another. Reverend Little kept no weapons in the house, for he had always placed his faith in God. Just now, however, as he approached the door and pressed one eye against the peephole, Little would have settled for a .38.

Two men in business suits, both white, clean-cut. Not Klansmen, by the look of them, unless their sheets and overalls were in the laundry. Little waited for the taller of the two to ring the bell, then cracked the door.

"Who are you?"

He thought his heart would freeze inside him when the tall man reached inside his jacket like a movie gangster going for his shoulder holster. It was just a wallet, though, not a pistol, that he held up with a flourish.

"Reverend Little? FBI."

THE OTHER MEMBERS of the wrecking crew were still arriving when Mack Bolan parked his car behind the meeting hall. The battlewagon and another dark sedan stood side by side, mud liberally smeared across their license plates, although the cars themselves were spotless. Safe from view by passing motorists, the Klansmen were inspecting shotguns, rifles, pistols, double-checking loads and setting safety catches, making ready for the night's festivities.

"You packing?" Bob Shelton asked as Bolan approached. Bolan pulled back the left side of his jacket to show the Browning in its shoulder harness, and the leader of the hit team handed him a sawed-off Ithaca. "You'd better take this, just in case."

"Expecting problems with the reverend?"

"I'm just like you. I like to be prepared."

"Suits me."

He looked the shotgun over, pumped the slide to put a live one in the firing chamber, flicked the safety on. The buckshot would not have much chance to spread if he was forced to make his move inside the battlewagon, but it wouldn't hurt to have the scattergun along. In case.

"Let's saddle up."

He counted five men in the second car, McCullough driving. In the back of the battlewagon, Bolan had a window seat this time, with Jackson driving and Shelton riding shotgun, as before. Bolan sat beside a Klansman he had never seen before, with Thorndyke topping off the sandwich on the driver's side.

They let the other car lead out, the battlewagon trailing, Bolan once again noticing street signs as they rode. The nameless Klansman tried to keep a conversation going with some ethnic jokes, apparently to camouflage his nervousness, but finally gave it up. It might not be his first time out with Shelton's team, but he was definitely showing signs of stage fright, which made him doubly dangerous when the chips were down. A frightened man was unpredictable, unstable, prone to fire at anything that moved—including friends. It did not help to see the nervous Kluxer carrying an Ingram MAC-10 submachine gun fitted with a 32-round magazine.

When they were fifteen minutes out, they passed the blackened ruins of the church. Shelton cocked a thumb in that direction.

"Bastard should have learned," he said. "Some niggers just can't take a hint."

"That ought to wake him up, all right," Jackson said.

"Too bad the fucker isn't going to live so he could learn from his mistake."

"Ain't it a crying shame?"

Four blocks beyond the church, the battlewagon slowed and moved toward the curb. As McCullough killed the lights, the car kept on rolling, nosing in across the street some fifty feet beyond.

"What are we doing?" Bolan asked.

"We're backup," Shelton said. "They won the toss for who should take him. We stand by in case he's got some of those union boys along for company."

The nameless Klansman looked relieved, and tried to hide it with a show of mock belligerence. "I thought you said that we was gonna take him!"

"Keep your shirt on. They're not going to dust him *here*. We'll all be at the party once he's in the bag."

"Okay, that's better." But the nervous tension was sounding in his voice again, and Bolan saw the Ingram trembling in his grasp.

Downrange, four Klansmen were unloading from the other car, McCullough hanging tough behind the wheel. They struck off in a flying wedge across the minister's lawn and were halfway to the house when floodlights blazed to life behind the hedges, trapping them at center stage.

"FBI! Lay down your weapons!"

One of the excited Klansmen fired a shotgun blast at Little's house, and suddenly the night was cleft by thunder, muzzle-flashes winking from the shadows, members of the raiding party dodging, weaving, sprawling as they tried to hold their own. McCullough dropped the point car into gear, tires smoking from a standing start, but men in navy coveralls with "FBI" emblazoned on the backs were charging from the bushes, peppering the car with automatic fire. Absorbing hits, the wheelman lost control and veered across the street, colliding with a car parked on the other side.

"Get in there!" Shelton bellowed at Jackson. "Let's get those Klansmen out!"

The battlewagon dug for traction, tortured rubber moaning on the pavement. Bobby Shelton was already craning through his open window, aiming his M-1 carbine at the FBI men, squeezing off before the agents recognized their danger. Then they were returning fire, the battlewagon taking hits, her windshield etched with graphic spiderweb designs.

A rifle bullet clipped the rearview mirror, plowing on to strike the nameless Klansman squarely in the face. A portion of his flabby cheek was sheared away, blood spurting everywhere, and he went crazy, holding down the trigger of his Ingram as he clapped the other hand against his face. It took a second and a half to empty out the weapon's magazine, and in that time he riddled Jackson, splattering his brains across the dashboard, tracking on to drill Bob Shelton in the back.

They were accelerating toward the house, a dead foot jammed against the pedal. Bolan did not have to think about his move before he made it, leaning hard against the door and rolling clear. He heard a muffled curse from Thorndyke as the Klansman tried to emulate his move and blew it. Then the pavement rushed to meet him, flaying palms and knees. The Ithaca was jolted from his fingers, skittering across the pavement, lost.

He rolled and came up running, well aware that members of the SWAT team would regard him as the enemy and cut him down if they were given half a chance. Behind him, riot guns and automatic rifles strafed the battlewagon, but they could not slow it down with Jackson slumped across the wheel. There was a rending crash as Little's house absorbed the crushing impact, followed by the hollow rushing sound of flames. Some of the probing rounds had reached a hot spot, and the battlewagon was about to self-destruct.

Bolan ran, unmindful of the pain that jarred through his legs with every stride. Across the street, in shadow, he tangled with a rosebush, long thorns ripping at his clothing, furrowing his flesh. He scaled a wooden fence and came away with splinters in his bleeding palms, relieved to feel the pain that meant that he was still alive, still moving on his own. Behind him, there was no more gunfire. More important, there were no voices calling after him to halt.

Had he eluded them, against all odds? Or were they coming after him in silence, knowing that a terrorist in flight would not respond to calls for his surrender?

Bolan crossed the tiny yard and scaled another fence. More splinters, biting deep. He touched down in a narrow alley that ran east to west between the fenced backyards of smallish, well-kept homes. Around him, lights were coming on inside those houses, residents aroused by screeching tires and gunfire in the night. He listened closely for the sounds of hot pursuit, heard nothing and began his retreat along the alley.

Keeping to the shadows, Bolan covered several blocks unnoticed save for the attention he drew from family dogs. In the confusion of the shoot-out, canine warnings went unheeded, and the Executioner was not observed until he chose to show himself, three-quarters of a mile from Reverend Little's home.

The taxi was cruising aimlessly in search of fares, its driver half-asleep, when Bolan stepped out of a shadowed doorway, flagged it down. The driver of the cab was black, and he examined the disheveled soldier with a cautious eye before he said, "Where to?"

Without providing a specific address, Bolan named the intersection nearest to the meeting hall of the Teutonic Knights. If it meant anything to his chauffeur, the black man gave no sign.

"Rough night?"

"You might say that."

"This neighborhood can get that way, you know? Especially for folks like you."

"What kind of folks are those?"

"The pale kind."

"So I gather."

"Not that I got anything against you-all. The only color my eyes focus on is green."

"I hear you."

"Some folks, though, they see a gentleman like you down here, a night like this, they figure you're just asking for it."

"Maybe next time I should plan ahead."

"That might not be a bad idea."

He paid the cabbie double on arrival, checked the streets in each direction, walked back to his car. The other vehicles would still be there in the morning, waiting for their drivers to return, like faithful beasts of burden tethered to stakes.

How many of the Klansmen had survived the ambush? If there were survivors taken prisoner, would they turn on Ritter and the others, offer evidence to save themselves from prosecution? If it played that way, a portion of Bolan's job would be complete. He would be free to concentrate on Freeman and the Vanguard and their supporters in the upper crust of Little Rock society.

His absence from the scene of the fiasco would be noted and remarked upon in time. If he intended to avert suspicion and maintain his cover, he would have to get in touch with Ritter soon, tonight, before he got the word from other sources. Explanations might not do the trick, but neither would silence. If Bolan simply went to ground, he would attract suspicion that much sooner, blowing any hope of keeping up his pose as a devoted Klansman.

It was worth a try. And if he failed, the savages could only kill him once.

15

"So what happened?"

"I'm still working on the details."

Freeman counted it a victory of sorts that he could sit across the desk from Mason Ritter and discuss the catastrophe in normal tones, resisting the temptation to reach out and smash the wizard's face.

"Why don't you give me what you have?"

"Okay...well, uh, I got a call from Bowers, like I told you on the phone, and I went down to see him at the meeting hall. He said the FBI was waiting for them when they got to Little's place, some kind of SWAT team, from the sound of it. They got the drop on Jackson's crew, and someone started shooting. Their side, our side—I don't know. When Bobby recognized the trap, he tried to help them out and he got wasted."

"Bowers says."

"That's right."

"We sent ten men to do a relatively simple job," Freeman said, reiterating. "Six of them are dead now, two are in intensive care with bullet wounds, and one is in the fucking burn ward. And you tell me Bowers *walked away*?"

"Well, *ran* would be more like it, I suppose. He bailed out of the battlewagon when Jackson got it. Jesus, you should see his hands and knees from where he hit the pavement."

"Save your sympathy. I had a little powwow with a contact in the medical examiner's office. They aren't done with all of the butcher work yet, but they do know Jackson *and* Bobby were shot *in the back*. Do you follow me, Mason? They were shot in the back from *inside* their own car."

"What the hell?"

"Who was riding in back?"

"Well, Jackson was driving, and Bobby was riding up front. That puts Bowers and Thorndyke behind them, along with Bud Murphy."

"The fat boy?"

"That's Bud."

"Well, now, Thorndyke's in ICU, Bud's in the morgue, and I'd say that leaves Bowers."

"But *why*? I mean, he was the one set the bomb that took down Little's church. He'd been tested and proved. Why the hell should he turn on his brothers like that in the middle of things? I don't see it."

"Could be that you still have your eyes closed," he answered. "Could be he was never a *brother* at all."

"You were there when I gave him the oath."

"I was there. But the fact that he swore doesn't mean he was telling the truth."

"Jesus Christ, if you're right—"

"Then we've got an informer—or worse—on the inside. That's right."

"But the bomb..."

Freeman shrugged. "It's a small price to pay for acceptance if he could get next to the leadership, build up a case that would put us away. Ask the boys down in Selma and Jackson how far an informer will go to dig up the dirt that he needs. You can find them all cozy and warm in the federal pen outside Atlanta."

"I still can't believe it."

"Let's hear the alternatives," Freeman demanded. "You think the good reverend invited an FBI SWAT team for coffee and crumb cake? You figure *God* told him the boys would be paying a visit last night?"

"Could be one of the others."

"The dead ones, you mean? Or the ones that were shot up and fried? I've been fighting this war for a while, but I've never seen Federals so clumsy they'd shoot up their own damned informers. It's time to wake up, Mason."

"Okay, let's say it's Bowers, then. What should we do?"

"We take him out as soon as possible and minimize our losses. Keep your fingers crossed and pray he hasn't passed on anything a prosecutor might find useful."

"I can try and finish it tonight."

"Is he at home?"

"I'll have to call and check."

"Feel free."

He watched and waited while the wizard searched his pockets for a tiny address book and found the number he required. Behind the poker face, Freeman's mind was racing, seeking varied ways to save himself if Bowers had communicated with his sponsors, if incriminating information had changed hands. The thought of failure and betrayal turned his stomach. He would not live through that nightmare. Not again.

The Vanguard's chairman drew some consolation from the fact that Bowers was a member of the Knights and thus removed, to some degree, from details of the central operation. Still, if he had gathered evidence enough to bring about arrests, some of the Knights would doubtless point a guilty finger at their wizard, and from there...

Freeman studied Ritter's face, imagining it with a bullet hole between the piggy eyes. With Ritter gone, no one could ever hope to prove a working link between the Vanguard and the Klan. No matter that their memberships might overlap; a man's political affiliations were his own concern, and Freeman could not be expected to police what his members did in their leisure time. His first concern would be with heading off a serious investigation. If the probers looked too deeply, they might find some tattered remnant of his other life, the name he had been born with. And from there—

"Not home."

Be calm, he told himself. There's time. But was there?

"Friends? A woman?" He would not quite bring himself to voice his fear that Bowers might be with his sponsors, spilling everything he knew for court stenographers.

"I'm told he's getting cozy with the Halsey girl."

"The chaplain's daughter?"

Ritter nodded.

Women. They were a pathetic weakness he could do without. In this case, though, a woman just might be his adversary's strength. The Halsey girl ran Ritter's office, did his filing, took his phone calls. She had access to the information Bowers might require to build his case.

"Make sure."

Another call, and this time Ritter got an answer. "Reverend H.? Mason Ritter here. I hope I didn't interrupt your dinner. No? That's good. I'll tell you why I'm calling, Reverend. I've got a message for Mike Bowers, and I wondered if you knew where I could find him. Ah. They are? No, no, it's nothing urgent. Reckon I'll just catch him in the morning. Thank you kindly, Reverend."

He cradled the receiver, frowning.

"Bowers and the girl are out somewhere. He doesn't know where they went or when they might be back."

"It doesn't matter. Put a team on Halsey's place, and one on Bowers's. Either way, they have to come home sometime. You can take him when he shows."

"It may be tricky, with the girl."

"No trick at all. I don't want any witnesses."

"You mean . . . ?"

"I mean your ass is on the line! Your secretary has been snuggling up to an informer, and you don't know *what* she might have given him already. Cut your losses, Mason. Be a man."

"I'll give the order."

"Do that, Mase. You do that."

SITTING IN HIS PARLOR, Reverend Jacob Halsey eyed the telephone suspiciously, as if expecting it to slither off the table and attack him. He had been shaken by the call from Mason Ritter, though the wizard often phoned him after hours to discuss Klan business. It had been the sudden interest in Mike Bowers and his whereabouts that set alarm bells clanging in the back of Halsey's mind.

Because of Lynn.

How many times had he advised her not to get involved with members of the Vanguard or the Knights? Each time they had the conversation, Halsey suffered pangs of guilt, a feeling of hypocrisy that he could not escape. As Lynn had pointed out, *he* was a Klansman, one of those he had warned her to avoid. She worked for Mason Ritter—over his objections—and she came in daily contact with the Knights. It was entirely natural that friendships might develop, even something deeper, but the fact that it was natural would never put his mind at ease.

He recognized the violence simmering within the men he served as chaplain. They were soldiers in a holy war, and combat brought out the beast in a man. It was the chaplain's job to keep an army mindful of its link with the Almighty, mend the wounded souls that were a natural result of mortal combat.

Lately, though, he had begun to question his involvement with the Knights. He still believed in what they stood for, adamant resistance to the creeping socialism that was ruining America. His brother's life had been destroyed by bankers, tax men, leeches living off the sweat and blood of honest working men. If violence was required to break their stranglehold upon the national economy and salvage other decent lives from ruin, then it was a reasonable price to pay.

But what did burning churches have to do with banks and Jewish plots and all the rest of it? How could he reconcile his own vocation with a midnight arson raid against the house of God?

Last night the wrecking crew had taken after Cletus Little. Halsey knew that much from news reports, although he was never personally briefed on the actions of the paramilitary wing. He recognized the published names of those who had been killed or taken into custody, and realized that Ritter's plan had broadened from destruction of a church to the abduction and assassination of its pastor. Not that Mason would have dreamed up the plan on his own. He was a man of action, not a thinker. The idea would have originated elsewhere, and unless Halsey missed his guess, its author would be Freeman.

Had Mike Bowers been involved in the attack on the church or the raid on Little's home? It seemed probable. Halsey was all the more uneasy over Lynn's attachment to the tall, dark Klansman when he thought of Ritter's recent call. Did Mason have other secret work for Bowers? Was he simply checking on his man? Or had the new recruit somehow incurred the wizard's wrath?

If Ritter had it in for Bowers, Lynn would be in danger while she shared his company. Halsey's mind called up an image of her body torn by bullets, instantly supplanted by a vision of a house—*his* house—in flames. No coward, he was man enough to feel a primal terror for his loved ones, and his niece was all the family that remained to him in his autumn years.

Where were they now? If he recalled correctly, Lynn had mentioned dinner, but if she had named the restaurant, it hadn't registered. Halsey cursed himself for being such an absentminded idiot. The one time that he should have listened, his brain had been in neutral, idling over other bits of trivia.

A restaurant. He thought of scanning the yellow pages, finally gave up the idea as hopeless. Enough time had passed for them to finish dining, anyway, and then what good would it do if he managed to recall the name? Where would they go when they were done? Somewhere, perhaps, where they could be alone?

He did not wish to think of Lynn and Bowers doing any more than dining, sharing conversation, driving home. He realized that Lynn was an adult, suspected—logically—that she was not a virgin, and he knew he could not protect her from the world at large. But he had always thought he could protect her from the Klan.

There was a bottle of Kentucky bourbon in the kitchen, tucked away behind the china he had not used since Emily passed away nearly seven years ago. The bottle had been opened twice: the afternoon of Emmy's funeral, and the night he got the news about his brother's death. The liquor was a salve for private tragedy, and in his heart, Jacob Halsey believed that God would understand.

He might not understand the thoughts that Halsey nursed as he began to drink, however. Dark thoughts, streaked with bloody crimson, painful to examine. Thoughts of self-destruction and perdition, images of hellfire everlasting.

Images of what he might be forced to do if Lynn was harmed. By Bowers, by Mason Ritter or by any other man alive.

She was his only living relation, and God help any man who tried to take that vestige of his flesh and blood away. In thirty-seven years, since he had been drafted into combat in Korea, Jacob Halsey had not raised his hand in anger to another human being. Lately, though, since his involvement with the Knights, he had been feeling urges that he thought, upon reflection, were decidedly unchristian.

It would help to pray, but first he had to have another drink. And after that, another. While he waited for the liquor to take hold, he thought of Lynn, and what would happen if she did not make it home. After a while, he knew that it was time to find his gun.

"I HEARD ABOUT what happened."

"It was hard to miss, I guess."

She had been jockeying around the subject all through dinner, carefully avoiding any reference to the Klan or last night's violence, the coincidence of his abraded palms. At last, when the dessert plates had been cleared away and the coffee poured, she could contain herself no more.

"You've hurt yourself."

He glanced at hands scraped raw and smiled. "You ought to see the other guy."

"I'll bet. You know—"

"I'm sorry I had to break our date last night," he interrupted her. "As things turned out, I should have kept it, after all."

"Are you all right?"

"I seem to be."

"I'm serious."

The waiter had begun to hover near their table, and Mike stopped her with a frown. "We'd better let this wait until we get outside."

He settled the bill and walked her to his car, slid in behind the wheel. She took a chance and asked, "Where to?"

"I thought your uncle was expecting you at home."

"Oh, I imagine he's asleep by now."

"You know, Lynn..."

"Was it terrible?"

"How's that?"

"You know exactly what I mean."

He shrugged. "I've been through worse."

"Why do you do it?"

Bowers put the car in motion, driving aimlessly. "Sometimes I ask myself that question."

"And?"

"And what?"

"What do you tell yourself?"

"I can't decide." They drove for several blocks in silence, Bowers frowning to himself and struggling with some internal problem. Finally he asked her, "Lynn, how do you *really* feel about the Klan?"

"Is this a test?"

"A simple question."

"In the early days...after my parents...I was hurt enough and mad enough to think the anger and the hate made sense. At least the Vanguard and the Klan were doing *something*, even if some of it was against the law. But now it all seems such a waste. So many lives...and all for what? Has anything been gained?"

"And yet you stay."

"I told you, I can't leave my uncle. He'll agree with me someday, and in the meantime I just try and keep him out of trouble."

Bowers spent a moment pondering her words, then cleared his throat. "I'm not a Klansman," he informed her. Simple. Just like that.

She was confused. "I thought you took the oath."

"I did. But it was part of what you'd call my cover."

"Cover? You mean like a spy or something?"

"Something."

It was happening too fast. She knew what he was saying, but her mind could not absorb the import of his words. "Who *are* you?"

"Let's just say I have connections with the government."

"The FBI?"

He shook his head. "I'm more the unofficial type. A sort of troubleshooter."

"So you *are* a spy."

"I guess."

"What are you doing here?" She had to ask the question, but she was no longer certain that she wanted to hear the answer.

"I was sent to penetrate the Klan or Vanguard—both, if possible—and bring them down."

"Arrest them?"

"Some of them may be arrested, I suppose."

"My uncle?" Sudden terror, clutching at her heart.

"Right now he's clean, as far as I can see. I'm hoping that he'll stay that way."

And then, beneath the fear, a stab of pain. "I understand. And seeing me was all part of your job?"

He pulled in to the curb, along a darkened street, and parked. "It may have started out that way," he told her frankly, "but it isn't that way now. I don't expect you to believe me, but—"

"I do," she said impulsively. "Don't ask me why."

He smiled. "You know, Mason Ritter might be interested in what I've told you."

"He can go to hell. I hate the way he's used my uncle, kissing up to him and playing holy, laughing at him when his back is turned. He makes a mockery of everything my uncle stands for, everything that he believes."

"I think you ought to talk the reverend into taking a vacation."

"How?"

"That's up to you. If necessary, you could try the truth."

Lynn shook her head. "I don't know how he might react. I hate to say it, but he might tell Ritter."

"That won't be a problem in a day or so. I just don't want you standing in the fallout when it all comes down."

She felt the blush begin to tinge her cheeks. She tried to make light of it, stretching for the simulated accent of a Southern belle. "Why, sir, I didn't know you cared."

"Well, now you know."

She leaned into the kiss, lips brushing his at first, responding swiftly as the passion flared between them. Sliding both arms up around his neck, she gave herself to the sensation as his gentle hands began their exploration of her body. Moments later, when she broke the kiss, Lynn realized that she was trembling.

"Where to?" she asked again.

"I really think I ought to take you home."

"And wake my uncle?" She contrived to sound appalled by the idea. "I think we ought to let him rest, don't you? Let's go to your place."

16

"I'm tired of waiting for this bastard."

"Take it easy." Tom Neece flicked his Bic and used the light to check his watch. "It's only been an hour."

"*Only,*" Andy Carlyle echoed. "Asshole should be dead by now."

"We'll get him."

"Yeah, unless the others bag him first."

"And if they do, so what? Dead's dead."

"*I* want him, damn it! I was friends with Jackson and McCullough, just in case it slipped your mind."

Neece turned upon his fellow Knight with sudden venom. "*You* were friends! So how do you think *I* feel, Andy? Anybody here need a refresher on how tight I was with Bobby?"

Silence from the others, and Neece turned to scan the drab apartment complex once again. It did no good to think of Bobby Shelton cooling in a drawer downtown, his trim, athletic form disfigured by bullet wounds and ragged autopsy scars. Far better to remember all the good times— boozing, whoring, kicking ass and keeping niggers in their place—that they had shared. Fond memories that could never be erased, no matter what became of Bobby's earthly shell.

The two of them had gone through school together, finally dropped out together, joined the service as a team. Against all odds, they had secured duty postings that allowed them to commute and keep in touch on furlough, raising hell just like in the old days, looking forward to their discharge and the time when they could start to put their newfound skills to work.

It had been Bobby's bright idea to join the Knights, and Tom had gone along, as always, never once suspecting that the midnight fun and games would lead to final separation. It was enough to make a grown man weep, but Tom Neece had not cried since he was nine years old and some damned fool had run down his dog in the middle of the road. You learned to live with pain as you got older, but it never went away.

To pass the time, he checked the stubby shotgun he carried, making sure he had a live one in the chamber, fiddling with the safety like a nervous little boy. He caught the wheelman looking at him from the corner of his eye and knocked it off, embarrassed. Damn it, where the hell was Bowers, anyway?

Behind him, Carlyle was grumbling again. "We're stuck here, sitting on our thumbs, while that son of a bitch is out there getting laid. I get a chance, I mean to geld his ass before I blow his head off."

"Maybe next time," Neece responded. "If he comes our way, there won't be time for any entertainment on the side."

"Plain killing's too good for the son of a bitch."

"It'll just have to do."

"Fuckin' white nigger sold out the Knights, Tom. He shit on his oath."

"We've got orders. We'll carry them out, and that's *all*."

A sedan was approaching, and they ducked as it braked for the entrance to the parking lot of the apartment complex. Neece confirmed the make and license number, counted two heads in the car.

"Must not have got enough. He brought her home to finish up."

"Come on, let's take the bastard!"

"No."

"I don't believe I heard that, Tommy."

"Let them get inside and settle in. He won't be looking for us while he's playing hide-the-tubesteak. We can pop them both in bed and get it over with."

"I'd like to pop her ass in bed, all right. You sure we can't take prisoners?"

"Forget it. It's a simple in-and-out."

"That's what I had in mind."

"Just keep it zipped. You get your head shot off in there, it better be the one that's sitting on your shoulders."

"How much longer do we have to wait?"

"I'll let you know. They won't be finished for a while."

"I guess that's what they call co-ee-tus interruptus, huh?"

"I'll interruptus his co-ee-tus."

"Fuckin' right."

"I'm going to give that nigger-loving bitch a 12-gauge hysterectomy."

"I've got the gun she needs right here."

"Looks like a derringer to me."

"Your ass."

"I always figured you'd be swishy in a pinch."

"Pinch this."

Neece left the others to their banter, recognizing false bravado, knowing that his gunners had to psych themselves up for the kill. They all knew Bowers's reputation as a Green Beret and a killer; each of them was anxious for a chance to bring him down, but none would relish being first to cross his threshold.

Never mind. Neece planned to claim that honor for himself. It was the very least he could do for Bobby, and he planned to do a whole lot more before the night was out.

"I DON'T HAVE ANYTHING to drink except some beer."

"No, thanks. I don't need anything."

Lynn stepped into his arms, her body molding tightly to his own, and Bolan felt himself responding automatically. She moved against him and he savored the sensation, opening his lips to greet her tongue. His hands slid down to cup her buttocks, pulling her insistently against his loins.

They broke for air, and Bolan felt her heartbeat, strong and swift. He said, "The first time I saw you, I was sure you'd be spoken for."

"By who?"

He shrugged, rewarded by the pressure of her breasts against his chest. "Oh, someone at the office, I suppose."

"Mason Ritter? Honestly, he's old enough to be my father." Lynn appeared to be amused by the suggestion.

"Freeman, then."

"I don't see all that much of him. Besides, from what I hear, he's more a man's man, if you catch my drift."

A faint alarm bell sounded in the back of Bolan's mind, alerting him to something he should recognize, but Lynn was offering a sweet distraction now, and he surrendered to the moment.

"Listen, Mike, I didn't come up here to talk about the Knights or Jerry Freeman."

Jerry?

"No," he said. "Me, neither." When they kissed this time, it lit a fire inside that only friction of the flesh could quench. He lifted Lynn, hands cupped beneath her gently curving buttocks, and she locked her legs around his waist, skirt bunched around her hips. Deliciously encumbered, Bolan made his way into the bedroom, scarcely conscious of her weight, consumed by urgent need.

Reluctantly they separated long enough to shed their clothing, hungrily devouring each other with their eyes as skin was hastily exposed. The merging of their bodies moments later was electrifying, and they fell together on the bed, all straining flesh, searching lips and hands. The moment was too powerful to be sustained, and Bolan felt his climax building, closing in with the momentum of a runaway express train. Lynn was there to meet him at the crucial instant, arching her supple spine to form a living bridge beneath him, trembling on the brink of her explosion. When they collapsed together, endless seconds later, she began to giggle helplessly like a delighted child.

"You must be ticklish," Bolan teased her.

"No, believe me. I've just never felt...anything like that...before."

"We aim to please."

"You do a damn fine job of it, I'll give you that." The bright smile faltered as her stroking fingers traced a scar. "What's this?"

"Old business."

"From the war?"

"One of them."

"Oh . . . and here." She bent to kiss the faded, dime-size remnant of a bullet wound. "What's this?"

"I've had some problems with my interpersonal relationships," he said.

"I can't see why." She found an ancient track along his inner thigh, one fingertip pursuing it in the direction of his groin. "This must have hurt."

"It's feeling better all the time."

"I don't see any damage here, but it can't hurt to check." Her magic fingers went to work, reviving him. "You seem to be in working order."

"Sometimes I surprise myself."

"I love surprises."

"Be my guest."

He lay beneath her this time, and the view from his perspective was hypnotic.

"Oooh. Don't move."

"I wouldn't dream of it."

Lynn found her rhythm, taking time to get it right, her pace accelerating as she gave herself to the sensation. Bolan held himself in check as long as possible, then rose to meet her on a downthrust.

"Mmm. You weren't supposed to move."

"I lied."

"I'm glad."

They worked together, each with greater tolerance this time, less urgency to reach the culmination of the act. They had all night, and Bolan saw no need to rush.

"Okay, that's long enough."

"'Bout time."

"Stay here," Neece told the man behind the wheel, "and keep the engine running. On the way out, we won't have a lot of time to spare."

"I've got it covered."

Carlyle and the others were halfway across the street when Neece caught up with them. "Hold on a second," he demanded, reasserting his command. "This isn't any half-assed smash-and-grab. You run this like a Chinese fire drill and the chances are he'll hand your head back to you on a plate."

"I ain't afraid of any damned Green Beret."

"Afraid and careful are two different things," he snapped. "You'd best remember that. The man who screws this up will think the beltline is a Sunday stroll around the park."

They hesitated at his reference to the Klan's communal flogging punishment, reserved for members violating klavern rules and regulations. None of them had ever run the beltline, but they had participated in the chastening of others and had witnessed the results. No one had ever died from the experience, although a few would bear the scars until their dying day. The damage to a Klansman's ego was sufficient in itself to make most think a second time before they trampled on the rules.

"I'll go in first," he said when he was certain that he had their full attention.

"Tom—"

"You heard me, Andy. I'm in charge, and it'll be my ass if anything goes wrong. You're second if you want, but keep your finger off that trigger till you have a decent target—and I don't mean me!"

"No sweat. I hit just what I aim at."

"Right. We don't want any fancy shit, remember? In and out. Pop Bowers *and* the girl, and let it go at that."

"Suppose we wake the neighbors?"

"That's what these are for." So saying, Neece removed a lightweight ski mask from his pocket, tugging it over his head. The others followed suit, and he was startled by their resemblance to clowns, with brightly colored rings around their noses, eyes and mouths.

"I would've rather worn my robe and hood," Carlyle complained.

"Why not just leave a business card with your address? You got an urge to make new friends among the FBI?"

"All right, Tom, I was only saying—"

"Get a move on, will you? We can waste time jawing when we're finished."

He had scanned the layout on arrival, double-checking the location of their target on a map displayed outside the rental office. Bowers had apartment 213 upstairs, with only one way in and out. A balcony no bigger than a Ping-Pong table jutted off the sliding glass doors of his living room, but from the bedroom windows it would be a twelve-foot drop to thorny hedges, minus any kind of safety net.

The place was dark, and Neece allowed the fact to boost his spirits. Too damned much to hope that the two would be asleep already, but at least if they were going at it, Bowers would be slow reacting to the entrance of his unexpected visitors. They only needed seconds, time enough to crash the door and find the party, put a few rounds through the bull's-eye and retreat. It would be simple.

Should be simple.

The night was warm, but under his shirt the perspiration felt cold and clammy. Neece would not admit it to himself, but he was worried, even frightened, by the move he was about to make. He had reviewed the file that Freeman had passed along to Mason Ritter, with its notes on Bowers's military service, all the things he had been up to since his discharge. Tommy Neece had never killed a man, unless you counted Theo Brown—and everybody had taken a shot at him, so who the hell could ever say for sure they did the job? But he was up against a killer now, without a doubt. The record had been crystal clear on that. Neece was not encouraged by the nature of his backup, either. Carlyle did all right at whipping helpless niggers, but he talked a better battle than he fought, and Billy Putnam was an unknown quantity, the king who grinned a lot when there was nothing funny going on.

If I was smart, Neece thought, I'd let *them* take the point. But it was still his job, and Ritter was counting on him. More important, he was counting on himself, for Bobby's sake. He owed the bastard one, and it was time to pay the tab in full.

They climbed the narrow stairs in single file, Neece leading, Carlyle close behind, with Putnam bringing up the rear. As far as Neece could tell, the neighbors were asleep, but some of them were bound to put in an appearance when the fireworks started going off. He only hoped none of them got crazy, trying to play hero. All he needed was to get his ass shot off by some old lady with a blunderbuss. The perfect climax to a fucked-up evening.

They crowded on the landing, elbowing one another, three men occupying space that would have been uncomfortable for two.

"Give me room, goddamn it!"

"Ain't no room to give."

"Shut up, for Christ's sake!"

Pivoting to face the door of 213, Neece gripped his shotgun tightly, cursing his sweaty palms. He hit the panel with a solid kick, an inch or so above the lock and slightly to its left. Incredibly, it held.

Again.

And nothing.

"Jesus H., get on with it!"

Neece aimed his snubby 12-gauge at the doorknob, closed his eyes and fired.

BOLAN HEARD THE FIRST KICK and was moving by the second, rolling Lynn away from him and off the bed.

"Down! Stay *down*!"

His shoulder rig was crumpled on the floor beside the bed. Bolan was crouched with the Browning autoloader in his fist when sudden thunder ripped the silence of the small apartment and his shattered door flew open, slamming against the wall with enough force to dent the plaster. Muttered curses in the darkness, covered by the sounds of shuffling feet as his attackers rushed the bedroom.

Bolan nailed the first one through the door with two rounds in the chest, a stunning double-punch that lifted him completely off his feet and hurled him backward toward his comrades. On his way to impact with the floor, the dying man squeezed off another buckshot round that loosed a rain of plaster from the ceiling, the concussion numbing Bolan's ears.

Behind the leader, other shotguns roared in the darkness, firing high on the assumption that Bolan would foolishly be standing to meet his enemies. Beside him, Lynn was moaning softly, wriggling to hide herself beneath the bed. Bolan left her to it, squeezing off a round in the direction of the nearest hostile muzzle-flash. Impossible to say if he had missed or not until both weapons answered him together, spraying lethal double-ought around the tiny bedroom, peppering the walls and tacky furniture.

In other circumstances, Bolan might have held off the gunners indefinitely, but he knew police would soon be on the way, responding to the firefight and reports from frightened neighbors. Even if the riot squad's arrival scattered his assailants, he could not afford to linger and discuss the problem with detectives. Not with Lynn there and a dead man stretched out on the threshold. Not with weapons and munitions hidden in his car downstairs.

One item of his armory had been carried up, however, with an eye toward future need. Somehow he would have to reach the closet. Just six feet from the bed to closet door, but with a pair of shotguns blasting at him, it might as well have been a mile.

He had to pin the gunners down, discourage them enough to buy himself the second and a half he would need to duck inside the closet. Once there, he had only to find his weapon in the darkness, stay alive to use it and emerge to kill two shooters who were waiting for him, covering the only exit from his hidey-hole.

He found the Browning's extra magazine by feel and palmed it, braced himself to run. Beyond the bedroom door, he heard the gunners shifting, thought he heard one reloading. There would never be a better time to make his move.

He burst from cover, diving toward the closet, emptying the pistol through the open bedroom doorway in a single burst of rapid-fire. The startled shout from one of his assailants might mean anything or nothing, and he was not counting on an easy kill as he threw back the closet door and slumped inside.

A storm of shotgun pellets slammed the door behind him, faint illumination from the windows streaming in through random holes. He tugged the Uzi from its carrying case and drew back the bolt, thumbing off the safety. Counting down, he gave the gunners time to gain new confidence, then kicked the riddled door open, hunching lower in the closet as all hell broke loose.

He counted five new thunderclaps and saw the closet door disintegrate before he made his move, firing the Uzi for effect. Stark naked, Bolan felt intensely vulnerable, but there was no time to hesitate; a suit would not have stopped the buckshot rounds, and it was time to do or die in the attempt.

One of the raiders fell, a tumbling silhouette, his weapon spinning free of lifeless fingers, clattering across the chintzy coffee table. Tracking on, the parabellum manglers took a bite out of the doorjamb, chewed through plasterboard and found the sole surviving adversary on the other side.

The guy broke out of cover, staggering, already wounded, trying to defend himself. A rising figure eight snuffed out the final spark of life and punched him over backward, deadweight walloping the floor with force enough to set the ceiling fixtures rattling downstairs.

The Executioner snapped the lights on, ready with the submachine gun if his enemies showed any signs of life, relaxing slightly as he saw that they were finished. Stepping outside the door, he scanned the corridor, half expecting backup to arrive and finish the job. Instead, a sleepy-looking woman with her hair in rollers stood and gaped at

Bolan for a moment, hastily retreating toward the safety of her own apartment.

Back inside, he spent a precious moment stripping ski masks off dead faces, trying to identify his enemies. He recognized Carlyle from the fracas at the Blackboard, and the first man down was one of Mason Ritter's bookends, Bobby Shelton's friend. Tom something. Number three was new to Bolan, but it did not matter who he was. He had confirmed the Klan's involvement in the strike, and that was all he had to know.

Somehow, by luck or accident, the wizard had seen through his tale of last night's raid. His cover was officially defunct, and there was no time left to fret about mistakes he might have made along the way.

"Come on," he barked to Lynn. "Get dressed. We have to leave right now."

"I'm coming."

She looked ashen in the artificial light, but she was not in shock. Not yet. Her movements might be jerky, uncoordinated, but at least she had her wits about her. Dressing automatically, with an economy of motion that surprised him, she was done before the soldier, stowing underthings and stockings in her crowded handbag. Bolan bagged the Uzi, shrugged his shoulder harness on and grappled with his jacket en route to the door. He could afford to lose the clothing that he left behind, and all his other gear was in the car.

Before they reached the car they heard the wail of distant sirens. Though he had expected something in the nature of an ambush, he and Lynn saw no one outside the building. The wheelman must have cut and run when it had become apparent that his passengers would not be coming back. The word would get to Mason Ritter soon enough, but Bolan was not worried for himself.

Lynn Halsey was a different matter altogether.

"Uncle Jacob!" she said suddenly when they were under way.

"He should be fine. That crew was after me."

"But why?"

"Somehow they've cracked my cover."

"Then you'll have to leave."

"Not yet. I've still got work to do. But *you* should go."

"Go *where*?"

"Away. It really doesn't matter at the moment. Anywhere the Knights and Vanguard can't find you for the next few days. Beyond that, you should be all right."

"You said those men were after *you*."

"They have to figure I've been using you to gather information. Even if they didn't think so earlier, they can't afford a living witness to tonight's performance."

"So they'll have to kill me, too."

"If they can find you. But they won't have time to chase you very far."

"How can you be so sure?"

"Because, from here on out, I plan to occupy their time."

She hesitated for a moment, finally blurted out, "I have to see my uncle, Mike."

He recognized her iron resolve and nodded. "But we'll have to check it out before you show yourself."

"Don't worry," she replied. "I won't let Ritter get his hands on me."

His hands.

And suddenly he knew. Beyond a shadow of a doubt. The certainty was sudden, absolute. He had the answer.

All he had to do from this point on was use it to his best advantage. For openers, he had to stay alive.

17

"What do you mean, they *missed* him?"

"Well—"

"Goddamn you, spit it out!"

"I mean he got away. *They* got away. Tom Neece is dead, a couple of his boys. No sign of Bowers or the girl."

"You idiot!"

"Now just hold on—"

"Hold on, my ass! A simple tag inside the target's own apartment, and your men not only screw it up, they get themselves killed in the bargain! What kind of half-assed operation are you running?"

"He was waiting for them."

"Bullshit! If your men can't take a target while he's getting laid, they can't do anything."

Ritter bristled. "I don't see you offering troops from the Vanguard to help."

"You'll have backup, don't worry. I'm calling the shots from now on, and the first man who screws up his job or ignores his instructions is going to wish Bowers had blown his head off!"

"Don't threaten me, Freeman. I've got as much riding on this deal as you have."

You think so, he thought to himself. But you don't know the half of it.

"Fine. I can count on you, then?"

"Absolutely."

The plan had already been formed in his mind. From the moment he had learned of the Bowers fiasco, his brain had been racing to find an escape hatch, a sideshow to cover his tracks when he ran.

"Mason, we need a diversion."

"What kind of diversion?"

"Oh, I don't know . . . something involving the union, to take off some heat while we pin down Bowers and get rid of him."

"Him and his bitch."

"Absolutely." He feigned concentration, brow furrowed, and broke into a well-rehearsed smile as he hatched the idea. "Wilson Brown."

"What about him?" the wizard inquired.

"He's been gathering followers, trying to fill his son's shoes." He could see Ritter's mind working, small cogs attempting to mesh, not quite making it. "What say we take him out, just for the hell of it?"

"Take him out how?"

"Why not go with a full-dress affair? Let him be an example for all of his people. His boy was a 'martyr.' Like father, like son."

"That means more heat, not less."

"It means *different* heat, Mason. It means heat *somewhere else*. While the locals and Feds are out chasing their tails over Brown, wasting time with the leftovers, we can tag Bowers, and bingo! We're out of the woods."

"You don't figure he's talked?"

"In the past thirty minutes? I doubt it." In fact, he was not at all sure, but he no longer cared. One more day, at the most, and he planned to be out of the bigotry business, with cash in his pocket and time on his hands. He would have to arrange an appointment with Andrews, of course, lay his cards on the table, but Freeman was certain the banker would wish to provide the funds he needed for travel abroad. He was certain the man would insist.

"Doesn't take thirty minutes to put through a phone call," the Klansman reminded him.

"Not ordinarily, no. But it might if you're running and hiding, with men out to kill you, a broad on your hands and nowhere in the world left to go."

"He could run to the damned FBI."

"Which you're watching, of course."

"Yeah, it's covered, but still—"

"Don't be paranoid. One fucking Judas does not have to be a disaster."

"He's taken out thirteen good men in two days!"

"I'm aware of that, Mason. Thirteen or a hundred and thirty, I'm not rolling over because of a setback, and neither are you."

"No one said I was rolling."

"All right, then. I want every man you can raise on the streets in an hour. I'll roust out the Vanguard while you put the Knights on patrol. We'll have two thousand men tracking Bowers before he can make a decision to fish or cut bait."

"If you say so."

"I do. Now get after it. I've got my own calls to make."

And the first one belonged to the banker—oh, yes. Andrews would not enjoy being awakened from sleep on the high side of midnight, but it would be good for him, start getting him used to a long list of other unpleasant surprises. His instant response would be outright denial, of course; he would bluster and bluff for a while, until Freeman laid out the specifics, a taste of the evidence he'd compiled in the past eighteen months. If Andrews argued too long or attempted to talk down the price, a reminder of what lay in store for him should be enough to complete the transaction. Considering every alternative, Freeman regarded himself as a bargain.

A going-out-of-business sale, perhaps. And then again...

He had already proved it was possible to change identities, erase the past and start from scratch in old familiar hunting grounds. It was a tried-and-true technique. If he could do it once, there was a chance that he could pull it off a second time.

Except that he had yet to pull it off *this* time. He would not be home free until he had the cash from Andrews safely in his hand and he was out of Arkansas. No, make that out of the United States. He needed a vacation, and he had no time to waste. In another day or two, the atmosphere in Little Rock and Chatham County might be lethal for him.

For all the confidence he displayed to Ritter, Freeman had no doubt that they were blown. It mattered little whether they caught up with Bowers now or not. By now his sponsors would have a good idea of what was going on from periodic contacts, and the Vanguard leader's disappearance would be frosting on the cake. The necktie party Freeman planned for Wilson Brown was merely window dressing, more confusion added for the benefit of anyone who might come looking for him prematurely.

He would let the Knights and the Vanguard take care of themselves when they were done with Brown. A lynching carried out in full regalia should be just the kind of bonus Andrews would appreciate, a little something extra for the propaganda mill. Once he had dropped the tired charade that cast him as a closet racist, they could get around to talking business, man to man.

Although, in Freeman's reckoning, they might be one man short.

LYNN WAS RELIEVED TO FIND the back door open, thankful for her uncle's absentmindedness. She had not wished to raise a fuss by knocking, and she dared not go around in front. Not while the men out there were waiting for her in the darkness.

Passing through the kitchen like a shadow, moving cautiously along the corridor, she found her uncle in his study, huddled in his favorite easy chair. At first she thought he was asleep... and then she saw the bottle, nearly empty on his desk, within arm's reach. For a moment, in her surprise and consternation, she forgot her mission. She had known about the bottle hidden in the kitchen cabinet, but she was sure Uncle Jacob had not touched it since the day of her arrival.

Until tonight.

Her touch woke him, and she was frightened by the brief contortion of his features.

"Lynn? Thank God you're safe."

What did he know? "I'm not," she said. "I mean, I can't stay, Uncle Jacob. Neither one of us is safe."

A shadow seemed to pass across his face, as if he understood her words too well, but he was still compelled to ask, "What do you mean?"

"They tried to kill us. Mike and me. He's waiting for me now."

"*Who* tried?"

"Tom Neece, some others. Klansmen, Uncle Jacob."

"God in heaven!"

"There are others waiting on the street outside. That's why I had to come in through the back."

"Outside? Damned reprobates! I won't allow it!"

He was on his feet and moving toward the door before she caught his arm and held him back. "No, Uncle Jacob! They won't listen to you now. For all I know, you may be on their hit list, too."

"Don't be absurd." But as he spoke, a sudden doubt appeared to cross his mind. "Why did they try... what has he done?"

"Mike isn't what you think. He's working for the government."

"A spy?"

"You have to understand," she pleaded with him, desperate to make him see before it was too late. "The Knights have lost control, the Vanguard too, for all I know. You must see that."

He frowned. "What would you have me do, child?"

"Come away with us. Mike says he can protect you. You could testify, receive immunity for anything that may have happened... anything you may have seen... or done."

"I took an oath," he said.

"It doesn't matter now. The Klan opposed everything you stand for, everything you believe in. You don't owe them anything."

"It doesn't matter what they've done or how I feel about the movement, Lynn. I swore an oath before Almighty God."

"You think He cares about the Klan? These men have murdered in His name, burned churches to the ground. You can't be any part of that."

"I am. By virtue of my oath, I share whatever guilt may fall upon their shoulders."

"And you have a chance to purge that guilt. Come with us."

"No man has the power to absolve me of my sins."

"They mean to kill me, Uncle Jacob. If you stay here, I'm afraid they'll kill you, too."

"Don't worry, Lynn. I'm not a helpless child."

She felt a sudden urge to scream, to shake him violently and force him to believe. "They're maniacs," she snapped. "They have no more respect for you than for the other men they've killed."

"Before I walk away, I need to have a word with Ritter. To explain myself."

"For God's sake, why?"

"Don't take his name in vain. I'll not allow that in my house."

"I'm sorry, Uncle Jake." Their conversation had assumed a strange, surrealistic quality. Lynn knew that she was losing the contest, and still she could not turn away. "Why Ritter? *Why?*"

"I owe him that, at least. I owe it to myself."

"He'll kill you . . . or he'll have you killed."

"I don't believe so."

"Please!"

"I think you ought to go now. Out the back, the way you came. Is Bowers waiting for you?"

"Yes." She had already told him that. "He's waiting."

"Good. I trust your judgment, Lynn. If you believe that he's a good man, I believe it, too."

"Don't make me leave you, Uncle Jake."

"I still have duties here. So much to do."

"Stay clear of Ritter."

"Go, now—quick, before they think to check inside."

"Be careful?"

"Yes."

"You promise?"

"Promise."

"There are still some things I need, upstairs."

"All right."

She left the lights off in her bedroom, fumbling in the closet for her clothes, no longer caring if colors matched or not. She felt a sudden urgency, a need to be away and running, to leave the old, familiar house behind. Before it killed her and became her tomb.

Downstairs, she found her uncle seated in his easy chair once more. He seemed alert now but troubled, leaning forward, one hand resting on the telephone.

"I'm going now. I'll see you . . . won't I?"

"Yes." His smile seemed genuine. "Take care."

She closed the screen door carefully behind her to prevent its slamming. Nearly one o'clock. The night was warm, almost muggy. Suddenly she wished it would rain, a downpour that would rinse the city clean.

There was a gap between the hedgerows, and an almost hidden gate that opened on the alley behind her uncle's house. Somehow, Mason Ritter's hit team had forgotten it or else hadn't known about it in the first place. Mike was waiting for her in the car, a submachine gun in his lap.

"He wouldn't come," she told him, weeping softly even though she tried not to.

"His decision."

"Yes." As if that settled everything, absolved her of her own responsibilities. "It was."

She owed her uncle more than that—a great deal more, in fact—and if she could not save him from himself, perhaps she could avenge him. In advance.

"You got enough to keep you for a while?" Mike Bowers asked.

"Should be. Where are you taking me?"

"The Greyhound station fair enough?"

She thought about it, finally nodded. "Yes," she told him honestly. "That should be fine."

THE PISTOL WAS an Army-issue .45. Jacob Halsey had not fired it in a decade. In Korea, long before he found his calling, he had carried it in battle but had never been called upon to use it in his own defense. His bloody work at Chosin Reservoir had been completed with the M-1 carbine he was issued as an NCO. The Colt had never taken human life.

Tonight would be a first.

He had arrived at his decision after listening to Lynn, but he had found and cleaned the gun beforehand. Just in case. It had already occurred to Halsey that he might be forced to kill in self-defense before the Knights would let him go, and while the thought did not appeal to him, it did not terrify him, either. Christian soldiers were prepared to carry out their duty as it was revealed by God, and Halsey had decided that his duty lay outside the Klan.

His oath would be no problem, he had decided. He did not intend to testify against the Knights or use his privileged information to the detriment of any Klansman. If he spoke against the group in times to come, it would be as a minister, advising members of his flock to purge their hearts and minds of hatred, to seek their help in Jesus rather than in men who hid their faces to do "God's work." Convincing Mason Ritter might be difficult—the wizard would naturally be suspicious—but an Army-issue .45 could be a powerful persuader in times of trial.

Such had been his reasoning before this fateful night. But the conversation with his niece had altered everything. If Ritter and the wrecking crew meant harm to Lynn, it was his duty to protect her, at whatever cost. His own defection from the Klan no longer mattered. Halsey's duty to his flesh and blood transcended any oath he might have taken with a fellowship of men. Lynn's safety was a sacred trust, and any man who tried to harm her would be forced to deal with Jacob Halsey first.

He did not care to think about Mike Bowers at the moment. Halsey had no time for government informers, pimps and liars on the public payroll. But if Bowers could provide protection for his niece, then Halsey wished him well.

His confrontation with Mason Ritter would be rather different now from his earlier plan. It would be no use trying to persuade the wizard to abandon his attacks on Lynn and Bowers. Ritter was a stubborn man, unwilling to admit mistakes, and there were felonies involved now, witnesses at large. The only way to stop the Klan was to remove its leader, forcibly and finally, from his position of control.

The minister could have spoken to authorities, pressed charges on behalf of Lynn, but Ritter would make bail, and in the meantime all his gunmen would be on the street, still hunting. Swift and sure removal of the wizard was Halsey's only hope, and even then the word would take some time to filter through the ranks.

He tried to picture Ritter's face, the moment of surprise before he realized that Halsey meant to kill him, that the gun was real and not some out-of-character joke. Would he try to fight? Or would he weep and plead for life, a coward to the end?

It came to Halsey now that he had surrounded himself with cowards, men who masked their faces and concealed their actions under cover of night. He had become one of them, tainted with their sins against almighty God, and he could only pray for ultimate forgiveness, sincerely repenting of the blindness that had cloaked his eyes.

It was impossible to ask forgiveness for a future sin, so Mason Ritter's death would have to wait. There would be time enough, he thought, when all was done . . . unless they killed him first. The prospect of impending death was not as frightening as Halsey had expected it to be. His own life seemed immensely less significant then Lynn's, and if his soul was hanging in the balance . . . well, he had no one but himself to blame.

He would surrender to the sheriff later, after he was finished. If he had the chance. If not, he would be content to know that he had done his best, had fulfilled his duty to the limits of his ability.

But there was still his fear to deal with. Fear of failure more than of death, mortal terror that his chosen course of action was too little and too late. He had nearly followed

Lynn, a moment after she closed the kitchen door; it would have been so easy to pursue her, take Mike Bowers up on his suggestion in the guise of guarding Lynn. The tattered vestiges of Halsey's pride prevented him from running after her, and now he was alone with doubts and fears that stubbornly refused to die.

No matter. In Korea he had learned to forge ahead in spite of fear, refusing to be paralyzed by contemplation of his own destruction. It had been a valuable lesson, and in later life he had confronted lesser tribulations with a fortitude that frequently amazed the members of his flock. So now, with death not merely possible but likely, he refused to flinch from duty as he understood it.

It was late, but Ritter had been at the office when he had called Halsey earlier, and there was still a decent chance of catching him there. If he had gunmen on the streets, the wizard would be staying near his telephone, prepared to issue orders and receive reports from members of the wrecking crew.

No time to waste, then, Jacob Halsey decided. He would leave the house as he had always left it, through the front door, and walk to his car parked in the driveway. If the Klansmen shadowing his home had suspected Lynn was inside, they would have crashed the door long since to drag her out. They might have orders to prevent his leaving, but the minister knew he would have to wait and see. If they were primed to open fire on sight, he had no chance at all. And he was finished before he started. If the Knights attempted to detain him without killing him immediately...well, there just might be a rude surprise in store for anyone who tried to block his path.

He drew back the pistol's slide, chambering a round, and set the safety. In military parlance, the gun was "cocked and locked," ready to be fired as soon as Halsey flicked off the safety and squeezed the trigger. Slipping it inside his waistband, where it was hidden by the jacket of his suit, he pocketed two extra magazines containing seven rounds apiece.

If Mason Ritter wanted war, the Reverend Halsey was ready to oblige. One man against the Klan was sucker odds, but he could only try—for Lynn and for himself.

A GREYHOUND DEPOT SHELTERED half a dozen late-night travelers: three women, two with children, and a solitary man who dozed behind the sports page. None of them looked like Klan assassins, and the Executioner allowed himself briefly to relax.

"I'm sorry, Lynn, but—"

"You can't stay. I know. I'll be just fine."

She had the Colt Mustang .380 in her handbag, and she had been briefed on how to use it in a pinch. He hoped it would not be necessary. Klansmen searching for them would be counting on a devious escape; he did not believe any of them would suspect so obvious a method as the bus line. Lynn should be long gone before the hunters got around to thinking simple.

In the meantime, Bolan had a few distractions planned that ought to keep them hopping, running for their lives.

"Take care."

"You, too."

He kissed her lightly, turned and walked away, his mind already on the here and now before he reached the parking lot. A superficial scan revealed no onlookers as he slid behind the steering wheel.

The answer to the riddle, when it came, had been simplicity itself, but he had needed Lynn to point it out unwittingly. He had been blinded by appearances—the altered face and hair, the different style of dress—and he had missed the obvious, the things that never change.

Like Freeman's hands, so small that he had trouble with a handshake. So unnaturally small that he would favor the Detonics .45 above all other weapons, something he could comfortably manage.

Hands like Gerry Axelrod's.

Lynn's comment about the Vanguard leader's sex life had awakened something in Bolan's memory, allowing bits of unassimilated data to collide and synthesize Freeman rumored to be a homosexual. Lynn's reference to falling into Ritter's hands. Tiny hands. Freeman's hands. Freeman's lack of any verifiable past beyond the point in time when Axelrod had disappeared.

Axelrod.

He was the one who had gotten away, in spite of Bolan, Able Team and Phoenix Force. The setup in Zermatt had been aimed at bigger fish, with Axelrod relegated to the status of a side dish. He had escaped in the confusion, with Bolan unaware until his enemy was well away. In the meantime, analysts had speculated on his probable elimination by the sponsors he had served with something less than absolute efficiency.

But Gerry Axelrod was still alive. Still planting seeds of hatred, reaping profits from the sale of muscle, weapons, mercenary expertise. The Vanguard had succeeded Axelrod's Aryan Brotherhood after a decent interval, just long enough for "Freeman" to have undergone the plastic surgery required to make him new again.

Except for those accusing hands.

The fingerprints might well be different, Bolan knew, but he was not concerned with evidence that would convince a judge and jury. *He* was convinced, and he would execute the standing sentence on Axelrod at his earliest opportunity. But there were questions to be answered first.

Like motive.

Axelrod was mercenary to the core, and money was his motivator, but it was the motives of his sponsors that now preyed on Bolan's mind. In his first incarnation, Axelrod had played both ends against the middle, bilking lame "survivalists" and "superpatriots" for hard-earned dollars on the home front while he cut sweet deals with terrorists and agents of the KGB abroad. There was no reason to believe that, given half a chance, the new improved *reichsführer* of America would pass on such a deal today.

Were Freeman's sponsors in the Southern Bankers' Conference merely patriots gone sour, closet Nazis looking for a way to put their money where their mouths were? Was there more at stake in Dixie now than merely black and white?

Was there, perhaps, a touch of Red behind the scenes?

Before he executed Axelrod, Bolan would have some questions for his enemy, questions he would be reluctant to answer. But the Executioner could be persuasive when he tried.

And in the meantime, close to seven hundred Klansmen were scouring the countryside for Bolan, each determined to retrieve his head and win the wizard's gratitude. If Freeman had committed Vanguard troops—which was probable—that put the tally at around two thousand. Add police in Little Rock and Parrish, sheriff's deputies in two adjoining counties, members of the state police . . . and he was up against an army.

So what else was new?

18

Wilson Brown awoke in darkness, startled by a sound he could not identify. At first he thought it might have been an echo from his nightmare, distant gunfire snuffing out a scream, and yet . . .

Predictably, his dream had been of Theo. All his dreams these days revolved around the figure of his son, although he never actually *saw* the boy. Sometimes a shadow figure, glimpsed peripherally; more often—like tonight—a pleading voice that emanated from the shadows of a barren dreamscape, calling out to him for help, for mercy. He was never quite in time, of course. Each night he seemed to come a little closer, but the gunfire would inevitably shatter his illusion moments, seconds prior to contact. Sometimes the report would startle him awake, cheeks slick with tears that he could never shed in daylight. Other times, the blast would jar his dreams off track, propel him back to Vietnam, the reeking jungles where another portion of himself had been lost.

And what about tonight?

His cheeks were dry, which might mean anything or nothing. Kicking back the tangled bedding, Brown sat up in darkness, finding his prosthetic limb by touch and buckling it on with an ease that came from years of practice. Standing in his shorts and V-necked undershirt, he held his breath and listened to the night.

Had he heard breaking glass? A doorframe shattering on impact? Brown was certain he would have recognized a scream.

Downstairs, muffled voices now, interrupted by the sleepy, angry ranting of his landlady. "What are you-all doing here? Get out my house, I say! Get out before I call—"

The blow was audible in spite of distance and the door that stood between them. Weeping, she responded haltingly to her interrogators.

"Where's your roomie, bitch?"

"Where is he? Quick!"

"U-u-upstairs."

A second blow made tears superfluous, and Brown was dragging on his robe as boot heels hit the stairs. Unarmed, he cursed the grief and lack of foresight that had caused him to forget his training. Theo might have been nonviolent, but it was a trait that father had not handed down to son. Now, too late, the ex-lieutenant knew he should have come prepared.

He seized a handy chair, applied himself and wrenched a leg free, weighing it for balance in his palm. It would be of little use against a firearm, but if he could take the bastards by surprise...

He heard them, huddled just outside the door, perhaps believing that their prey had slept through the commotion. A whispered consultation as they tried to buck up their courage, and then one of them tried the knob.

Come on, you sorry bastards. Come to Papa.

Cautiously the door eased open and a head intruded, features covered by a stocking mask. Brown stabbed the chair leg laterally through the mask and deep into the socket of an eye, rewarded by a wild, unearthly shriek of pain. The prowler brandished a revolver, pumped a wild shot toward the bed and lost the weapon as the bludgeon cracked across his wrist.

"Don't kill him, damn it!"

Grinning at the knowledge that they needed him alive, Brown hit his sagging adversary with a savage backhand, flattening his nose and darkening the tattered mask with blood. Behind him others caught the body, wrestled it aside and crowded through the open door. He counted five before they hit him, though there might have been another in the hallway, but it scarcely mattered in the circumstances.

Lashing out with his prosthetic, Brown cracked a knee-cap, toppling another enemy. He made a point of stepping on the fallen gunner's hand, delighted with the feel of fingers snapping underfoot like pencils, as the others rushed him. Four-on-one was sucker odds, he knew, but he could maim a couple of the bastards as they took him down, and later, after he was dead, a few of them would bear his tokens of remembrance.

"Catch his arm!"

"I'm trying, damn it!"

"Jesus! Ow!"

A pistol cracked across his skull, and Brown was reeling when the boot exploded in his groin. With all his remaining strength, he whipped the chair leg down across the nearest skull and felt it crack despite the cushion of a ski mask.

Falling.

Falling.

Hammered to his knees by saps and gun butts, Wilson Brown embraced the darkness and escaped from pain.

"Don't kill him!" someone growled.

Wilson Brown no longer cared.

REVEREND JACOB HALSEY PARKED his vintage Chevrolet behind the Vanguard meeting hall, retrieved his pistol from the seat beside him, slipping it inside his belt. He did not lock the car. If he came out again and it was there, he would consider driving home. If he did not come out . . .

The lights were on in Freeman's office, as he had expected they would be. The boss man and his puppet would be huddled near the phones, awaiting fresh reports from hunters in the field. Some word of Lynn or Bowers. An announcement of their death, perhaps. And would they know Halsey was coming? Had the gunners stationed at his home phoned in a warning? They had made no move to stop him when he left, and he had not been followed, though he had been prepared to lose a tail if necessary. Obviously they were

under orders to remain in place and watch the house for
Lynn's return, but had they sent a runner out to make a call?

From habit, he had driven by Mason Ritter's office first
and found it dark. That left him only one alternative, for
Halsey knew that Ritter would not join the hunt himself.
The wizard was a coward at heart, and he would never lead
the way in any situation where resistance was expected.
Possibly, if Lynn had been alone . . .

The back door was unlocked, and Halsey slipped inside,
closing it silently behind him. Freeman did not pay a
watchman, but there might be Vanguard troopers on the
premises. He thought it likely they would all be committed
to the hunt by now, but there was no point in courting an
unnecessary risk.

Gun in hand, he passed on the elevator and took the
stairs. Without the background noise of daily business,
Freeman or his underling might be alerted by the elevator's
sound, and Halsey did not plan to give them any warning if
he could avoid it. Climbing swiftly, two steps at a time despite the protests from his knees and ankles, he arrived on
Freeman's floor before the first full minute had elapsed.

It was the third door on his right, and it was standing
open now. If he had used the elevator, they would surely
have been waiting for him when he stepped out blindly to be
met by guns. Immensely pleased with his success so far, the
minister dismissed the niggling voice of conscience reminding him that pride was a sin. He had murder on his mind,
and in comparison with taking human life, a little pride
would scarcely make a ripple in the lake of fire.

He flicked the automatic's safety off and curled his finger snug around the trigger, mentally prepared to open fire
at any sudden movement by his adversaries. Odd that he
should think of Freeman and the wizard in those terms,
when he had followed them for so long, feasting on their
every utterance as if it was the gospel. Feeling foolish and
betrayed, he stepped across the office threshold, scanned the
waiting room and found it empty, moved with grim determination toward the would-be führer's inner sanctum.

Here, too, the door was open, and he heard their voices well before he saw their faces. They were arguing—or, more precisely, Freeman was berating Ritter while the wizard made a churlish effort to defend himself.

"We should have had reports by now, goddamn it! What's the matter with those men of yours?"

"*My* men? Your guys outnumber mine by more than two-to-one. I don't hear *yours* reporting anything."

"This whole damned mess is your fault, Mason. If you hadn't sent incompetents to do the job—"

"I sent the best I had. Remember, it was your man who cleared Bowers in the first place. If it hadn't been for *your* okay, he would've never gotten in the Knights to start with."

"Listen, you—"

Freeman's bitter stream of words dried up as Halsey stepped into the office, covering them both without selecting either target as his point of focus. Military training was returning to him now, across the years. When covering a group of prisoners, don't point your piece at any single man. Cover the group and be prepared for sudden moves by any individual.

It was the first time in his life that Halsey had been called upon to use that sage advice. At Chosin there had been no time or opportunity for taking prisoners.

"You look a little peaked, Pastor." Freeman's smile was oily, something you might discover on the bottom of your shoe.

"What are you doing, Reverend?" Ritter sounded scared, and he did not possess the skill to hide it.

"I've got business to discuss with both of you," he said. "It won't take long."

"That's good," the Vanguard's chief replied, pretending not to see the .45. "We are a little pressed right now."

"I have the answer to your problem."

"I don't think so, Chaplain."

"You might be surprised."

He sat down, uninvited, in a chair that let him cover both of them at once. His back was to the wall, the open doorway on his left, preventing any late arrivals from surprising him.

"You tried to kill my niece," he said to both of them at once. Mason Ritter paled beneath his tan, but Freeman merely leaned back in his chair, content to wait and see what Halsey might be working up to.

"Have you gone crazy, Jacob?" Ritter's hands were shaking, and there was a tremor in his voice. "Why would we do a thing like that?"

"I'd like to hear your answer on that point myself," he said, "before I kill you."

"Jesus, Reverend!"

"Take it easy," Freeman purred. "There must be some mistake."

"You made it."

"Have you spoken to your niece this evening?"

"I have. Your jackals missed her, by the way. Seems like the four of them together couldn't find the back door to my house."

He saw a spark of anger deep in Freeman's eyes and knew that he had scored a telling point.

"What did she tell you?"

"Nothing but the truth. I'll ask you one more time: why did you try to kill her?"

"Nobody tried to kill her, Jacob. Not deliberately. The word was out on Michael Bowers—he's a government informer, did you know that?—and your niece was with him. In his bed, I might add."

"Never mind that, Freeman."

"Don't you want to know the facts? Your niece, in bed with an informer who's been selling out the Knights for federal gold. If I was a suspicious man, I'd say that gives me cause to wonder about *you*, Pastor."

"I never betrayed my oath. *Never*. It's you two who twisted the Knights, turned them into a criminal gang at your own beck and call. What became of the values we stood for? What happened to justice for common men? Help for the innocent? Alms for the needy? You've ruined the movement with personal avarice, living like leeches and sucking the hope from your followers."

"Well," Freeman drawled, smiling thinly, "I'd say that we've smoked out our Judas. You think so, Mason?"

Ritter was trembling too much to put faith in his tongue, but he nodded, the jerky response of a spastic.

"Yes, sir, I've been wondering just who the traitor might be," Freeman said, speaking casually, drawing attention away from his hands in his lap. "I'll be honest and say that I never suspected the reverend here. Hell, if you can't trust a minister, who can you trust?"

Ritter shrugged, held his tongue.

"You were foolish to think I wouldn't react when you went after Lynn," Halsey told them. "She's all that I have."

"That's the truth," Freeman growled. "And you sure as hell don't have the Knights anymore."

"I'll survive."

"Will you? What do you think, Mason? Will he survive?"

Ritter's move came from nowhere, a lunge, not toward Halsey but rather away from him, diving for cover. Instinctively turning, Halsey squeezed off a shot at Ritter, saw blood on the sleeve of the wizard's jacket before he was slammed over backward, propelled by a blow to the face.

On his back, tasting blood in his mouth, Halsey heard dim echoes of gunfire and knew that the second shot must have been Freeman's. A gun in his lap or beneath the desk—somewhere—and now he was pushing away from his desk, standing up, looming huge above Halsey, the squat automatic impossibly large in his fist.

"Better luck next time, Jacob. Of course, there won't *be* any next time."

Halsey's fingers were numb, unresponsive, as he attempted to raise his own weapon. He saw Freeman's smile through a fine ruby haze, watched him stoop to retrieve Halsey's weapon.

"You're out of your league. See you in hell."

Halsey closed his eyes, began to pray. "The Lord is my shepherd, I shall not wa—"

"GET UP, MASE. You're not hurt."

The Bible-thumper's blood was on Axelrod's shoes and slacks, but he was not concerned. He kept an extra suit on hand for such emergencies, and he would change before he kept his rendezvous with Michael Andrews at the bank. Just now, his mind was on removal of the human refuse from his office, a distasteful chore that could not wait.

"Get up, I said!"

The wizard had his jacket off, examining the bloody crease that Halsey's slug had etched across his biceps. Ritter had been luckier than he deserved; a few more inches and the bullet might have cracked his ribs to drill a lung.

"I'm hit!"

"You're grazed, goddamn it. On your feet."

"Is he dead?"

"If he's not, he'll be nursing one hell of a headache tomorrow."

"For Christ's sake, he ruined my jacket."

"Forget about that, will you? Go bring your car around, then get back up here and help me get rid of him."

"*My* car?"

"You heard me."

"But . . . what should I do with him?"

"Who gives a shit? Drive him out to the country, for all I care. Dump him on Main Street. But get him the hell out of *here*."

"Jesus Christ."

"Move your ass!"

He was trembling with rage by the time Ritter left, sorely tempted to make it two corpses and drag them both down by himself. As it was, he would have to save Ritter for another time. His meeting with the banker was in an hour, and Axelrod did not intend to miss that session, not at any price.

In fact, his price would be a cool one million dollars, and he thought Andrews would consider it a bargain. Axelrod had not played any of his aces on the phone, referring merely to their "urgent business," hinting that it might be catastrophic if the banker failed to show. He tried to put himself inside the other's mind, to imagine what Andrews must be thinking. Clearly there was blackmail in the wind, but nothing would prepare his pigeon for the shock of final revelation. When the banker realized he *knew*, knew *everything*, he would be more than happy with the price of silence. He would be ecstatic.

Axelrod was being generous, all things considered. With the dirt he had on Andrews, he would easily have asked five million, even ten. He could have cleaned out the frigging vault, claimed the banker's wife—except that he had seen her several times, and she possessed nothing that would have changed his attitude toward the opposite sex. Or he might have claimed the banker's firstborn son, a more delicious thought, and one that made him smile.

He found a box of trash-can liners in the closet, pulled one out and worked it over Halsey's leaking skull. The job was nearly finished when a whirring sound distracted him. The elevator. Knowing it was Ritter but refusing to take chances, Axelrod covered the open doorway with his Detonics .45, enjoying Ritter's expression when he came face-to-muzzle with the gun.

"Be careful with that, will you?"

"Always."

"Well, I got the car. You gonna help me with this thing or what?"

He took the dead man's feet, left Ritter with the head and shoulders. Halsey had seemed thinner when he was alive, but then, deadweight was always heavier. A corpse was inconsiderate that way, refusing to cooperate around the corners, sagging in the middle, hauling on your arms until it felt as if they were ripping from their sockets. They released their burden in the elevator, riding down, a respite that was only long enough to make the clergyman's body that much heavier when they picked him up again.

Outside, the muggy night was finally cooling off, an indicator of the hour. Ritter had to drop his end of the body to find his keys and open the trunk, and he was groaning by the time they got the huddled form inside. The trash-can liner made a liquid sloshing sound as Jacob Halsey was laid to rest.

"Go on now, and when you're finished, meet the boys to settle up with Brown. They're waiting for you."

"Don't remind me."

"Do you have a problem with that, Mase?"

There was deliberate menace in Axelrod's voice, and Ritter got the point.

"No problem."

"Fine. I'll see you later. Maybe we can meet for lunch and you can tell me how it went."

"Okay."

They would not meet for lunch, of course. When Ritter called and got no answer, curiosity would set to work. It would be hours more before anxiety broke through, and by the time his stooge came looking for him, Axelrod would be long gone. If anyone should take a fall for killing Halsey or the niggers, Ritter was the man on tap. What did it matter if he sang his heart out in a cell and coughed up everything he knew? The beauty of it was that he knew *nothing*; every "fact" the wizard knew about his cohort, "Freeman," was false. The more he sang, the more he made himself appear duplicitous, a scheming killer trying to escape his just desserts by laying the blame on shadow men.

Upstairs, Axelrod kicked off the bloody shoes and trousers, retrieved fresh clothing from the closet and began to dress. Once he had put the touch on Andrews, he would stop by "Freeman's" home just long enough to gather his belongings—things with which he did not care to part just now—and then he would be off for parts unknown. A set of extra plates were waiting for him in the trunk of his car, ready to replace those registered in Jerome Freeman's name. If he was stopped for any reason on the first leg of his journey, the plates and a bogus driver's license would agree that he was Peter Thomas of West Memphis, free from wants and warrants in the state and federal crime computers. How could anyone be looking for a man who never did exist?

He heard the sound—or the suggestion of a sound—as he was zipping up his trousers. Taking time to smooth the fly, he turned to face the doorway of his private office, startled by the figure framed there, gun in hand.

"This is a nice surprise." He forced a smile. "We've all been looking for you."

"Here I am," Lynn Halsey said.

ONCE BOWERS LEFT HER at the Greyhound depot, Lynn had ducked outside to flag a cab. Her first stop had been the meeting hall of the Teutonic Knights, but it was all in darkness, and she had paid off the driver outside Vanguard headquarters, noting the light in Freeman's office window. She had no concrete plan in mind; invasion of the Vanguard stronghold would be tantamount to suicide, but with the automatic pistol in her purse she felt somehow invincible. She had been moving toward the door with long, determined strides when something captured her attention in the parking lot.

Her uncle's Chevrolet.

She would have known it anywhere, a classic '65, with paint and bodywork in mint condition. Uncle Jacob did not love the car, as young men sometimes idolized their wheels; he simply liked it, treated it with care and offered his apologies when some collector tried to buy it out from under him.

Her stomach lurched. If Uncle Jacob was inside—and, obviously, no one else had parked his car behind the Vanguard meeting hall—what did it mean? She tried to reconstruct his words, their last conversation, but she managed only fragments. He had spoken of his work, of a duty yet to be fulfilled. What duty? And to whom? Was he delivering an ultimatum to the leaders of the Klan, or reaffirming loyalty to the order? Had his mind been so eroded by their hateful doctrines that he could have turned against her after all?

She was ashamed for even thinking such a thing. If he had meant to harm her, she would not have been allowed to leave his house. In fact, he had encouraged her to leave with Bowers. A dreadful certainty was growing in her by the moment, telling her beyond a shadow of a doubt that Uncle Jacob had not driven here to pledge support for Freeman or the Vanguard.

He had come to settle an account.

As she was fumbling for the automatic in her purse, the back door of the building opened, spilling light across the pavement. Dodging to her left, she crouched behind her uncle's Chevy, peering cautiously around the fender. Two men shuffled through the doorway, burdened by an object slung between them. In the flare of light, she recognized Mason Ritter, picked out Freeman's face in profile as they labored toward a waiting car. With sudden terror, accompanied by nausea, she recognized their burden as the lifeless body of a man.

The corpse's head was covered by a bag of some sort, but she recognized the clothing. Uncle Jacob's Sunday suit, the one he had been wearing when they had spoken, no more than forty minutes earlier. Half blinded by her tears, consumed by a desire to rush at her uncle's murderers and shoot them where they stood, she watched the men stuff him inside the trunk of Ritter's car. The wizard mumbled something to his master, climbed behind the wheel and drove away, conveying Lynn's only relative to some secluded resting place.

She had no way of following the car, and so she waited, watched as Freeman headed back inside. She gave him time to reach his office, dabbing at her eyes and checking the pistol, as she had been taught, before she followed him. Unmindful of the noise, she used the elevator, and the killer's own distraction allowed her to reach the threshold of his office undetected. She let him hear her then, her weapon leveled at his chest from twenty feet away.

"This is a nice surprise," he said, strain visible behind the phony smile. "We've all been looking for you."

"Here I am."

"Is there a reason for the gun?"

She took another step into the room, noting that he had changed his clothes. The slacks that lay beside his stockinged feet were wet with blood. Her uncle's blood.

"There is. I mean to kill you."

"Ah." If anything, his smile appeared to widen. "And I don't suppose we could negotiate?"

"Too late."

"I have a lot of money in the safe," he said. "I'm on my way to get a great deal more right now. Feel free to name your price."

"I'm not for sale."

"What will your uncle say?"

"I doubt if he'll say anything now that he's dead."

That wiped the smile away, and Freeman took a step in her direction, freezing as she thumbed the automatic's hammer back.

"Be careful, will you?"

"I'll be careful not to miss."

"You don't look like a killer, Lynn."

"Not yet."

"I've known some killers in my time."

"You see one in the mirror every morning."

"Others. Men—and women—who can kill without a second thought. For money, pleasure, any cause at all. I'd say that you don't have it in you."

"Bet your life?"

"I might." He glanced across her shoulder. "Take her, Mase."

It was the oldest trick around, and Lynn fell for it. While she was turning, she realized her mistake, the empty doorway yawning at her, mocking her. Before she could recover, bring the pistol to bear on Freeman again, he had closed the gap between them, clubbed her from behind. The floor rushed up to meet her, giving way to darkness, and she seemed to fall forever, knowing she had to hit bottom soon.

19

He awoke to pain, ignored the urge to moan and bit his lip instead. So many different kinds of pain: the jagged, shattered feeling in his groin, the dull ache in his back and ribs, the incessant rhythmic throbbing of his skull. He had forgotten, in the years since Nam, that pain could wear so many faces, could have so many textures and degrees.

In darkness, Wilson Brown began to take an inventory of his battered body, tensing muscles in his arms and legs to check for broken bones, and finding none. The artificial foot was still in place, and from the feel of things—no sticky patches on his clothes—he had not bled except from wounds to his face and scalp. As for his face, his eyes still opened— barely—but his nose was broken, sure as hell, and his exploring tongue retreated from a painful gap where one of his incisors had been snapped off at the gumline.

Bastards going to pay for that, he thought, and was reminded instantly of his absurd position. Bound and beaten, waiting to be carved up like a Christmas turkey, he was logging mental threats against his captors. It was funny, if you thought about it, but somehow he did not feel like laughing.

What time was it? he wondered. His wrists were bound behind his back, and in any case, he had taken off his watch before going to bed. No way of even estimating how long he had been unconscious. It was dark outside; he saw that much by peering under the door of the prefabricated shed in which he lay. Brown knew it was a shed and not a room inside some larger building, from the breeze that reached him, slipping in around the door and carrying the smell of grass and forest.

Forest.

Theo had been murdered in the woods. Perhaps his killers had conveyed him to that very spot, to wait upon their pleasure as he counted down the final moments of his life. Beneath the pain, fresh anger came to life, and Brown began to test his bonds judiciously, first straining, then relaxing, giving knots and twists of rope a chance to gradually expand.

How much time did he have before they dragged him out to get the party rolling? Minutes? Seconds? Certainly not hours; they could not afford to linger at their work, not after the commotion they had created at the rooming house.

Brown thought about his landlady, wondering if she was still alive. If so, she might have called the police by now. If not, the melee could have roused light-sleeping neighbors, sent them to their telephones. But not in time. Assuming that a call was made and deputies responded promptly, they had still been too late to interrupt the kidnapping. Closing the barn door after the horses were gone, they would make their reports, question neighbors, dispense all the normal assurances. No stone unturned. Don't call us; we'll call you.

Would the FBI be involved yet? Did it matter? The G-men were sharp, but they followed the book and went through all the motions, the same as the locals. His body might well be discovered before all the various agencies had covered the same narrow leads. If they finally picked up his killers on some charge or other...well, what would it matter to Brown?

In the jungle, survival had been top priority, second to none. He had learned on the job, and the lessons were all coming back to him now. Keep your cool. Panic kills. Take it easy and go with the flow. When you see a chance, take it, and make all you can of the moment. It may be your last.

Brown heard a murmur, the sound of human voices. Two sentries on their rounds, taking time for a smoke outside the door of his stockade. He wriggled toward the wall and pressed his ear against the corrugated metal, catching only snatches of their conversation.

"...wizard get here?"

"I don't know. A while."

"...the nigger...fun."

"Should be."

"Not like his boy."

At once the pain was gone, replaced by deep, abiding rage. He had a little time, at least—"a while"—before the leader of the mob arrived to open the festivities. If he could free his hands, meanwhile...

Then what?

He was alone, unarmed, against a hostile force that he could not begin to estimate in size. They plainly meant to kill him—after having "fun" at his expense—and they were definitely armed. Assuming he could free himself, surprise one of his guards and seize a weapon, did he have a chance?

No matter. Trussed up in the dark, he had no chance at all, but he had never been a quitter. Not when he'd been a blocker for the hot dogs in the NFL, not when he'd led a combat team in Nam, not when they had told him he would learn, in time, to live without his foot.

Not when the Executioner had trusted him in Monaco, against all odds.

The rope was nylon, slender and resilient, knotted tight around his wrists and ankles. Taking turns, he flexed his legs and then his arms, not caring which gave first, refusing to believe that neither rope would yield to his determination. He would free himself, or he would still be trying when they came to haul him out, a bull to the slaughter. But he would not make it easy for them. No damned way at all.

While he lived, he would resist with every ounce of strength remaining, and he would make them work for everything they got. Their "fun" would have a price, if he had anything to say about it.

And if he survived, somehow, he would delight in pissing on their graves.

THE PHONE AT WILSON BROWN'S rang seven times before an unfamiliar voice came on the line. "Detective Howard. Can I help you?"

Bolan felt his stomach rolling. "May I speak to Wilson Brown?"

"He isn't in just now, sir. If you'd care to leave your name and message..."

"No. No message."

Breaking the connection, Bolan held the telephone receiver in a death grip as he gazed out of the phone booth at the filling station gas pumps. Brown was "out" and the police were in, which meant there was major trouble at the rooming house. Had Brown been kidnapped? Would the officer have framed his cagey answers differently if the onetime football pro was dead?

"God*damn* it!"

Punching up the operator, Bolan rattled off the number of a private line in Washington. He paid the toll by credit card, a card registered to a dummy name and number in San Diego that was billed each month and never failed to pay the tab in full. He would be waking Leo up, but there was nothing else to do, and he was running out of time.

"Hello?"

The little Fed did not sound sleepy. Rather, there was agitation in his voice.

"They've taken Wils."

"I know. We caught the squeal from Little Rock just now. The office patched it through. What's happening down there?"

"My cover's blown, and Ritter's people fumbled when they tried to take me down. My best guess is that Axelrod is running a diversion."

Turrin hesitated. "You mean Freeman."

"I mean Axelrod."

"Aw, shit."

"Exactly."

"All this time I didn't see it? Christ, I must be getting old."

"I barely figured it myself. No time to run it down right now."

"What's on with Wils?"

"They'll ice him if they can." The Executioner refused to let himself believe that Brown was dead already, lying in some roadside ditch. "I have to try and get him back."

"You still believe in miracles?"

"Somebody has to."

"Yeah, I guess. You'll keep me posted?"

"When I can."

"Watch out for interference, okay? The Bureau's fielding every man in Little Rock on this one."

"I'll be watching."

"Yeah. I wouldn't want to see you tagged by one of ours."

"I'm out of time."

"Okay. Stay frosty, huh?"

The line went dead, and Bolan backtracked from the booth to his waiting car. If Brown had been abducted by the Klan, then it could go in one of two directions. Either he was dead already, driven somewhere for a speedy execution, or they were holding him for something more elaborate, a ritual of sorts, to be performed before the klavern as a whole. Assembling the Klansmen would require some time, he knew, especially with hit teams on the street patrolling for himself and Lynn. If he could find the meeting place, before it was too late...

But who would show him, now that "Michael Bowers" was officially an outcast, banished from the Klan? The mobile hunting parties would be primed to kill on sight, and if he managed to surprise one of them, take a living prisoner—then what? The odds were fifty-fifty that his captive would deceive him, lead him on a futile chase around the county, while his cohorts went to work on Wilson Brown.

He had one chance. Beyond a shadow of a doubt, if he was not too late, one man could lead him to the killing ground. He put the rental into gear and left the filling station with a squeal of rubber, standing on the accelerator, jumping the lights when they turned red against him.

He was running late for his unscheduled appointment with a wizard.

DESPITE THE BODY in his trunk, the feeling that each motorist he passed must surely recognize his guilty burden, Ritter had been forced to detour by the office on his way to Chatham County. He could not appear before the Knights without his regal robe and mask, the uniform of office that he wore with pride. Tonight, however, trepidation mingled with his usual enthusiasm.

Ordinarily he got a kick out of the Klan's infrequent necktie parties. Lynchings were a rarity these days, but once or twice a year the hard-core members of the klavern got together for a little sport, abducting some black sheep off the street at random to serve as a sacrificial lamb. The disappearances went unexplained, the bodies—what was left of them—disposed of with an eye toward permanent concealment. There were abandoned bauxite mines in Southern Chatham County where remains could lie undisturbed forever. Ritter thought that Reverend Jake would like it there just fine with Wilson Brown to keep him company.

It made him nervous, though, to ride around with Halsey in his trunk. Suppose he got pulled over for a moving violation and the officer could smell his fear? Some cops were gifted that way, able to detect a liar by his looks, his smell. What if he got a flat and had to change the tire with Jacob resting right beside the spare?

Sweet Jesus, what if he was in an accident?

Aware of every rut and pothole in the road, he drove like an old woman, holding to the limit, even shaving some off that when there was other traffic. It took twice the usual time for him to reach his office, and he knew they would be getting restless at the meeting ground. But they would wait, because they had to. A wizard did not have to offer his apologies to any man among the rank and file.

Upstairs, he took his robe and hood out of the closet, folded them until they fit his leather briefcase, checking to make sure he had forgotten nothing in his haste. The pistol in his pocket seemed to weigh a ton, but he would keep it with him, just in case. He might be needing it before the endless night was over.

Ritter started for the stairs . . . and froze, as shadows near the outer door revolved themselves into a human shape— Mike Bowers, leveling a pistol at his face, with bloody murder in his eyes.

"You're running late there, Mason."

"I've got time." But could he reach his pistol, draw and fire before the big man took his head off? No. It was impossible.

"We're going for a ride," Bolan told him.

"Oh?"

"I'd hate to miss the main event."

"You think that's wise?"

"I'll take my chances."

"For a nigger?"

"For a friend."

"I knew it."

"Shake a leg. You're wasting time."

He summoned all the courage that remained, and forced the words out through his teeth. "What makes you think I'd take you anywhere?"

"Oh, I don't know. I've got this sneaking hunch you want to live."

"I don't believe you'd kill me in cold blood."

"I think you do."

And he was right, of course. The wizard *knew* that Bowers would be pleased to kill him, given any small excuse. He might be dead already, if he did not hold a precious secret locked inside his mind.

"Let's make a trade."

"I'm listening. You've got five seconds."

"I play guide, and then you let me walk."

"Depends."

"On what?"

"On how much time you waste, and whether we arrive before the party starts."

"We'll be there."

"You should hope so."

"Twenty minutes. Thirty, tops."

"You're wasting time."

Before they left the office, Bolan took Mason's gun away. Downstairs, the wizard was about to slide behind the wheel when he was halted by the pressure of a pistol in his ribs. "Just give me the directions," Bolan ordered. "You can take the rumble seat."

A sudden nausea enveloped Ritter. If the trunk was opened, Halsey's body found, all bets were off.

"I can't do that."

"Wrong answer."

Bolan had the pistol pointed at Ritter's forehead. He could see the soldier's finger tightening around the trigger, and he folded. "Jesus, wait a second!" Babbling, he had to reel the roads off three times in succession, letter-perfect, to convince his captor that he was not pulling any kind of scam. When Bolan had it memorized, he prodded Ritter toward the trunk and waited while his captive fumbled with the keys.

The blood was leaking out of Halsey's garbage bag. The threadbare carpet in the trunk had turned into a swamp.

Bolan didn't need a moment to assess the situation. Reaching in, he tugged the plastic bag away, revealing Halsey's face, the bullet hole precisely centered in his forehead, nothing much in back.

"Get in."

"I can't!"

"I'll bet your life you can."

He did, the carpet squishing underneath him, sticking to his hands. He vomited, another contribution to the stew, and then Bolan planted a foot in his kidneys, forcing him in beside his lifeless bunkmate.

"If you're lying to me, Ritter—"

"No, I swear! You'll see."

"*We'll* see."

The lid came down, and he was trapped in darkness with the corpse. The engine caught a moment later, and the makeshift hearse began to roll. The pastor's body jostled him defiantly, an otherworldly subway rider staking out his space. The wizard would have vomited again, but he had nothing left inside.

If Bowers followed his directions, he was in for a surprise. The Knights would welcome him with open arms, and no mistake. *Fire*arms, that is. The cocky bastard would not last a second and a half against the Klansmen who were gathering to deal with Wilson Brown.

It would be something to behold, provided that he lived that long. And if they recognized his captor while the car was still in motion? If they opened fire while Ritter was still locked inside the trunk with Halsey's corpse?

Then he was finished.

Eyes closed against his waking nightmare, breathing through his mouth in an attempt to mask the stench of death, he wondered if the leaking minister remembered any prayers.

THE BANKER CHECKED his Rolex, found the time approaching half past one o'clock. He sipped a cup of coffee purchased from a convenience store en route and cursed the day he had chosen Freeman as his latest tool. The man had seemed to have potential, but in retrospect he had been trouble from day one.

Now this. An urgent call demanding that they meet within the hour, near the bank, no questions asked. When Andrews attempted to postpone the meeting, Freeman had grown abusive, snapping orders like the two-bit psychopath he was, demanding strict obedience. It might have been amusing, but for his repeated reference to a "secret" that he would be bound to share with members of the press—as well as federal agents—if the banker kept him waiting.

Andrews never had responded well to threats, his temper taking over, tending toward retaliation rather than submission. But he had to know what "secret" Freeman knew—or *thought* he knew—before he set about the business of reminding his employee who was boss. The time had come for Freeman to be chastised, and severely, for his insolence. It would be pleasant to devise a fitting punishment and put it in effect himself . . . but not tonight.

He traveled armed, for self-protection, but he did not plan to murder Freeman here, this morning. He had already marked another member of the Vanguard, one of Freeman's up-and-coming young lieutenants, as a possible replacement if and when it came to that, but he was not prepared to kill on such short notice, almost on the doorstep of his workplace. Not unless it was absolutely necessary.

Of course, if things went sour at the meeting, and he was forced to act in self-defense . . .

The Vanguard's leader was a minute late when Andrews spotted headlights, watched them turn in from the street and go out as the car rolled up close beside his own. Freeman sat behind the wheel. In the back seat of his car, a form vaguely human was wriggling beneath a blanket.

"Company?" He had the pistol in his hand, concealed below the window.

"A spy. My problem," Freeman told him. "You've got problems of your own."

"Such as?"

"Your cover. It's about to spring a leak unless you patch it in a hurry."

"I'm afraid you've lost me."

"Really, *comrade*? Have I?"

A lump formed inside Andrews's stomach, but he held the poker face. "You're babbling nonsense."

"Am I? Let me try again. I should be able to explain. After all, it's as simple as KGB."

The lump became a block of ice. He knew. Somehow, impossibly, in spite of everything, *the bastard knew*.

"What are you saying?"

"I believe we understand each other now, Mikhail Andreivich. I'd bet a million dollars that you know exactly what I mean."

"You think that *I*—?" He forced a laugh that came out sounding brittle, harsh. "You must be mad."

"Not yet. I'm hungry, though. That million dollars ought to fill me up just fine."

"Assuming what you say is true— "

"Assuming."

"You must realize that I don't have that kind of cash available tonight."

"I'm looking at a bank right now."

"You're looking at a bank that has a time lock on its vault. Unless you have a jug of nitro in the trunk, that lock will open at its normal time. That's eight o'clock tomorrow morning."

"Listen, comrade—"

"No, *you* listen!" Andrews put the edge of steel back in his voice, attempting to disguise his sudden fear. "At home I have one hundred thousand dollars in a wall safe. I can let you have that much tonight. If you want more, you will be forced to wait. It does no good to threaten a machine or curse at tempered steel."

"You'd better not be jerking me around!"

"One hundred thousand dollars now, or take your million in the morning."

"I'll be waiting when you open up at eight o'clock. If I'm not out and running clear by 8:15, a nasty little package will be posted to the FBI."

"I'll see you then, together with the package."

"Right. If I were you, I'd leave the fancy tricks at home."

"How could I hope to trick a man of your perception?"

"Never in a million years, and don't forget it."

"I assure you, nothing is forgotten."

Freeman let him have a sneer in parting, put the Continental through a tight U-turn and powered out of there. As Andrews watched the taillights wink, then disappear, he let the ice block in his stomach slowly melt, regaining his composure. Somehow, Freeman had found out his secret. Given time and opportunity, Andreivich would have enjoyed debriefing his subordinate, discovering the methods he had used to crack a cover that had been decades in the making. But it scarcely mattered now.

The "package" mattered, definitely. Freeman's evidence against him, ready for delivery to the authorities or to the media if he refused to pay the designated ransom. He would pay, of course, and gladly. What was money, in the last analysis, except confetti that had been assigned an arbitrary value by society?

But he would *not* leave his "fancy tricks" at home.

Oh, no.

He had a very special trick in mind for Freeman, one that would eliminate his threat forever, and in style. He thought the redneck mercenary would appreciate it, if he only knew. In fact, the sleeper thought that he would have a blast.

20

The country road was dark and rutted, winding through a grove of cottonwood and oak. Each time a pothole rocked the car, Bolan heard a muffled protest from the trunk as Ritter made contact with his leaky traveling companion. Bolan smiled, content that this time out the wizard would not have an opportunity to keep his hands clean.

Just ahead, the narrow road swung left and opened into a wooded glade. The trees were thinner here, more widely spaced, and vehicles were parked between them, three rows deep. He counted forty cars and pickup trucks before he finally gave up. No matter what the odds, he was going in, and there was no point fretting over numbers he could never change.

He parked behind a station wagon sporting a gun rack in the rear and killed the engine. Swiveling to scan the open meadow thirty yards distant, he could pick out several dozen Klansmen, ghostly in their raiment as they helped erect a giant wooden cross. Brown shirts were scattered through the crowd, as members of the Vanguard mingled with their brothers of the sheet.

The problem of his actual approach was solved as Bolan parked the car. A Klansman, all in white, had been assigned to keep an eye on traffic, and he was approaching now, his mask thrown back, a curious expression on his face.

"Hey, there!" he called. "Ain't that the wizard's car?"

"You've got a good eye, brother. Mason had me bring it on ahead. He's right behind me, coming in with Freeman."

"Freeman's coming?"

"Absolutely. You're surprised?"

The Klansman shrugged. "I saw some of his Vanguard boys check in a while ago, but no one told me it was going to be a combination deal."

"They wouldn't want to miss this kind of action."

"No, I reckon not." The man was eyeing Bolan quizzically. "Do I know you?"

"It's possible."

"I'd swear I've seen your face somewhere."

Before he could pursue the matter, his attention was distracted by a muffled groan that emanated from the trunk.

"Now, what the hell—"

He made it halfway there before the edge of Bolan's rigid hand impacted at the juncture of his skull and spine, obliterating conscious thought. Before the guy could fall, his head was captured in a vise of flesh and muscle, one twist separating vertebrae and snuffing out his life.

The soldier left the straw man draped across a fender and doubled back to free his captive from the trunk. It took a moment for the wizard's eyes to focus, but he recognized the close proximity of death and made no move to run.

"Get dressed," the soldier ordered, dropping Ritter's briefcase at his feet. "We're going in—together."

Moving swiftly, knowing they might be surprised by new arrivals any moment, Bolan stripped his recent kill of robe and hood, depositing the body in the trunk of Ritter's car with Jacob Halsey. Keeping one eye on the wizard as he dressed, Bolan slipped into the satin robe, placing the conical hood on his head and lowering the mask to hide his face. The robe had snaps in front, providing easy access to the hardware underneath, but Bolan cut a slit below one arm to let him reach the Uzi submachine gun in its armpit swivel rig. Spare magazines were tucked inside his belt, with two grenades clipped on in front.

The snow-white robe could hide a multitude of sins.

"Nice and easy, now," he cautioned. "Any deviations from the normal script could be hazardous to your health."

Another line of cars was pulling in to park as Bolan followed Ritter toward the meadow, trailing several paces back and covering his Judas goat, prepared to cut the wizard down if he attempted to alert the others. Off to one side, near the tree line, Bolan spied a shed with sentries on the door. It was a safe bet Wilson Brown would be inside there, and he thought of veering off to take the guards immediately, make a break without delay, but knew it would be suicidal. If the prisoner was under guard, it meant that he was still alive, and any chance they had lay in following the ritual . . . to a point.

The ranks of robes and brown shirts parted for them, Ritter leading, nodding to the faithful as they called his name, some of them raising stiffened arms in salutation. As he mounted the dais, Bolan took up station on the wooden steps, assuming a position where his field of fire would cover Ritter and the crowd. Behind them, someone touched a match to kerosene-soaked burlap, and the giant cross erupted into rippling flame.

Mason Ritter tapped the microphone and waited for the feedback to subside. Across the meadow, stragglers were hurrying to join the throng. Two hundred men, give or take, and Bolan knew he could not kill them all. With luck, he would not have to.

"Brothers!" Ritter bellowed at his audience. "We have assembled here to celebrate a victory against the nigger-loving, Jew-backed farmers' union!"

"Damn right!"

"Lay it out!"

"Our guest of honor probably would like to slip away somewhere," the wizard said, and waited for appreciative laughter to subside, "but he's been called in here by popular demand!"

"All *right*!"

"Let's do it!"

"Bring the nigger out!"

"You all know why we're here, and I assume you came prepared." This time, the wizard cast a sidelong glance at Bolan as he spoke. A murmur of assent ran through the crowd as Klansmen dug beneath their robes, producing knives and razors, blackjacks, lengths of pipe, revolvers. Here and there, a sawed-off shotgun was in evidence.

"I see you still know how to throw a party," Ritter drawled to the approving hoots and rebel yells of his constituents. "I won't waste any more of your valuable time, then, except to say... *bring out the nigger!*"

"Bring him out!"

"Bring out the nigger!"

Bolan slipped a hand inside his robe to grip the Uzi, bringing up his free hand to the snaps in front. Downrange, the sentries were emerging from the shed, supporting Wilson Brown between them like a prisoner en route to execution.

STRUGGLING WITH HIS BONDS and getting nowhere, Brown had listened to the mob as it assembled thirty yards away. It was impossible to count the vehicles or voices, but he thought there must be hundreds of the rednecked bastards, waiting for an opportunity to cut themselves a slice of dark meat for the party. Sensing it was hopeless, knowing that the nylon ropes would never yield in time, he kept on trying anyway.

The sons of bitches might destroy him, but he would be damned before he let them make him quit.

The Klansmen had been gathering for something like a quarter of an hour when a sudden hush fell on the crowd. He knew, without the need of being told, that someone in the upper crust of kluxdom had arrived. A moment later, and the troops were calling out his name.

Mason Ritter.

He would finally meet the bastard face-to-hood, at any rate. Brown prayed that he would have the strength and spittle left to plant one in the wizard's eye before they started carving on him. And if not, he had in mind as backup a few choice quips about the ranking Klansman's ancestry, just in case they kept him out of range.

He heard a hollow tapping in the distance, as of someone drumming fingertips against a microphone, the momentary feedback squealing like a banshee in the darkness.

"Brothers!"

It was show time. He closed his mind to the infernal diatribe, refusing to eavesdrop on his own death sentence. It was ridiculous, if you thought about it: after Nam, the syndicate and all the other shit he had been through in forty-some-odd years of living, he was going to be lynched by morons living in a bygone era, dreaming of the "good old days" that never really were. It made him want to laugh, except that he was too damned angry. Too damned scared.

Why not? He was about to be the main course at a feast of ghouls, and he was reasonably certain that the Klansmen did not have a quick, clean kill in mind. Allowing for the time, assuming most of them had jobs to go to in the morning, they could spare a couple of hours for the torment of a fellow human being. Something they could talk about in years to come, a little bit of hell on earth to help them feel superior.

"Bring out the nigger!"

That was it. They were playing his song, and the damned ropes were still tight enough to cut grooves in his flesh. If he had a while longer, a few days perhaps...

Sudden light in his eyes from the two-story cross that was burning outside in the meadow, surrounded by blood-thirsty ghosts in their shrouds.

"Time to go, boy," the sentry informed him, and then there were two of them, grabbing his arms in an effort to haul him erect.

Brown fought back as much as the ropes permitted, letting one Klansman carry his weight as he kicked at the other with feet bound together. He missed the guy's groin, knocked him flat on his ass with a blow to the hip, but he bounced back and swung with the butt of his shotgun, releasing a fountain of blood from Brown's cheek. He collapsed in their arms, cursing bitterly, unable to fight anymore as they dragged him outside.

Ragged cheering broke out on the fringe of the mob, spreading swiftly as Klansmen and storm troopers got a first look at their prey. In the firelight, he caught sight of ax handles, hatchets, machetes, a cavalry saber. The bastards had bought out a hardware store. Business was good.

"Bring him here!"

"Let me at him!"

"You want a piece, brother?"

"I got dibs on his head."

In the crowd now, conveyed by his captors between rows of white robes and brown shirts. The few exposed faces were seething with hate, spitting four-letter filth as he passed. For perhaps half a heartbeat, he pitied the poor stupid bastards, then anger surged up again and he wished them to hell.

One last shot. Put one throat in my hands.

One would do, if he couldn't kill twenty or thirty. Just one of the jackals to join him. One bastard along for the ride.

They were close to the dais now, Ritter in purple on high, regarding his prey with the eyes of a vulture, the head of the microphone close to his mask.

"Are you ready, my brothers?" he purred to the crowd.

"You're damned right!"

"We *been* ready!"

"All right, then—"

From nowhere, a knife blade slid down through the ropes that secured Brown's wrists. Hesitation, and then it repeated the move at his ankles, enabling him to stand on his own. He was free for the moment, aware that it must be a part of the game. Yellow scum that they were, they preferred the illusion of "fighting" a man who could try to defend himself, bare hands against the two-hundred-odd bludgeons and blades in the crowd.

"Motherfuckers!" he rasped. "You want me? Come and get it, you bastards! *Come on!*"

As the first wave surged forward, Mack Bolan ripped open the snaps on his robe and cut loose with the Uzi, a burst punching waist high through satin and khaki. The robed Knights and storm troopers toppled together, the second rank wavering, wondering what had gone wrong.

Bolan held down the trigger and sprayed the assembly from left to right and back again, raking the ranks as he emptied that first magazine. They were jammed in so closely, all hot for a chance at their prey, that he could not have missed if he had tried. In the crowd, those with firearms were searching for someone to shoot, one or two of them squeezing off practice rounds into the mob. Klansmen fell, thrashing helplessly, bright crimson blossoms defacing their robes.

On the dais, Mason Ritter was down on all fours, seeking cover where none was to be found. Bolan thought about shooting him, decided not to as he snapped a new magazine into the Uzi and ripped off his mask, moving forward to guard Wilson Brown.

"What the hell—?"

Recognition, in eyes nearly closed by the beating Brown had absorbed. He grinned, revealing missing teeth.

"I'll be damned!"

"Find a weapon, Lieutenant! I can't do this all by myself!"

Scattered shots from the crowd, bullets droning like hornets around them as Klansmen and men of the Vanguard began to catch on. Bolan backpedaled, hosing the crowd with another long burst, watching several go down in a tangle of arms, legs and sheets. On the fringe of the killing zone, Brown found a pistol discarded by one of the fallen and made it a cross fire, selecting his targets from those who were armed, fighting back. Bolan crouched by the dais and waited, his stuttergun poised, for the stampede to thin.

They were breaking en masse for the cars, shouts of warning replacing the curses and catcalls of moments before. Bolan tugged a grenade from his belt, pulled the pin and let fly, overhand, pitching hard, for the point of the crowd. Smoky thunder enveloped a half dozen Klansmen, and others were dropped in their tracks by the shrapnel that sprayed in a circular killzone, away from ground zero.

The lynchers were wavering now, undecided, a few of them breaking away for the trees, others ditching their robes as they went to ground, seeing concealment in the tall grass of the meadow. A handful were answering fire with more zeal than success, wild rounds snapping a yard above Bolan's head, gouging the wood of the dais.

Mason Ritter was winged by a stray, and he leaped to his feet, crying out, "Don't shoot *me*! I'm on *your* side!"

A shotgun blast out of left field sent him spinning, robes flaring out behind him like Dracula's cape as he fell, arms outstretched, toward the cross. With a shriek he embraced it, arresting his fall as the sleeves of his robe and his mask caught the flames, going up in a flash. One more scream and he slid down the pole like an animate shish kebab, sizzling his way to the ground. Bolan watched him impact, his broken legs thrashing, refusing to carry him, blackened hands straining for mercy from heaven. Instead, what he got was a bullet to silence his cries.

"Too damned good for him."

Brown was beside him now, armed with a shotgun and scanning for targets.

"Could be."

They were fresh out of candidates, tattered survivors escaping, their outlines like ghosts in the forest, and all out of range. On the field dead and dying lay twisted together, two dozen or more, their regalia discolored by bloodstains and soil. Weapons littered the meadow, discarded as owners took flight for their lives.

Brown was grinning through split, swollen lips. "Looks to me like the Ku Klux have gone out of business."

"Not quite," Bolan answered. Across the dark meadow, a few cars and pickups were pulling out, running dark, spewing up dust from their tires. The thirty-foot cross cast its shadow across the field, flickering dimly, preparing to die.

"You got more? Hey, I'm game."

"You're a mess, Wils. I'll find you a medic before I move on."

"Listen, Sarge, I don't want to pull rank. If there's more of these birds, I'm not hanging it up till they're finished."

"*One* more, and he's not worth your time."

"Well, in that case . . . thank God! You got wheels?"

"I've got wheels and a half. Would you care for a lift in the Klanmobile?"

"Solid."

Dead eyes watched them pass from the field, Bolan still in his robe and supporting the black man who hobbled beside him. The meat wagons would not arrive for an hour yet, running with red lights and sirens to search in vain for survivors. Meanwhile, the dead were alone with their dreams.

21

The shackle had been specially designed to offer limited mobility. Its four-foot chain, secured to a central upright of the metal hut, permitted access to a cot and folding chair while falling well short of the door. The collar bit Lynn Halsey's ankle when she moved, and after several fruitless bids to free herself, she sat immobile, studying her prison.

She was locked inside the smaller barracks at Camp Nordland, near the compound's southernmost boundary. The Quonset hut accommodated eighteen men, but none was currently in residence. The live-in guards, perhaps a dozen of them, were bunked in Barracks 1, and thus far they had left her alone on Freeman's orders.

He would have her killed before another day was out; of that much she was certain. She could link him to her uncle's murder, send him to the death house with her testimony, and he was in jeopardy as long as she survived. The mystery, to Lynn, was why she had survived this long. It would have been so simple to eliminate her, put a bullet in her head and dump her body in the woods, along the highway—anywhere, in fact, where it would not lead back to Freeman and the Vanguard. Keeping her alive implied that he had some use for her, and Lynn was not certain she wished to contemplate what that might be.

Her stomach growled, and Lynn immediately tried to think of something else. There was a toilet in the barracks, but she could not reach it, tethered as she was. In an emergency she would make do, but in the meantime she would fight the need while she could, denying Freeman and his men the pleasure of debasing her.

He had not taken her alive for personal amusement; Lynn was confident of that, at least. His interest in the female sex was seemingly restricted to the typing speed of this or that potential secretary. Neither would he have abducted her to please his men, although they might abuse her if they had the chance. From all appearances, the Vanguard's chief regarded his subordinates with thinly veiled contempt, and was not prone to offering them "treats" of any kind. Her presence at the camp would suit his purposes, and no one else's.

After running through the possibilities, Lynn knew that only two explanations made any sense. If Freeman meant her for a hostage, something he could bargain with if he was pursued by the authorities for Jacob Halsey's murder or some other crime, then it was in his own best interest to keep her reasonably healthy. On the other hand, if he intended to extract some information from her—possibly about Mike Bowers—then she could look forward to a rigorous interrogation, no holds barred. She thought Freeman and his goons would happily resort to torture, and she wondered how long she could hold her tongue once all their talents were applied. An hour? Two? Was she exaggerating her own stamina?

Escape was critical, not only for herself but for the damage it would do to Freeman's plans. If she could not contrive a way to free herself, then she must think in terms of an alternative that would deprive her captor of his hostage, of the information that he might desire.

The shackle held her firmly tethered; she could not dislodge it from the upright where it was anchored, and the clasp around her ankle left her no possibility of working herself free. Without a tool of any sort, she could not hope to cut or pry it open. No part of the cot or folding chair was strong enough to break the manacle or snap the links of chain.

By walking to the far end of her leash and straining forward, stretching out her arms until her shoulders ached, Lynn found that she could reach the nearest window with her fingertips. The glass was frosted to prevent anyone from seeing in or out, but she believed she could break it with her fist if she applied herself. The broken pieces would be sure to fall outside, but others would remain. If she could free a jagged shard, put it to use before her guards responded to the sound of breaking glass . . .

The thought of death was sobering, but Lynn had seen so much of it already tonight that she quickly grew accustomed to the notion. Death was preferable to the pain that Freeman and his soldiers might inflict in the pursuit of information she did not possess. And if he chose to keep her as a hostage, it would be at best a temporary stay of execution. When he finished with her, after his escape had been accomplished, she would be a piece of excess baggage, something that would merely slow him down. He would eliminate her with the same disdain a man might show while stepping on an insect. The disdain that he had shown for Uncle Jacob.

Better, Lynn decided, to deprive him of the opportunity, the pleasure. If she killed herself, not only would he lose his shield, his source of information, but he would be inconvenienced by another body on his doorstep. Not precisely what she might have called a victory, but at the moment it was all she had.

She tried to calculate the force required to break a windowpane. It would not do to simply crack the frosted glass, but neither did she wish to smash it into smithereens. A happy medium would leave her several shards to choose from, any one of which would nicely do the job.

Lynn was about to try it, straining at her tether, one arm cocked to strike, when she was startled by a shuffling step outside the barracks door. She retreated to her cot and sat demurely, eyes downcast, as one of Freeman's brownshirts entered with a plastic tray in hand. Approaching her, he hooked the camp chair closer with a boot and set the tray down on its seat. She saw a glass carafe of coffee with an empty cup, a plate of sandwiches with pickles on the side.

"Commander says you need to keep your strength up," he informed her. "I'd say you look pretty fit right now."

When she did not respond, he masked his irritation with a leering smile.

"Them dills are kosher. Like commander says, the only thing the Jews are good for's making pickles."

"What does Freeman want with me?"

"I couldn't rightly say. But me, I'd settle for a piece of what you're sitting on right now."

"I'll see you dead first."

He was stung by her response, and his face went dark with rage. "I think you got it backward there. You'd better eat up while you can. Commander just might change his mind about the need to keep you healthy. When he does, we'll talk again."

She let him have the last word, and he left her, smirking as he closed the door. His parting glance had made her flesh crawl, and she felt a sudden urge to shower, cleanse herself, as if from contact with a pair of unclean hands. Instead, she poured a cup of hot black coffee, drank it to help herself relax. A fleeting thought of drugs or poison crossed her mind, but Lynn knew she was being paranoid, and in any case she no longer cared.

The coffee cup was thick, but she believed she could break it on the metal frame of her cot. Once shattered, it would adequately suit her needs, without the noise of breaking window glass. But first, a gnawing trace of hunger made her give the food a second glance. It made no sense, devouring a sandwich moments before committing suicide, but the condemned were always offered food, and why should she refuse?

Deferring self-destruction to a later moment, Lynn began to eat.

AFTER DROPPING WILSON BROWN outside the entrance to Emergency Receiving, Bolan drove directly to the home of Gerry Axelrod. A rich two-story modern in the suburbs, it was set back from the street behind a spacious lawn, with hedges and a chain-link fence in front, a wooden fence in stockade style behind. A narrow alleyway out back provided access for sanitation trucks and the men who came to service swimming pools and manicure lawns.

He made a drive-by, saw a dark sedan parked in the drive and pulled around in back. The stockade fence was barely six feet tall and posed no challenge as he vaulted over, clad in blacksuit, and merged with the shadows of the shrubs in Axelrod's backyard. An oval pool reflected moonlight and the glare from kitchen windows.

Bolan crossed the patio to peer through sliding doors. Inside a pair of Vanguard troopers dressed in street clothes sat across from each other at the dining table, killing time playing nickel blackjack. With the upstairs windows dark, he took them for the house force, gambling that Axelrod had left them to secure the premises while he was occupied with business elsewhere. It was risky, barging in on gunners when there might be others dozing in the parlor or in any one of several rooms upstairs, but Bolan had no options left. He wanted Axelrod—would have him this time—but he needed information first.

He tried the sliding door and found it locked. With his Beretta 93-R in his fist, he took a long step backward, picked up a wrought-iron chair with his free hand and propelled it toward the broad expanse of glass. It struck dead center, crashing through and bringing down the window like a frozen waterfall, its jagged pieces jingling on the flag-stones of the patio.

He followed through without a heartbeat's hesitation, low and fast, the silent handgun leading, tracking into target acquisition. At the dining table, Bolan's targets were re-sponding awkwardly, the dealer clinging to his cards, his partner scrabbling at the buttoned flap of his leather GI holster, getting nowhere fast. If there were any other gun-ners in the house, his entry should have brought them on the run, but only ringing silence echoed from the living room, the darkened stairs beyond.

He needed only one of them alive, and so he took the nearest gunner with a round between the eyes, opening a keyhole on the bridge of his nose and punching him back-ward out of his seat. His heels drummed briefly on the vinyl floor as Bolan held his weapon steady, pointed at the dealer's face.

"Your choice," he said.

"Wh-what choice is that?"

"It's easy. If you talk, you live—provided you're convincing."

"Jesus . . . I don't know."

"Goodbye."

He was already tightening his finger on the trigger when the trooper broke. "*No, wait!* What do you want to know?"

"I'm looking for your boss."

Relieved. "He isn't here."

"Wrong answer, guy."

"Oh, yeah, okay. He's at the camp."

"Camp Nordland?"

"Yeah. He took the girl out there a couple hours ago."

"What girl?"

"The preacher's daughter, niece . . . whatever. Halsey. I don't know her first name."

"You said two hours?"

"Give or take. I didn't check the time, you know?"

"Okay."

"That's it?" The trooper plainly smelled a rat, as if he knew that he was getting off too easy. "Nothing else?"

"Don't press your luck."

Bolan was backing toward the exit when his adversary did precisely that. The gunner was no faster with his awkward holster then the other guy had been, but Bolan let him haul the automatic clear before he fired. Round one impacted on the junior Nazi's chin, evaporating bridgework as it burned up through his palate toward the brain. The second round was probably unnecessary, but it couldn't hurt: a second head shot while the guy was twisting, plunging toward the floor.

There were no brownshirts left to challenge Bolan as he backtracked to his car. Camp Nordland. Thirty minutes out, if he caught all the lights and pushed his rental to the limit in between. That made two and a half hours, at least, since Lynn had been seen alive, and he could feel the apprehension gnawing at his gut like starving rats inside a bamboo cage.

How had she managed to connect with Axelrod, and why was he now holding her? It never crossed the warrior's mind that Lynn had run to join his enemy by choice, that she would voluntarily remain in "Freeman's" company. Somehow she had acquired a means of transportation from the Greyhound depot and had traveled to the Vanguard offices, the office of the Knights—it scarcely mattered now. She had surprised Freeman doing something, going somewhere, and the savage had decided he could not afford to let her walk. It was encouraging that she had not been killed immediately; on the other hand, he did not wish to think about the treatment she might receive from Axelrod or his companions in captivity.

There was a chance, however slim, that Axelrod suspected her of working with "Mike Bowers," helping gather information on the Knights for future prosecution. If that proved to be the case, Lynn could expect a full "debriefing" from the Vanguard's chairman, even though she had no answers for him, had no secrets to divulge. Her very silence might convince her captors that their first suspicions were correct, and they would never rest until they broke her spirit, crushed her will. If they had any skill at all—and Axelrod, at least, had dealt with masters of the art—Lynn would confess to anything from childhood foibles to the Kennedy assassinations, and it would not be enough.

He closed his mind to images of lacerated flesh and screaming nerves laid bare. There were too many turkeys on his soul already, and the soldier did not know if he could bear the weight of yet another. Not this time. Not here. Not Lynn.

She was in jeopardy because of him, and for no other reason in the world. The lady had not asked to be a part of Bolan's war; he had inducted her, with sex and sympathetic words, intending all the time to use her as a source of information, extra eyes inside the Klan. No matter that the plan had been revised along the way, her role eliminated after Bolan recognized the nature of his feelings for this inno-

cent. She had been nearly murdered once, while sharing
Bolan's bed. For all he knew, she might be dead—or
worse—because he had allowed the shadow of his everlasting war to fall across her life.

If so, it was a burden he would carry to his grave. But in
the meantime, there was hope while life remained, and Bolan was not giving up by any means. There was a great deal
he could do for Lynn if she was still alive. And if she
wasn't... well, there was a great deal he could do on her
behalf. Sweet vengeance might not ease the pain he felt inside, but he could let her killers know a taste of hell on earth
before he sent them on their way.

He would give them a preview of coming attractions, with
Death in the starring role and a supporting cast of corpses
from the Vanguard and the Teutonic Knights, all filmed in
bloody, dying Technicolor.

And the projectionist was ready to roll.

GERRY AXELROD CHECKED his watch against the wall clock
in his office, cursing under his breath as he saw they agreed
on the time. Still five hours to go, and he wondered if Andrews was sleeping. He hoped not. The bastard deserved to
be pacing and chewing his nails while he waited to make the
delivery.

The cash could be trouble at customs, but Axelrod had all
the rough spots worked out in his mind. He would charter
a flight to Mexico, then disappear and resurface with one of
his backup identities, taking his time before booking for
Europe, the Orient, anywhere he could be free to relax for
a while.

When he thought about Europe, memories of Switzerland sat in his stomach like stones. He had nearly been killed
there, along with Ramirez, his KGB contact, and others; his
final escape had been damned near miraculous—or pure
dumb luck. The hell of it was that he still did not understand what had gone wrong; he had no idea *who* had been
trying to kill him or *why*. There were rumors, of course.
CIA. SAS. KGB. He had listened to each in their turn and
rejected them all while he waited for brand-new incisions to

heal on his face. In the end he had given it up, but he hated the feel of another disaster-in-waiting that came to him now when he thought back on recent events.

He had covered his tracks like an expert, preparing his own resurrection in style. Even if his cover was shaky close up, he had known there would be few occasions for long, in-depth scrutiny. Aware of the risks, he had taken a gamble . . . and he had come *that* close to losing it all. If he had not seen Bowers for what he was—

Damn the man, anyway! He had appeared out of no-where, slipped through Axelrod's best defenses, to strike at the heart of the Knights. Had he shown up days earlier, Theo Brown might still be alive. As it was, both father and son had been removed from the scene, and his hold over Andrews was stronger than ever.

The telephone's shrilling startled him. Axelrod's stomach was weighted with lead as he grabbed the receiver.

"Hello?"

"Let me have the commander." A breathless voice. Desperate.

"Speaking."

"Oh, Christ, sir, I'm sorry. It's Tucker. You'll never believe it."

"Slow down, Charley." Tucker was one of his sergeants, and one of those chosen to join in the rally where Brown would be dealt with. "Just tell me what happened."

The trooper obeyed his instructions, and Axelrod felt his blood turn to ice as he listened, reliving the chaotic scene in his mind. Somehow, someone had started a shoot-out in place of the nice quiet lynching that Ritter had planned. Charley Tucker had run for his life, showing more sense than Axelrod would have expected, but he had seen close to a dozen men dead on the ground, and the battle had still been in full swing when he had taken to his heels.

"Could you see who was shooting?"

"No, sir. He was wearing a Klan robe, and all. Just the one man, at first, but then others got in on it, trying to stop him, I guess. It was hell on a Ferris wheel!"

"Charley, I think you should take a vacation. The sooner the better. Get hold of the others—the ones who can answer—and tell them to get out of town. There'll be no end of heat after this."

"I've been packing already," the sergeant responded. "I'll get on those calls...but I don't think I'll have too much luck, sir."

"Just do what you can, Charley."

"Yes, sir."

He broke the connection and stared at the phone for a moment, the wheels of his mind spinning aimlessly, digging for traction and throwing off sand. For an instant his vision was clouded by fear, followed closely by rage—and then Axelrod had his first great revelation.

Of course.

Bowers.

Who else, for Christ's sake, would show up in full Klan regalia and shoot up the party? Who else had a stake in preserving Brown as a witness in upcoming trials for conspiracy? Who had already defeated the best guns Mason Ritter could field?

It was strange for a government man to react with such violence, but "strange" did not count anymore. If the evidence Bowers secured had been gathered illegally, it would be thrown out of court by the judge—but it wouldn't mean shit to the men he had killed in the process. A dead man was just so much meat, and before he lay down with the rest of them, Axelrod had it in mind to resist. With his last ounce of strength. With the last breath of life in his body.

If worse came to worst, he could still use the girl as a shield, compel Bowers to give him a running head start. And if that did not work . . . well, then, Axelrod thought that he just might have something to trade.

Make that some*one*.

A KGB sleeper, for instance, with twenty-odd years of subversion behind him. What Fed in his right mind would pass on a bargain like that?

And if Bowers was not in his right mind? What then?

He needed information, and quickly, before he met Andrews. Before he went back on the street. He would have to know more about Bowers from *inside*: the way he reacted to pressure, the way he thought, *anything*. And, as he glared at the telephone, Axelrod knew where to get everything that he needed. The answer had been right there under his nose all along.

IN BLACKSUIT, BOLAN STALKED the razor-wire perimeter of Axelrod's encampment, counting heads and logging numbers in his mind. Two sentries on the gate, another four assigned to walk the wire in pairs, with lights on in the camp commander's office and the smaller of the barracks buildings. Bolan played a hunch: assuming that the visible security would be reduced in daylight, that left three or four men from the day shift sleeping in the larger, darkened barracks. Axelrod would be inside his office, possibly with backup, probably alone. Inside the smaller barracks, he would find the prisoner, perhaps alone.

He chose a spot along the wire and waited for the roving guards to pass before he cut an opening and slithered through. From visits to the camp as "Bowers," Bolan knew the fence was not electrified or linked to any sensitive security devices. It was just a fence, defended by a force that would be much too small—and much too tired at 3:00 a.m.—to keep a lone, determined man from gaining entry to the compound.

Once inside, he knew that Lynn was not his first priority. The barracks was not soundproof, and he heard no screams or other sounds from its interior. It crossed the soldier's mind that he might be too late, she might be dead, but if he bought the absolute worst-case scenario, then there was nothing he could do for Lynn in any case. Alive or dead, the prisoner could wait a few more moments while he dealt with other business.

If he meant to help Lynn, or avenge her, he would have to pin the Vanguard troopers down, eliminate as many of the hostile guns as possible in one deft stroke. The less resistance he encountered when he went for Lynn, the better he would like it.

It was easier to kill a sleeping man than one awake and armed, so Bolan took the day shift first. The barracks was not locked, and no one saw him as he slipped inside, the Uzi dangling from its shoulder strap and his sleek Beretta, with its custom silencer, in hand. The larger barracks had the capacity to sleep twenty-eight, but only four bunks now were occupied. He passed among the sleeping neo-Nazis like a nightmare molded into flesh and gave them each the benediction of eternal sleep. The third one struggled for an instant, woke the man beside him, but a silent parabellum closed the trooper's startled eyes before he had a chance to shout for help.

Four down, a minimum of seven left to go, including Axelrod. It had been easy so far.

Too damned easy.

Stepping from the silent barracks, Bolan nearly ran into a sentry who had deviated from his rounds en route to the latrine. The trooper had a semiautomatic shotgun in his hands, and after half a second's hesitation, realizing that he did not recognize the man who stood before him, he was stepping backward, leveling his weapon.

Bolan shot him in the face, short-circuiting the fire command and knocking him off balance, but he could not halt the reflex action of a dying trigger finger. Angled toward the stars, the 12-gauge blasted empty air, then discharged again on impact with the ground.

He might as well have taken out an ad to tell the Vanguard he was coming. With a shout from one side and a whistle from the other, Bolan heard the gunners coming for him, primed to kill.

A minimum of six against one man.

Against the Executioner.

22

"Who's firing? What the hell is going on out there?"

One of his troopers faltered, glancing back at Axelrod. "Intruder, sir!" he answered, sprinting off to join the sweep. Across the compound, from the general vicinity of Barracks 1, the muzzle-flash of automatic weapons laced the night with fire.

Mike Bowers? Who else could it be? Somehow the Fed had traced him back to camp, and he was closing for the kill. But had he come alone? Was he that stupid, to attack a dozen men without some kind of backup?

And why not? There had been twenty times a dozen at the rally earlier, and Bowers had apparently come out of that all right. The bastard was some kind of one-man army, a machine, but he was not invincible. One of the sentries might get lucky, blow his ass away...but Axelrod was not prepared to take that chance.

He tugged the squat Detonics autoloader from its shoulder rig and sprinted for the smaller barracks, keeping one eye on the action to his left. The compound was not lighted, but he saw the silhouettes of running, crouching figures, gunfire winking in the darkness. Moonlight showed him that the door to Barracks 1 was open. The day-shift troopers should have been responding, but they showed no sign of life. A nagging apprehension gripped him as he stared at that vacant doorway, and he started running faster. Toward the light.

The girl was on her feet when Axelrod burst in, eyes wide with fear and hope. "What's happening?" she asked, a tremor in her voice.

"Sit down!" He shoved her backward toward the cot, and kept her covered as he fished the key out of his pocket, dropping it in her lap. "Unlock the iron and come with me."

She did as she was told, taking a moment to massage her ankle. He grew impatient, reaching out to tangle fingers in her hair, jerking her to her feet and dragging her toward the door.

"You're hurting me!"

"Tough. My car's around in back. We're going for a little ride. If anybody tries to stop us, you're my cover, understand? You try to run, I'll kill you like I would a cockroach. Do you hear me, woman?"

"Yes."

"All right, then, you go first, and take it slow unless I tell you otherwise."

He killed the lights—no point in giving Bowers any easy shots—and followed Lynn outside. Upon arrival, he had parked his car in back of Barracks 2, providing easy access to the lockup, and he had not moved it afterward. It was unlocked, and Lynn was forced to enter from the driver's side. He kept her covered as he slid behind the steering wheel, fumbling his key into the ignition. He reached across in front of Lynn to lock her door from the inside.

"Nothing fancy, now," he cautioned her. "I know you've got the nerve to jump, but it won't get you anywhere. Nowhere but dead. You understand?"

She nodded, fighting back the tears that glistened in her eyes. He felt encouraged by the minor victory, her gesture of submission. In a few more moments, he would be away from here and running free, beyond the reach of Bowers or his sponsors. In a few more hours, he would have the cash from Andrews and would be on his way to Mexico. To freedom.

But he was not ready to retire. Not yet. There was no reason to retire once he had proved his cleverness a second time, escaping from the snare that had been laid for him. Twice, now, his enemies had tried to bring him down, and twice he had outwitted them. In fairness, it was time for

Axelrod to turn the tables, let the hunters know precisely how it felt to be the hunted.

Starting, possibly, with one Mike Bowers, federal agent.

First, however, it was necessary to complete his getaway. He turned the engine over, slammed the car into reverse and cut a sharp 180, aiming for the gate. It would be locked, of course, with no one left on guard to let him out, but he could crash the chain-link barrier without impairing the performance of his vehicle. The paint job did not matter anymore.

"Hang on!" he barked at Lynn, pleased to see her flinch and cower in her seat. "It gets a little rough from here on in."

A BULLET WHISTLED PAST his ear, and Bolan went to ground. He tracked the hostile muzzle-flashes with his Uzi, squeezing off short, measured bursts in answer to the fire from running sentries. On his left a trooper stumbled, arms outflung to welcome death before he plowed the soft earth with his face. Behind the fallen gunner, two more separated, breaking off in each direction, firing as they ran.

He took the nearest of them first, a rising figure eight of parabellum manglers riddling the man from crotch to throat and knocking him off stride. He staggered, reeling like a vaudeville imitation of a drunkard, finally sprawling on his back, spread-eagled in the dust.

His partner used the opportunity to close on Bolan, firing with a semiautomatic rifle from the hip, his hot rounds chewing up the sod a yard to Bolan's right and creeping closer, slapping into mother earth. The Executioner responded with a burst that cut the sentry's legs from under him, and held it as his target fell across the line of fire, a dozen bullets ripping through his chest and face before he had an opportunity to scream.

Then Bolan was on his feet, already moving as the hunters tried to flank him, emptying the submachine gun in a ragged burst designed to hold the opposition back while he looked for cover. Finding it against the near wall of the larger barracks, he took time to feed the Uzi another magazine, prepared as two more challengers assaulted his position.

They were shouting, firing as they came, and Bolan wondered who had taught them that maneuver. It was something from a grade-B movie, obviously meant to terrorize the enemy, but shouting would not make the troopers bulletproof. He fired a burst around the corner, left to right and back again, too close for aiming to be necessary. The intimidating shouts immediately turned to screams as Bolan's two assailants toppled, gut-shot, writhing on the ground. He spared them each a mercy burst before he stepped from cover—and he nearly lost his head as a surviving sniper brought him under fire.

The first round missed his cheek by a fraction of an inch and rang against the corrugated metal of the barracks wall. A second round was dead on target, square between the eyes, except that Bolan had already gone to earth, avoiding death by a fraction of a heartbeat. Clinging to the shadows as the automatic fire ripped overhead, he tried to spot the sniper, finally succeeding as a muzzle-flash betrayed his enemy.

The guy had found himself a place atop the camp command post, flattened on the roof and using altitude to his advantage. Bolan gauged the distance, made it something less than forty yards. It should have been an easy shot, and he assumed that shadows must have spoiled the gunner's aim, preventing him from scoring with a first-shot kill.

It would be suicide to rush the sniper over open ground, no better to retreat and leave him in position to command the compound. Searching for a third alternative, the soldier found it quickly, snapping off a burst to draw the gunner's fire and simultaneously backing toward the open barracks door. He slipped inside, moved past the leaking brownshirts in their bunks and eased a window open halfway down. It was a short drop to the ground outside, and Bolan scuttled toward the cracking sound of rifle fire, the barracks now between him and his enemy.

The sniper obviously thought he had his prey pinned down, continuing to squeeze off random probing rounds at ten- and fifteen-second intervals. He paused at one point to reload, but Bolan waited for the firing to resume. He wanted both eyes fastened to a gun sight when he made his move.

His new location was a few yards closer to the camp command post, better shielded from the sniper's view. The final twenty yards would still be open ground, but Bolan did not plan to rush the sniper. Unclipping two frag grenades from his military webbing, he gripped one tightly in each hand, removed the pin from each and stepped into the open.

Twenty yards. An easy pitch. The first egg wobbled slightly in its flight and disappeared inside the CP's open window. Shifting hands, he dropped the safety spoon from number two and let it fly, a looping overhand that dropped it on the roof behind his prostrate target.

Now the sniper saw him, swiveling with startled, jerky motions, squeezing off a hasty burst that missed him easily. He ducked behind a corner of the barracks, counting down the doomsday numbers, waiting for the end.

His first grenade went off inside the CP shack like muffled thunder, blowing off the door and rattling the walls. The sniper screamed, aware of what was happening too late to save himself, and then the second thunderclap erupted at his back, hot shrapnel ripping through his flank and side, blowing him off the roof like a scrap of rag in a hurricane.

Bolan saw him crumpled on the ground and knew a mercy burst would be a waste of time. There was an outside chance that Axelrod had been inside the CP when it blew, but he could not afford to take the chance. Before he left the compound, he would have to find his prey, make doubly sure.

But first, to Lynn.

The grating sound of tires on dirt and gravel startled Bolan, brought his heart into his mouth. Too swiftly for conscious thought, he recognized the sound for what it was: disaster in the making, failure laughing at him, mocking his defeat. Before he had a concrete plan in mind, he was moving out to intercept the car in a final, desperate effort to prevent his quarry from escaping, dragging Lynn along to certain death.

To Bolan's left, the headlights blazed to life like dragon's eyes, the engine's snarl eclipsing every other sound. He sprang the silver AutoMag from military leather, braced it in both hands and stood his ground.

ACCELERATION PRESSED Lynn Halsey back against the cushion of her seat as Freeman gunned the heavy car, tires spewing dirt and gravel in their wake. Despite his warning, she was tempted to escape, unlock the door and leap before he had a chance to raise his gun and fire. If she succeeded, would he chase her? Back up over her, perhaps? Would the incessant gunfire from the center of the compound drive him off before he could make good his threat?

Her hand was on the door latch when the double-punch of rapid-fire explosions ripped the night apart. Ahead and to her right, she saw the camp command post spewing fire and twisted sheets of metal, smoke already pouring from the open door and windows. In the firelight, twisted bodies cast their abstract shadows on the earth, dark bloodstains soaking through the tunics of their uniforms.

A running figure, tracking from their right and closing on a hard collision course, erupted from the shadowed hulk of Barracks 2. A man, no more than eighty yards away as Freeman flicked the headlights on and kicked them into high-beam.

Bowers.

Standing like a rock, a silver handgun leveled at the hurtling car as if its puny rounds could stop the juggernaut from crushing him to pulp beneath its wheels.

Lynn knew precisely what she had to do. Unmindful of the danger to herself, she lunged at Freeman, struggled with him for the steering wheel and felt the car begin to drift. Another yard or two should do it, and—

His elbow struck her squarely in the forehead, stunning her. Before she could react, his arm was locked around her throat and he was hauling her into his lap, wedging her body between himself and the windshield, the gunman outside. Unable to breathe, she saw colored motes spinning in front of her eyes, and she knew sne was dying. Prevented from speaking, her mind still cried out: *Kill him, Mike! Kill him! Kill him!*

BOLAN WATCHED the charging vehicle swerve left, then back on course, its headlights boring toward him through the night. Unable to observe the struggle for the steering wheel, he supposed Lynn must still be inside the car, and he dropped his aim, eyes squinting in the glare, until his sights were centered on the Caddy's grille.

He squeezed off three in rapid-fire, the hammer strokes impacting on his target with a sound like someone pounding on a kettledrum. A cloud of steam erupted from the punctured radiator, turning black with oil smoke as his rounds drilled through the engine block and stalled it out. The hood flew back, a flapping alligator's jaw obscuring the windshield, as the vehicle's momentum kept it rolling.

Thirty feet from Bolan it began to veer, the driver losing confidence, the power steering frozen in his hands. Bolan circled, closing, as the Caddy jolted to a halt against the flaming hulk of the command post. He had the driver's door and window covered when his adversary called him from the dappled, firelit shadows on the other side.

"Mike Bowers?"

Bolan kept the car between them, giving up his view of Axelrod to keep his enemy from gaining the advantage of an open shot.

"I'm listening," he said.

"Why all of this? Why *me*?"

"I missed you in Zermatt. Let's say I owe you one."

The spokesman for survivalists was silent for a moment. When he found his voice again, there was a tremor in it, rippling the surface of his cultured tones.

"So that was you?"

"I had some company."

"And this time?"

"You and me."

"What's your percentage, Bowers?"

"No percentage. And the name's not Bowers."

"Yeah, I figured. Want to share it with me?"

"Bolan."

Silence on the dark side of the car while Axelrod mulled that one over. And the tremor in his voice was more pronounced a moment later when he said, "What put you on to me?"

"You did it all yourself. You're a deserving case."

Emerging from the shadows, two forms merged as one. "I've got a little something here you might be interested in."

Lynn Halsey stared at him with pleading eyes, but Bolan knew she was not pleading for her life. She wanted Axelrod—or Freeman, as she knew him—dead and in the ground for murdering her uncle.

"Want to make a trade?"

The soldier shook his head. "Not this time."

"I could kill her."

"Sure you could. And what's your encore?"

"I've got information you could use!"

"I'll settle for a bird in hand."

"A sleeper, damn it! KGB! Don't tell me that's not worth a little slack."

"I couldn't say."

"You know the Southern Bankers' Conference?"

Bolan nodded, holding his sights on the visible half of Axelrod's face. It would not be an easy shot, and yet—

"The local honcho. Michael Andrews. He's your man."

"You say."

"I've got a briefcase in the car. The evidence is all inside. It's yours, the skinny and the girl. Just let me walk."

"No sale."

"But I thought—"

"Your mistake."

"You bastard!"

"Right."

He saw the move before his adversary made it, felt the anger boiling out of Axelrod, preparing to explode and sear Lynn's life away. He stroked Big Thunder's trigger, rode the recoil, squeezing off again before the rolling echo of his first shot died away, and Axelrod leaped backward like a puppet yanked on strings, dead before he hit the ground. His body twitched, the reflex action of his dying muscles simulating life, his one eye open, staring at the heavens.

Lynn came to Bolan, sobbing, and he clasped her in his arms, allowing her to cry it out. They were alone beneath the friendly stars, and Bolan's work was finished.

Almost finished.

There was one more IOU awaiting cancellation, one more bit of refuse to be swept away before the Executioner was done in Arkansas.

The sleeper had a nightmare coming to him, and he didn't even know it, yet.

EPILOGUE

The news of Freeman's death preempted the morning farm reports. It followed a description of the slaughter at a Ku Klux lynching party outside Parrish. Twenty-eight were dead, at final count, and agents of the FBI were scouring the countryside for stray survivors, interviewing all known members of the Klan in search of a reliable eyewitness. Meanwhile, someone with a grudge against the Aryan Vanguard had killed two men at Freeman's home and then moved on to kill another ten—along with Freeman—at Camp Nordland.

All in all, it was a bloody morning's work, and very possibly the finish of the Klan in Arkansas. According to reports, one of the rally dead—a body burned beyond immediate attempts at recognition—was believed to be the "wizard," Mason Ritter. From appearances, a member of the Knights had gone berserk and sprayed the crowd with automatic fire. The only witness presently on record was the Klan's intended victim, Wilson Brown, who had described his ordeal from the hospital bed where he lay under twenty-four-hour guard by federal agents.

Michael Andrews had been disconcerted by the morning's news. He was relieved, of course, to know that he had heard the last of Freeman, but there was the "package" to be thought of, and the possibility that it might be in federal hands right now. Did evidence of his identity exist, in fact? Or had the mercenary racist been relying on a bluff to earn himself an easy payoff? At the moment, there was nothing for Andrews to do but wait and see.

He would go through the motions of a normal day, for starters. Business at the bank, an early lunch with two of his associates from the Southern Bankers' Conference. They had already called, inquiring as to the details of the Freeman matter, and he had promised explanations when they met at noon. At the moment, their worries were the least of his concerns.

There had been calls to make, arrangements to be canceled after he received the news of Freeman's death. The two assassins he had hired to follow Freeman from the bank would still be paid, as promised, even though their work—or part of it—had been performed by someone else. They had been hired to follow Freeman from the bank, dispose of him and mount a thorough search for any evidence he might have hidden on his person, in his car or in his home. No searches would be possible now, with the police and the FBI investigating everything the dead man had ever touched, but Andrews would not quibble over twenty thousand dollars. The assassins were reliable, good men and he might well have need of them again before too long.

His contacts in the prosecutor's office and the sheriff's homicide division would inform him of developments, if there was time. His major worry was the FBI. If they laid hands on Freeman's evidence, the locals might not know about it until news of his arrest was printed in the daily papers.

He could leave, of course, but even that took time. There was one hundred thousand dollars in his bedroom wall safe, ten times that securely stashed in Switzerland—the funds he had embezzled from his clients over the years. He could catch a flight to anywhere on earth with two hours' notice. But evacuation was a signal of defeat, and Michael Andrews had himself convinced that he could still fight on to victory.

He was a Marxist in his heart, beneath the layers of comfortable capitalism that he wore as a grand disguise. Not suicidal, but committed to the cause of revolution, which he had served all his adult life. Perhaps a dozen men in Moscow knew of his existence, although few would ever have thought about him in the course of normal daily business. Serving as the spearhead of the revolution, he was naturally alone.

If he should be arrested, brought to trial, the revelation of his long career would be another victory of sorts for Mother Russia. The humiliation that Americans would suffer, their embarrassment throughout the world, would almost justify the sacrifice. Of course, the blacks would not believe it for a moment; they would charge the FBI or CIA with covering for racists in the government, red-baiting as a smoke screen for their own covert activities. Dissension would be multiplied throughout the land, and it would be his fault.

His glory.

Still, the idea of a life in prison—or the thought of execution as a spy and saboteur—did not appeal to Michael Andrews. He seldom thought of himself as Mikhail Andreivich these days. In fact, it was years since he had consciously thought in Russian, although he remained fluent in his native tongue through deliberate private practice.

No, the idea of a prison cell did not fit in his plans at all.

Tomorrow he would leave. Announce a personal emergency to members of his staff this afternoon, a false itinerary they could follow and accept, while he prepared to fly off in the opposite direction, bound for parts unknown.

Tomorrow.

But today it would be business more or less as usual. One last chance to dip his fingers in the bank's supply of ready cash. The money he had planned to siphon off for Freeman would do very nicely for himself. By the time the auditors discovered it was missing, he would be long gone, beyond their reach. Beyond the reach of sheriff's officers, police or FBI.

Tomorrow.

Straightening his tie, the soon-to-be-ex-banker smiled at his reflection in the mirror. What he saw there was success—at several levels. He had done his duty for the revolution, and he had prospered as a direct result of his attention to duty. After more than twenty years of service to the cause, he was retiring to enjoy the good life for a time, and no one had the power to stop him.

Andrews doubted that the KGB would even miss him, let alone attempt to find him. If his disappearance caused a ripple in the Kremlin, they would notice that his exit had been made in character, a capitalist banker absconding with the hard-earned money of the proletarian clients who had trusted him with their life savings. It was perfect, a fitting culmination to his career as a sleeper.

Locking the front door behind him, he strode briskly down the walk, across his lawn, in the direction of the waiting limousine. A different driver held the door for Andrews, smiling deferentially, and he supposed that Thomas must have called in sick. No matter. Nothing could be less significant than the selection of a new chauffeur.

He settled back into the leather-upholstered seat, contemplating the future with mounting enthusiasm. Somewhere tropical, perhaps—at least for openers. And later, Switzerland. Or Liechtenstein. Perhaps the Orient.

He missed the usual landmarks, did not recognize the storefronts sliding past his tinted window. Leaning forward, he pressed the button on the intercom that linked him with the driver.

"Why are we going this way? Thomas never comes this way."

The driver's eyes were studying him, not without a trace of curiosity, in the rearview mirror.

"Shortcut," said the Executioner before he put the pedal to the floor.

Available soon!
SuperBolan #11

Bolan tracks nuclear fuel across the stony wastes of the Sudanese Sahara to thwart the plans of a powerful consortium to attack the Middle East.

**A secret arms deal
with Iran ignites a powder keg,
and a most daring mission is
about to begin.**

THE BARRABAS STRIKE

JACK HILD

**Nile Barrabas and his soldiers undertake a
hazardous assignment when a powerful top-
secret weapon disappears and shows up in
Iran.**

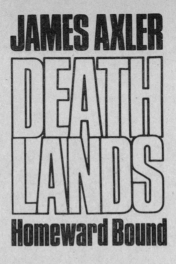

JAMES AXLER
DEATH LANDS
Homeward Bound

**In the Deathlands,
honor and fair play are words of the past.
Vengeance is a word to live by . . .**

Throughout his travels he encountered mankind at its worst.
But nothing could be more vile than the remnants of Ryan's
own family—brutal murderers who indulge their every whim.

Now his journey has come full circle. Ryan Cawdor is about
to go home.

GOLD EAGLE

DL5-R